THE GENERAL'S MATE

THE BLUE SOLACE: BOOK THREE

C.W. GRAY

❀ Created with Vellum

BORAL SYSTEM, PLANET DERELICT

"Thank you for joining us for this most important event," Leti Ando addressed the crew and passengers of The Blue Solace. His soulmate, Captain Will Hackett, stood at his side, yawning and trying to keep his eyes open. Leti's infant sister, Pepper, had kept him awake every night for the past week.

"Captain ordered us to listen to you," Finn said. "We have no choice." The Cardinal's tail twitched behind him and his cat-like ears drooped sadly. "Leti, come on. I want to go shopping."

Leti ignored him. "I know everyone is eager to leave the ship and visit the planet while we refuel, so I really appreciate that you've taken time to share this moment with us."

"Can we go yet, Hack?" Dru asked the Captain. "I'm really hungry and want market food. Like, yesterday."

"Today," Leti continued, "is the day that my best friend in the whole galaxy becomes a freeman." Leti held up Draif's slave contract for his audience to see. "I remember when I first met him…"

"Leti, can you hurry? Morgan and I want to get to the bar sometime today," Draif said, rolling his eyes. "Just tear it up and come on."

"Oh fine," Leti said, frowning. "I wanted to make it special, but no, let's just tear it up like nothing important is happening."

Dru groaned. "Fine, finish your speech."

Leti smiled brightly at the ship's lieutenant. "Thank you, Dru. I always knew I liked you best. Anyway, when I first met Draif, I didn't realize how important he would become to me. Through the years, he's been my best friend, my confidant, and truly the most important person in my life."

"Uh, standing right here, baby," Hack said. "You know, your *soulmate*? The father of your unborn child?"

"Draif is the most capable and talented person I know," Leti said, ignoring his mate.

"I still surpass him in fighting," said Selene, the ship's weapons master, her voice monotone and flat as usual.

"Not for long, Selene," Draif said in a singsong voice.

"I don't know if I'd say he's the *most* talented cook," Juniper, the ship's cook, added. "So, he can cook a couple of dishes, but who makes those little squirrel-shaped chocolates you like so well, huh? I don't understand why you want them squirrel-shaped, but do I question you?"

"Don't question him," Draif said. "You don't want to know."

"He deserves so much in life," Leti said, tearing up. "He deserves the best of everything—"

Hack's snores interrupted Leti's speech. His mate leaned against the wall, still standing, sound asleep.

"Okay, I'm out," Draif said. "The Captain fell asleep. Come on, guys."

The crewmembers staying behind quickly left the cargo bay, and the rest ran down the ramp, escaping while they could.

Draif hugged Leti tightly. "I love you, Leti, but I'm just a guy. I don't need a fancy speech. I know you love me, and I love you just as much. Come on. Let's rip up those contracts."

Leti lay his head on his best friend's shoulder. "Okay, Draify love," he said.

Together, the two held up Draif and Pepper's contracts. They ripped them into little pieces, grinning at one another as the pieces fell to the floor. A cleaning bot zipped by, sucking up the remnants of paper.

"Now, remember to file that in the system, so it's official," Draif said, smiling.

Morgan waited at the ramp, watching the two in amusement. Draif and his new friend quickly left, heading to the planet for some fun.

Leti looked at his sleeping mate. His long, narrow ears twitched. His poor mate deserved some rest. Since they found out Leti was pregnant, Hack was determined that Leti get as much sleep as possible. He was only one month pregnant, but he did get tired a lot. Still, it wouldn't hurt him to get up to take care of Pepper during the night so Hack could sleep.

He poked his sleeping mate, hard.

"*What?*" Hack startled awake, standing straight, eyes blank. "You finished your speech, baby? Did you already tear up the contracts?"

"Yes, Will," Leti answered. "Now go to bed. Selene, Ava, and Dannol are staying with the ship, and the Yellow Solace and Green Solace are docked on either side of us. You need to get some rest or you'll be no good to anyone."

"You wanted to go to the market though," Hack protested. "I don't want you to miss it."

"Oh, I won't," Leti said. He nodded to his two shadows, Maia and Silas. They were former prisoners on a Concord mercenary ship. After surviving a battle alongside him, they had decided that their sole purpose in life was to keep Leti safe so Hack could do his captain stuff without worrying.

At least, that's how it felt to Leti.

Maia was a pretty Dedril with purple scales, dark skin, and black hair. She was also very good with a vibro-blade. Silas was Betonize, massive and fanged, with the green eyes and dark brown skin of most Betonizes. He was still a little malnourished, but Juniper was doing his best to keep the man fed.

"Maia and Silas will come with me. Lilah didn't want to leave the ship, so she's watching all the little ones in the commons." Leti turned his mate toward the door and gave him a little shove. "Get to our quarters and go to bed."

"Fine, but only if you take Princess Buttercup and Gravy with you," he said, yawning.

Leti knew that was probably the best deal he was going to get. "If you insist," he said.

Back at his room, Leti put a leash on Gravy and handed him to Maia. Then he looked at Princess—all eight feet of him—stretched out on the bed, eyes sleepy, happy, and relaxed.

"Come on, baby boy. You're going with us today."

Princess yawned widely, sharp teeth gleaming in the ship's bright lights. The Fire Veil Dragon crawled out of the bed and walked to Leti, shrinking as he went. Leti picked him up—the dragon now one foot long and two inches wide—and stuck him on his shoulders.

"Go to bed, Will," Leti said, pointing to their bed. Hack kissed his cheek, then fell face-first onto the bed, moaning in happiness.

Chuckling, Leti and his shadows left the ship. Gravy looked around the spaceport, happy to sniff everything he could reach with his nose. The Newfoundland mix was a big dog, and his nose reached a lot of things.

"Hey, watch your dog, lady," a stranger yelled at Maia when Gravy's nose poked his butt.

"Sorry, sir," she said, trying to keep a straight face. Silas smiled, fangs gleaming, and the stranger squeaked, then ran off.

"Behave, you two," Leti said.

"Hey, I didn't do anything," Maia said.

"I was talking to Gravy and Silas," Leti said, sharing a smile with the small woman.

They left the spaceport, and Leti immediately figured out why the planet was named Derelict. All around him stood shabby buildings falling and rotting. The ground of the planet was hard, jagged rock. Strangely enough, it resembled the buildings that squatted on it, slanted and crumbling.

"So, this is Derelict?"

"It's not the most impressive planet in the system," Silas said. "But, it's not the worst either."

"It's one large city with several spaceports," Maia added. "Sort of like Vextonar, but with a lot more grubbiness and grit."

"They have a really nice trade market," Silas said. "All sorts of ships stop to fuel up here, so lots of interesting stuff makes its way to the market."

Leti grinned, excitement building. "Let's go see what they have. You all have your money, right? If you see something you want, let me know and we'll stop. You don't have to be *on duty* today, okay?"

Silas and Maia looked at one another and grinned.

"We're always on duty, Leti. The Captain will kill us if you get hurt," Maia said. "We'll let you know if something catches our eye though."

"Why, hi there, Leti," said Caspian Juren, captain of the Green Solace. "What a surprise! I didn't expect you here at all."

"Cas," Leti said and nodded with a scowl. "Will called you?"

The large blue Grell smiled sheepishly. "He couldn't sleep until I agreed to watch out for you too." He grinned at Silas and Maia. "No offense to you both. He knows you would do anything to keep him safe."

Maia smiled softly. "Yes, but you're his brother. That'll make him feel better. I really didn't expect to get off the ship without him."

"He does love his honey bunches here," Cas said.

Leti ignored the three of them and looked around the market, which spread out for miles. Stalls were set up along each side of the cluttered streets, selling everything imaginable, including the usual things like clothes, jewelry, and art, but they also had some unusual things. One stall held artifacts dug up from several planets across the galaxy. Another held actual physical books, while yet another held exotic pets. The pets drew Leti's attention, but he forced himself to look away, heading toward the artifacts.

The stall for the artifacts was actually three stalls, loosely combined. A large tarp covered the top, protecting shoppers from the cold rain. Leti walked slowly up each aisle, admiring every item. There were some fakes, of course, but Leti spotted some genuine pieces. Catching the vendor's eye, he pointed to the three genuine and intact pieces.

Time to put on his snooty Vextonian Prime face. "How much for these three," he asked casually.

"Good eye, sir," the man said. "These three are highly rare finds."

"Rare?" Leti gave the man a skeptical look. "If it's actually genuine, that one is only two thousand six hundred years old, at the most. If it is indeed rare, there are several good pieces for sale that come with documentation. Several," he said, looking down his nose. "Are you telling me you have notarized and sealed documentation for each piece you're selling?"

The man winced. "Well, no, but what about the bowl here? It's from Siren's Lament, Pre-Human Diaspora."

"Perhaps, but again, hardly rare—if it is indeed genuine—and you have no documentation. Fifteen hundred credits for all three? That's more than fair."

The man gave him a sharp look. "Twenty-one hundred credits for all three. I won't sell them for one credit less."

Leti sighed. "Fine," he said. He waved to Cas. "Carry those carefully, and try not to be so clumsy."

"Yes, sir," Cas said deferentially, picking them up after the man wrapped them.

"Come along," Leti said, moving away from the stall. As soon as he was out of the vendor's sight, he stopped and wiggled in happiness, clapping. "Oh gods, I can't believe I just paid twenty-one hundred for these three. Those are all Pre-Human Diaspora artifacts. Do you know how rare they are?"

Cas laughed. "No, and I doubt the vendor really does either."

They moved on, and Leti stayed way too long at the book stall. He found journals from different time periods across the galaxy, old copies of novels, and a few more rare finds, one of which was in ancient Crellic. Maybe it would be useful. After haggling, he piled Cas down with more bags and continued on.

He averted his eyes away from the exotic pets stall,

forcing himself to look at the ground as they walked past. Looking away from the stall, he noticed a small man about the size of Draif, perusing a clothing stall. He was very young, only seventeen or eighteen years old.

The man's eyes traveled over each member of Leti's group, sizing them up. Leti recognized that look. Selene had the same one right before she sparred with one of the other crew. A practiced, knowledgeable assessment of an enemy. The man's cold, black gaze met his, sending a shiver down his spine. The man nodded, then called the vendor over, holding up a beautiful green silk robe with golden roses stitched throughout it.

"You alright, Leti?" Maia looked around the market, then back at him, eyes questioning.

"I'm fine," Leti answered, shrugging and shaking his head. So a man was looking at his friends like they were prey. Nothing to worry about. Really.

Looking over the next stall, Leti promptly forgot the stranger when his gaze met a pair of green, Betonize eyes. A small toddler was crouched under a jewelry stall. A thick chain circled his neck, the other end tied to the leg of the stall. The cold rain had soaked through his clothes, and he was shivering. The boy had his small fist bunched in his mouth, and his big eyes watched Leti's every move. *Oh no!*

2

*L*eti stopped at the jewelry stall, forcing his eyes from the boy's. The vendor smiled widely.

"Greetings, sir," the man said. "Are you looking for something in particular? I have a lovely selection of rare opals from Beton and some gorgeous golden pearls from Fallow."

Maia and Silas casually browsed the man's wares, while Cas stood at the corner of the stall, loaded down like a packhorse. Leti leaned closer. "Why do you have a child chained to your stall," he whispered. He didn't want Cas or the others to talk him out of this.

The man gave him an uneasy look. "It's my daughter's pet," he said quietly, waving to a young girl, about ten, who sat in the corner, far from the rain, eyes glued to her tablet. She looked completely disinterested in being there. "I didn't want to leave him at home. My son was furious when I bought the child, because I wouldn't buy him a bed-slave. Honestly, I'm afraid he'll hurt him. Why I thought dabbling in slavery was a good idea alludes me."

Leti closed his eyes and breathed out slowly. Princess hissed, claws digging a bit into his shoulders. He opened his eyes and tried for a friendly smile. "How much for him?"

The man's eyes widened. "You'd buy a child?" He kept his voice low, eyeing his daughter nervously.

Leti rolled his eyes. "You did. At least I'll free him after buying him," he said quietly.

The man smiled. "In that case, I suddenly have a sale. You buy two pieces of jewelry, and you get a free child. Pick out your pieces, and I'll go break the news to my daughter." His expression soured. "She'll take it so well."

"What's her favorite piece here?"

"The Fallon pearls, why?"

"Tell her I'll buy the pearls for her if she doesn't complain."

The vendor laughed. "That might work." He leaned down near her and whispered in her ear. Her face screwed up in anger, then consideration, then indifference. She shrugged and went back to her tablet. He came back. "I offered to give her half the profit from your purchases too. Have you decided?"

"Yes," he said. "The pearls for your daughter. I'd like that amethyst hairpin my friend is looking at, and the leather and jade bead bracelet there." He considered the man's wares for a moment. "I'll also take five of those gold hair beads." He smiled. "I'm kind of impressed at the variety you have here."

"Thank you, sir," the man said, smiling and bagging up his purchases. Maia frowned at him when he pulled the hairpin from the display, and Leti gave her an innocent look. The vendor handed the wrapped purchases to Cas, then unchained the child. "You'll need to get him in some dry clothes fast. My daughter is a bit heartless, and I'm ashamed to say I've done my best to not think about it."

"What's his name?"

Leti pulled the little Betonize child into his arms, and the boy wrapped his legs and an arm around him with no hesitation. He was soaked to the bone and burrowed into Leti's warm coat. His little fist stayed firmly in his mouth as he laid his head against Leti's shoulder. His dark brown hair was soft and tickled Leti's nose. Princess sniffed at his head, then went back to relaxing on Leti's other shoulder. Gravy wandered over and sniffed the boy, woofing softly to say hello.

"I honestly don't know. He's almost two years old. He can't talk yet, and his contract had nothing on it. Oh, his contract," the man said. "Wait, I have the paper copy here. Apparently, you're supposed to carry it with you if you take a slave anywhere. If you'll wait just a moment, I'll enter it into the system and make it official."

"Thank you," Leti said. It took only a moment, and Leti owned a child. He knew he'd free him as soon as they got to the ship, but it shouldn't have been this easy to buy and sell a person.

"No, thank you," the man said. "This planet doesn't deal in slavery, and I really didn't understand the reality of it. I'm glad not to have to worry about it now."

Cas grinned when he saw the boy in Leti's arms, and Maia just rolled her eyes. Silas though... Silas smiled brightly, green eyes soft. "Not many would take on a Betonize child," he said. "We have fangs, claws, and get pretty big. You sure about this?"

"Of course I'm sure," Leti said, huffing. "It's like you don't even know me."

Silas nodded solemnly and took off his coat. Together, he and Leti took off the little boy's clothes and wrapped him in the coat. He was all warm and snuggly, but Leti was quite aware he wasn't wearing a diaper. That was their first stop.

The group continued through the market, shopping and enjoying the loud chaos. So many different species were gathered in the market, more species than Leti had ever seen. They stopped for lunch and sat at a covered table. Silas went to get their food, and Gravy settled under the table, sitting on Leti's feet.

"I can't believe you're adopting another kid," Cas said. "I know you just bought him to free him, but you can't tell me you'll hand him off to someone else now."

The little boy sat on Leti's lap, staring up at him with big, trusting eyes. "No, he's my son now. Will's too."

"Can I tell Dad?" he asked. "Please?"

Leti rolled his eyes. "Sure. Oh, get out the stuff I got at the jewelry store."

Cas pulled the bag out and laid it on the table. Leti handed the hairpin to Maia. She glared at him but took it, immediately putting it in her hair and preening. "You didn't have to buy me anything, Leti."

"Of course I didn't," he said. "I wanted to though." He handed the gold hair beads to Cas.

"What are these?" Cas asked.

"Hair beads, dork," Leti said, smiling. "You have such long, pretty hair. These will look great in it."

"Aww, his hair is pretty," Maia said, laughing at Cas's face.

"I'm a warrior, Leti," Cas said. "Warriors don't wear jewelry in their hair."

Leti stared at him in disbelief. "Oh, you have no idea what ancient warriors wore. Besides, I think they'll look really good."

The Grell sighed. "Okay, I'll wear them."

Silas brought a large tray of food to their table. "I got some pulled meat here for the little one. Meat is one thing every Betonize child loves." He reached over and pulled the boy's fist from his mouth. "Looks like his fangs are coming in too. You'll want to make sure he has something to chew on."

"Do you think they'll have something here?" Leti looked around their little section of the market. He dished up some pulled meat and got a small spoonful. The little boy gobbled it up, opening his mouth for more. Leti gave him more, then slipped a bite to Gravy. Princess was a vegetarian so none for him. Besides, his new son was hungry. Leti didn't like how skinny he was.

"I'll look around for you after lunch," Silas said. He spied the leather and jade bracelet on the table. "You'd best either put that on or put it up. You don't want to tempt thieves."

"It's yours," Leti said.

"I got hair beads," Cas said dryly.

"Well, you do have really pretty hair," Silas said as he caressed the bracelet. "This is really for me?"

"Yep," Leti said, watching his son wolf down his lunch.

"Why?" Silas looked puzzled. Pleased, but puzzled.

Leti smiled at the big Betonize man. "You're my friend. I thought it'd look good on you."

Silas blinked a few times and put it on. "Thanks," he said quietly.

"No problem," Leti said, finally getting in a bite of his own. Damn, that meat was good. No wonder his son loved it so much. "How do you know so much about kids, Silas?"

"I have a lot of younger brothers and sisters," he said, smiling wide, his fangs flashing in the light. "They're all on Beton now, but I remember watching them for my mother. She had to work a lot since my dad died right after the youngest was born."

"I'm sorry, Silas," Leti said. Even though he didn't like his father, he still would hate for the man to die. He couldn't imagine losing a father that you cared for.

"It's fine. I was really young. I have a few good memories, but mostly, I remember my stepfather. He came along about five years after my father died. He's a good man."

"Why didn't you choose to go back to Beton after we were rescued?" Maia asked, curious. Most of the former prisoners had no family to return to. For Silas to have a family, but still choose to stay, was unusual.

Silas shrugged. "I want to help fight the Concords. When I was taken, it could have been any one of my siblings in my place. What they do is wrong, and they need to be stopped. Kidnapping non-human species just to torture them for fun in their downtime is a shit thing. Captain Hackett wants to stop it. I want to help. That simple."

Leti patted the man's arm. Silas was a good guy. "We're glad to have you, Silas."

"Hell yeah," Cas said. "We're going to need all hands on deck to take them out, that's for sure."

A small figure in the shadows caught Leti's attention. The man was back, staring at Leti's group. He wasn't sure how long the man had eavesdropped on them, but a puzzled look covered his face when he saw Leti's new son. The man frowned, backing away from the area. Soon enough, he'd disappeared around the corner.

The afternoon passed quickly. They found some teething toys for Leti's new son. Leti learned not to call them chew toys or vendors would give him horrified looks. Finally, they headed back to the ship.

As they passed the exotic pet stall, Leti's son yelled, holding his hands out. Leti followed his eyes to a large cat sitting in a cage. It was *very* large, definitely not a housecat. It was just a little smaller than Gravy. One ear was missing the tip, and there were scars here and there, showing off a bit of a violent past. He did not purr. He did not look cute and cuddly.

Leti wanted him. Badly.

Leti's son was also in love. His baby gibberish was excited, and his arms remained in the air, reaching for the animal. *He takes after me*, Leti thought, smiling.

"Oh, this is great," Cas said. "Hack's never going to let you go to a trade market without him again."

Leti sighed. "Sir, how much for that cat, there?"

The vendor looked at the cat, looked at him, then looked at the cat again. "It's yours. For free. Please take it."

"Seriously?" Silas looked surprised.

"Uh, okay," Leti said. "Cas, can you get it?"

Cas groaned and tried to lift the cage, but it was too heavy for one hand, and he carried a lot of packages. "Um, I may need some help here."

"I'll carry it," Silas said. He opened the cage and pulled the large feline out. The vendor jumped back, getting as far away from the animal as he could. It did nothing, though, letting Silas pick it up. It took both arms to carry it. "Do you have a collar and leash?" he said. "I don't think I can carry him all the way to the ship."

"Sure thing," the vendor said, hurriedly handing him the leash. "Good luck."

"Well, uh, thanks," Leti said. "Are you sure you're alright with giving it to us?"

"Gods, yes," he said. "That thing has been a menace since it came three shipments ago. I've been trying to give it away for the past week."

"Okay, well, thanks again." Leti led the way to the

ship. "What kind of animal is it? It's feline, but it's so large."

"It's a Betonize hunting cat," Silas said. "I didn't want to tell the vendor or he might have charged you. They're usually really expensive, but most wealthy families try to purchase one for their sons when they're young. The cats bond with them, growing up with them, and make fine companions." He grinned. "Your boy has good taste."

Leti's son leaned over his shoulder, watching his cat with a surprising intensity. "Oh yeah," Leti said. "He's in love."

"Definitely your son," Cas said.

Gravy walked next to the cat, tongue hanging out, looking proud of the new family member. He reached over and licked the cat's cheek. It grumbled and shook its head, hair slicked up with slobber. The cat gave Gravy a hateful look and stalked along after Leti and his son. Gravy wagged his tail and gave the cat another kiss. A small, delicate, plaintive meow escaped the large cat. Leti and his son both started giggling.

Hack met them at the ship, Pepper strapped to his chest. He looked awake and aware for the first time in at least a week. Rizzie, their adopted daughter held his hand, waving as the group approached.

"Will," Leti said, smiling softly, glad to see his mate looking well-rested. "Meet our son, Sami, and his hunting cat, Pax."

3

EN ROUTE TO CHARYBDIS STATION

*H*ack watched his new son chew on his teething ring. The large hunting cat curled around the little boy protectively, rumbling at anyone who approached. Their little boy definitely took after Leti.

"Cas told me this morning that you had another one, son." His father's purple face grinned at Hack from the vid-screen. Admiral Fasi Juren looked like a fierce warrior, but when it came to his family, he was a softie. "He looks like a cutie too, but what's that beast with him? I've never seen anything like it."

"That's his hunting cat," Hack said, sighing. "He takes after Daddy Leti."

His dad laughed, eyes bright with joy. "I can see that. If you're gone much longer, your mate's going to adopt an army."

"True. Can't say I mind though," Hack said, happiness settling inside him. He'd be fine with an army of kids if that was what Leti wanted. "We stayed longer than planned at Union Station, but it couldn't be helped. We couldn't leave the Concord's prisoners unprotected, and they needed sorting and medical aid. How's it going on your front?"

"The Council understands why the Concords need to be wiped out. They stand in full support," Fasi said solemnly. "We're making plans now. I think we'll wait until you all get home to make a move. We do have our scouts out, gathering information."

"I'm glad the Council supports the decision. It's a big step to declare war on another mercenary group."

"That wasn't the hard part," his dad said. "They've been pressing me..."

"Pressing you for what?"

"Charybdis Station's changed quite a bit over the centuries," he said. "A change is coming, a big one. I had hoped to put it off onto the next admiral, but it's time."

"What change?" Hack asked. His father looked both excited and worried.

"Don't worry about it," Fasi said with a smile. "We'll deal with it when you get home. Tell me about Sami there."

"Leti bought him in the trade market on Derelict. We'll free him and officially adopt him as soon as we're out of the system. He's a sweet boy," Hack said, picking up his son. Pax allowed it, nodding. "Sami, this is your grandpa."

The little Betonize boy looked at the screen, sharp teeth gnawing on his toy. He waved shyly, then buried his face into Hack's neck.

"He's pretty smart," Hack said. "He's not talking yet, but he seems more responsive than other kids."

"Every parent says that," his father said, smiling. "Everyone thinks their child is a genius."

"But he is, Dad," Hack said. He hugged his son closer, love filling him. Three months ago, he never would have imagined he'd have three kids—four counting his brother—and one on the way. He never would have imagined he could love this much, or that he'd have a mate he adored.

"Sure, son. Sure," his father said dismissively. The foolish man didn't realize his grandson's true genius. "So, have you told Leti yet that I'm the admiral for the station?"

Hack winced at the question and at the sharp teeth digging into his neck. Sami liked to bite sometimes. "No biting," he said gently but firmly and set his son down.

Sami blew him a kiss in apology and crawled back over to Pax, leaning on the large feline and chewing his toy.

"See what he did?" Hack pointed to Sami. "He said sorry without saying sorry. I told you he's smart."

"Uh huh. Don't avoid my question. Have you told Leti yet?"

Hack groaned, sitting and throwing his head back. He stared at the ceiling. "No. He thinks I don't notice, but he's already so nervous about meeting everyone and settling down at the station. I don't want to make it worse." He sat up, eyeing his father. "It's not like you're one of those snooty leaders who insist on royal treatment. He'll be fine."

"Sure, son. Sure he will," his father said drolly. "Really, though, don't worry too much about it. Renee and I will make sure he settles in just fine. I also already got him a little present I know he'll like."

"Thanks, Dad," he said. "Anything you want me to work on from here?"

"Maybe the artifact? Has that other doctor… Franklin was her name, right? Has she found out anything about it?"

"I'm not giving her the chance," Hack said. "I don't trust her, Dad. The way she was taken prisoner, her attitude toward non-humans, it just seems off. Maybe when Dr. Manning can keep an eye on her at the station, I'll feel differently."

"Alright. I'll go ahead and talk to Orsla. I know she's looking forward to getting her hands on the element. She was pretty upset to hear about Dr. Morrick though. She said he was a good man, and she hated for him to die like that. They were rivals, but apparently got along much better than I thought."

"Anything else you want me to work on? I can start reaching out to my contacts in the spaceports to track the Concords as they dock."

"Good idea, son," Fasi said. "The other captains could do the same. I'll let them know. Now, there's one more thing you could do. Well, not you really, but Beck. One problem we're running into as we plan is the fact that most, if not all, of the Concord ships will have prisoners onboard. Realistically, most of our battles will be in space, not on the ground," he said. "Beck's the most inventive engineer we have, aside from his father, and he has more practical fighting experience then Pops does. Ask him to start brainstorming ideas for how to get the prisoners out alive. Right now, all we can come up with is disabling every ship instead of destroying them. As it is, that takes a lot of maneuvering, and it ties our hands in battle, which increases our own casualties. The Concords have numbers on their side. They're the largest mercenary group in the galaxy—not the most skilled, but the largest."

"I'll talk to him. If anyone can come up with something, he can."

"Thanks, son. I'll get back to work and talk to you tonight, okay? Mo is enjoying your nightly chats. I haven't told him about Sami yet, wanted to give you the honor."

"Good idea," Hack said, smiling. "Love you, Dad."

"Love you too, son," his father replied and nodded.

The call ended, and Hack looked over at Sami. The little boy had fallen asleep against Pax, his mouth wide open. His soft snores blew the cat's fur back and forth. At first, Hack had worried about Pax being around Sami, the boy wasn't even two years old, but Pax was a lot like Princess Buttercup—scary as hell, but loyal to his person, and also, a little too smart for an animal. After observing them and talking with Silas, he grudgingly accepted the fact that Pax was a permanent addition to the family.

The door opened and Dru walked in. "What's

wrong with you?" she asked, sitting across from him. Monty, her Vexal newt, was perched on her shoulder, judging him with his little black eyes.

"What makes you think there's something wrong? I'm perfectly fine." He wasn't worried about anything. He didn't stress over keeping his family safe or worry about the upcoming war. What was her problem anyway?

"You look like you want to blow something up," she said, smirking. Her brown eyes tracked his every move.

Damn it! Why'd he have to have a smart lieutenant?

Hack sighed. "It's so damn strange. On one hand, I've never been so happy. Leti is simply amazing, and the kids are great. I never really thought I'd have my own family, and yet, here I am. On the other hand, I'm worried sick. Declaring war on the Concords is a big deal. We've never fought another mercenary group when we weren't being paid to. It seems like everyone back home is just rolling with it. I don't understand how they don't see the ramifications."

"What do you mean?"

"We have allies," he said. "Other mercenary groups that we get along with, call in for aid when we need it. What happens when they see us fighting with another group? It's not like there's some agreement that says we can't, but what's it going to do to our reputation with the others?"

"You have a good point, but I don't think they'll be surprised," Dru said and shrugged. Damn it, another person who didn't care.

"Seriously? They won't be surprised?"

"Hack, Charybdis Station isn't your typical mercenary group. We've been changing for a long time, and the other mercs aren't blind. They know it too."

"Dad said a change was coming," Hack said, baffled. "I don't get it."

"We'll see when we get back. I have an idea what he means, but I don't want to say anything. I could be completely off base."

"Oh, come on, Dru. You can't *not* say something now."

She laughed. "Fine. I think Charybdis Station's about to become more than a mercenary group. Maybe a lot more."

"Like what?"

She sat back in her seat and smirked. "That's up to your dad and the Council."

"Damn it, Dru," he said, frustrated.

A little voice piped up from the corner. "Damn it, Dru," Sami said, or at least it sounded like what he said.

"Oh fuck," Hack said. "Leti is going to kill me. Those were his first words."

"Fuck," Sami repeated. That was much clearer.

"Oh gods, Leti is definitely going to kill me."

Dru shook with laughter. "Oh gods. That is just perfect."

"Can you watch Sami? Thanks!" Hack didn't wait for an answer and jumped to his feet. Retreat was sometimes the best action. He ran out the door and fled to engineering.

Beck banged around his workshop, angry grumbles echoing in the large space. The large green

Grell was the most even-tempered and gentle man Hack knew.

"What's wrong, Beck?"

The Grell startled, yipping and spinning around, tail clutched in his hand. "Damn, Captain," he said. "You scared the shit out of me."

"Why are you banging around? I don't think I've ever seen you in a bad mood."

Beck shrugged, looking baffled. "I don't know. I just feel jittery and annoyed all the time. It started about a week ago. I shifted and ran around Derelict when we were there, but that didn't seem to help at all."

The Grell weren't just big furry humanoids. They also shifted into large wolf-like creatures. He remembered the first time his dad had shifted around him. He had just moved in with them and thought his dad's new shape was the most amazing thing in the world. So, of course, for at least a week, he'd insisted his dad stay in that shape anytime he was home. It made his stuffed wolf, Milo, even more special.

"I spent all week making two of those energy nets you liked so well. They should have taken me a full month to make, but I can't sleep and I can't seem to stop moving."

Hack thought about Beck's words for a moment. "I think I know how you feel. You feel like there's something you're supposed to be doing? Your feet need to be moving constantly? Everyone pisses you off?"

"Yeah, that's it exactly!"

"You have itchy feet, Beck," Hack said. "You remember what that means?"

His big, plain face lit up with joy. "I'm gonna meet my mate soon?"

"Sounds like it. It took me a while though, so I don't know if it'll be soon."

"It doesn't matter," Beck said. "I can't believe I'm gonna have a mate. I'll finally get to have sex!"

"Whoa there, buddy. TMI," Hack said. "Wait, you haven't had sex?"

"No," he answered. "I wanted to wait to be with my mate."

"Gods, you're so sweet, Beck," Hack said. "Your mate had best know how lucky he or she is."

"He," Beck said. "At least, I hope so."

"So, how will you know when you meet him?"

"Scent. Grell know by scent."

"Do you think it's anyone onboard?"

"No, I'd have smelled him by now. I've been aboard the other two ships too," he said. "I went to talk to their engineers on Derelict. It doesn't have to be someone I've met yet. It just means I'm getting ready to meet him. You started feeling it when it was close to the time you were meant to find Leti. I'll find my mate. He'll be beautiful and sweet. It'll be perfect. You'll see."

"It had best be perfect. You deserve only the best," Hack said.

"Oh, whatever," Beck said. "You're starting to sound like Leti when he talks about Draif. So, did you need something? You don't usually visit my workstation."

"Oh, yeah. The admiral wants you to try to come up with a way to deal with Concord ships that carry prisoners onboard. We can't easily disable every ship without putting our own ships at too much risk, but we want to save as many Concord prisoners as possible."

"Hmm, I'll think on it. That's a tall order, but I like a challenge."

"Thanks, Beck."

"Not a problem," he said.

"Will, you had best get your butt to our quarters right this instance!" Leti's exasperated voice came over the ship's comm system.

"Well, someone's sleeping on the couch tonight. At least you have a couch now," Beck said, smiling. "Get going, Captain. You don't want your mate to get any angrier."

4

Hack slowly walked toward his quarters. He stopped at Wobble's room, petting the llama and making sure he had food and water. Most of the time the older refugee kids took care of him. They adored the fuzzy critter.

Speaking of the older refugee kids, Julia, a young Wello hybrid, stepped through the door as Hack finished refreshing Wobble's water. She clutched a brush, a bit of red knitting, and an apple in her hands. Her wide eyes focused on him as if he was a predator hunting for prey. The poor girl hadn't relaxed around him since she boarded.

"Hey, Julia," Hack said softly. He knew she'd been through a lot. She didn't have to like him, but he'd damn sure do his best not to scare her.

"Captain Hackett," she said and nodded. "I was just going to play with Wobble."

"That's good," Hack said. "He likes you kids an awful lot. Leti appreciates you helping out with him."

"He's nice," she said and started feeding the apple to the llama. "Ava taught me how to crochet, and I made him a hat."

"Is that what you have there? It'll match his scarf perfectly. Want to put it on?"

She nodded hesitantly, and the two of them worked together to pull the knitted beanie on Wobble's head. She had made holes for his ears, and a long braided piece hung down each side. She smiled when they finished. Hack had to admit, Wobble looked kind of cute… for a llama.

"He looks good, Julia," Hack said. "I'll leave you to play, but it was nice seeing you."

She nodded shyly and moved to Wobble's other side, disappearing behind him.

Hack left Wobble behind and went to check in on Lucas and Alois. Alois was still unconscious, and Nettle didn't understand why. He was completely healed, but he wouldn't wake up. Lucas was finally stabilized and off the pain meds. He'd be measured for prostheses when they got to the station.

"Hey, Captain," Lucas said, setting his tablet down. Draif sat beside his bed, frowning at his own tablet.

"How are you feeling?"

"Okay," Lucas said, grimacing. "I shouldn't complain because it's a shit ton better than before." He smiled wide. "Are you dragging your feet back to Leti?"

Hack shrugged. "Maybe."

Draif snorted, not looking up from his tablet. "Don't put it off too much longer, or he'll be even angrier. Hey, by the way, these investments I made are looking good. Tell Leti that if he ever decides to leave you, he and the kids will have plenty of money."

"Yeah," Hack said drily. "I'll be sure to mention that to him. Especially since he's mad right now."

"That's okay. I just messaged him," Draif said. "Oh, he says that he's staying with you forever and that nothing could drag him from you. He also says he really wants to hit you with something hard right now. And… he likes your penis." Draif looked up from his tablet. "These are our conversations now. I hear more about your penis than I ever wanted to, and Leti threatens to hit you a lot."

Hack grinned, standing straight and proud. Leti liked his penis. He had suspected he did, but they hadn't had sex in over a day, so he couldn't be a hundred percent sure.

"Uh oh," Draif said. "Leti says you better get home right now, or he won't let your penis visit him. Honestly, though, I think he's bluffing."

"Well, I'll see you two later," Hack said, spinning and sprinting out the door. He went to his room to face his fate. Princess Buttercup was at his food bowl, crunching away on his kibble. He gave Hack a look, and he swore the dragon was laughing at him.

Leti sat on the couch with Rizzie and Sami, watching a cartoon on the vid-screen. Gravy and Pax sat on either side of the pile of cuteness. His darling mate glared at Hack and slowly got up, untangling himself from the kids. Rizzie moved into his spot and cuddled with Sami. She settled her head on his, hauling his wiggling body close.

Leti pulled him into the bathroom, the only place they had privacy anymore.

Leti growled. "Why was our son's first word *fuck*?"

"It was actually 'damn it, Dru,'" Hack said, wincing. "I can't help it that he's so damn smart. I tried to explain that to Dad, and he didn't believe me."

"Don't distract me with our son's genius, Will," Leti said. "Everyone really needs to watch what they say or our kids will be potty mouths. What would your parents think?"

"That I must be their father? Trust me, baby, they were worse when they adopted me. Mom in particular was pretty bad. Somehow, we all survived, and they raised three good kids. We'll do the same," he said. "I know you're nervous about meeting my parents and getting to the station, but I promise, they *will* love you. The station's great too, full of good people."

Hack cupped Leti's cheek in his hand and leaned down to kiss his mate. Leti moaned and Hack deepened the kiss, pulling his mate's soft body to him. Gods, he was addicted to his taste.

"Daddy Leti, Daddy Will," Rizzie called. "Sami's hungry. I can hear his tummy go grrr, and he's chewin' on the couch."

"That boy is all you, baby," Hack said, grinning as he pulled out of their kiss.

Leti groaned and tried to hide his smile. "He's terrible and adorable all at once."

Hack leaned down and kissed his sweet mate's cheek. "Just like you." He laughed and darted out of the room before Leti could smack him. He got Pepper from her bassinet. "You, baby girl, are all mine. You and my Rizzie are Daddy Will's girls." Pepper's wild red hair and bright green eyes looked like Leti, but she was his baby. All his.

They gathered up the kids and the pets—minus Princess, who decided to enjoy the solitude—and went to the commons for dinner. Maia met them at the door, grinning at the kids.

"You know, I'm with Hack and on the ship," Leti said. "Do I really need a guard?"

She looked around the hallway. "I don't see a guard, Leti," she said. "What're you talking about? Let's go get dinner."

Quite a few of the crew and refugees were already there, sitting at tables and on couches, enjoying Juniper's beef stew.

Gravy and Pax went to the pet bowls for water and kibble. A few pet beds were strewn about the room, and Hack could see Fluffle and Marmalade already in one, curled up together. Hector, Dannol's rooster, strutted around the commons, letting everyone know he ruled the ship.

Juniper himself darted around, making sure drinks were full and everyone was eating enough. He waved at Hack and his family, then continued his path around the room. Hack saw an empty table and led everyone to it.

Leti sat, putting Sami on his lap. "I feel bad, but I just noticed a lot of the younger kids have to sit on the couches to eat."

Hack looked around the room. There were a lot of

children, varying in ages, and Leti was right. The younger ones couldn't eat well at the tables. The older children, adult refugees, or other members of the crew held them in their laps or made sure they were seated at the couches.

His friend Morgan, a big brute of a man, fed a toddler on his lap while the ship's diplomat, Ava, sat in the middle of a group of five children under the age of seven. She made sure they each had a plateful and were eating. Her gentle, melodious voice drifted through the room, calm and kind. Two of the oldest children sat with Lilah and fed four more of the youngest children, while Nettle, the ship's doctor, hovered over Lilah. She'd be giving birth any time now.

"I wish I had thought of it while we were on Derelict," Hack said, feeling guilty. "I could have gotten some better seating. We'll be home in a few days though."

Selene brought a tray full of food to the table, then sat next to Maia. "Leti, you missed training yesterday." She passed out plates and dished up her own.

Leti took a page from Sami's book and blew her a kiss. "I got busy going through all the stuff I bought at the market. Oh, by the way, I found you a pretty, Pre-Human Diaspora bowl from Siren's Lament. It's in great condition."

Selene blinked. "You're giving it to me? Items from that period are expensive."

"Of course. I thought of you when I saw it and knew you'd like it," Leti said, shrugging.

Hack smiled. His mate didn't realize how big his small acts of kindness really were.

Selene nodded, going back to her food. "I think Rizzie could start self-defense training if you wanted her to. She's too little for the phaser, but she could start learning some basic moves."

"Already? Really?" Leti looked at their daughter, watching her daintily eat her chicken and broccoli.

"Most kids on Charybdis Station start learning basic self-defense around four. We make it a fun game, and it gives them a chance to meet the other kids too," Hack said.

"Do you think she needs to, Selene?" Leti stuffed chicken in his mouth but looked thoughtful. Thoughtful and hungry.

"It couldn't hurt," Selene said. "I've already started working with the other kids too. Some of them needed it to give them a little control again."

Maia nodded in agreement. "I wish I had known more myself. It might have made it harder for the Concords to take me."

"Xu really likes it, Daddy Leti," Rizzie said. Hack hadn't realized she was paying attention to their conversation. "I wants to learn to protect folks too. I gots Pepper and Sami to protects. I'm the big sister."

"Ladybug, you know me and Daddy Leti will protect you, right? You don't have to be worried or scared," Hack said. He didn't like the idea of his little girl being afraid.

"I know," she said, shrugging. "The galaxy's scary sometimes, and I wants to help."

Leti looked at him, nodding his permission. "Okay then," Hack said. "You can start with Selene tomorrow. She's the best, you know."

"Yeah," Rizzie said excitedly, bouncing in her seat. "Xu really likes her." Xu was a little Dedril boy, a couple of years older than Rizzie. He seemed to follow Selene around like a puppy. She was patient with him though.

"Has Fasi found homes for the other children?" Leti bit his lip, looking around the room.

"We've found homes for almost every child. Dad said that by the time we get home, he'll have placed everyone. When the ship docks, we'll be met with a lot of happy people." Maybe Hack needed to talk to his dad about Xu. Selene would make a good mother, if that was something she wanted.

Leti nodded, frowning and poking at the carrots on his plate.

"Leti," Hack said. His mate looked up, expression conflicted. "What's wrong?"

"I know it would be easier to let someone else take Sami in, but I love him so much, Hack. He's ours, just like Rizzie, Pepper, and Mo."

"He's my little brother," Rizzie agreed, nodding and giving Hack a hard look. "He's family. I'm gonna share my bed with him too. Unless he bites me, then he sleeps with Princess."

"Thank you for sharing, Rizzie. You're a good big sister," Hack said. He looked closely at Leti and Rizzie, making sure he had their attention. "Now, let me be clear, I know he's ours. I already love the little monster too much to give him to anyone else."

Sami held his mouth open like a baby bird for Leti to shovel little bites of meat into. The boy loved meat. He was perfectly content with his place in the world, and Hack planned on keeping it that way.

He looked around the room. "Each of these kids is going to make a family just as happy as you, Sami, and Pepper make me," he told Rizzie, then looked at his mate. "I love our family, baby, just as much as I love you and that's… Well, that's a lot."

Leti smiled, heating something inside Hack, something he never knew he had until he'd met his mate.

Trouble was coming, true, but looking around the room, he knew why it was necessary, why they had to fight, no matter the consequences. No one deserved to be stolen and tortured for amusement. These people deserved justice. They deserved better than what they'd gotten. Everyone did.

5

"We need to hurry, Will," Leti told his mate. "The kids will be back in thirty minutes."

"I swear, if I'm not inside you in the next five minutes, I'll go crazy."

"Yeah, yeah. Shut up and get over here," Leti said. He loved his mate, he did, but they hadn't had sex in two whole days, and that was a really long time. How Leti had gone twenty-five years without his mate was beyond him.

Hack wasn't a stupid man. In seconds, he had Leti spread out on their bed, his freckled body on display in his gold, filmy robe. Hack's mouth went to work, tasting each and every freckle he came across, leaving a brand of heat behind him.

"What are you doing? My dick's down there."

"I need these freckles, baby. I have to taste them. Each. And. Every. One." He punctuated his words with soft kisses.

"Thirty minutes, Will," Leti reminded him through his moans.

Leti arched toward his mate. He grasped Hack's head in his hands, pressing him close, while Hack licked at one of his pebbled nipples, nibbling and flicking the sensitive nub. Leti's body burned from his mate's touch. He still didn't understand how he got aroused so quickly any time they touched, but it wasn't like he minded.

Hack lifted his head and slid the gold robe off Leti's shoulders.

"Why'd I even put that on?" Leti teased.

Hack grinned, then stilled for a moment, staring at Leti's body. His eyes burned as they moved over him. Leti knew his pink birthing line was a stark contrast against his pale skin.

"What are you staring at?"

"You're so beautiful, Leti," Hack whispered. "Hard where you need to be, soft in all the right places, all those damn distracting freckles. How did I get so lucky?"

Heat boiled through his body at his mate's words, and he thrust his hips up, hoping Hack would touch him. Hack growled low and stroked Leti's warm, bare legs, moving his big body between them. He rested his erection against Leti's bare dick, pushing against him. Leti moaned and thrust toward him in desperation. He needed him so badly.

"Will, please," he begged raggedly, slipping his hands to his mate's pants.

Hack suddenly pulled back from him. "I want to taste you," he said huskily.

Leti eagerly spread his legs wider, and Hack moved down his body, enclosing Leti's dick in his mouth. After a few sucks, he released him with a pop, giving him a long, slow lick. Leti moaned as Hack began to lick and tease his hard flesh, eventually closing his mouth around him again. Leti tangled his hands in his mate's soft hair and exploded inside his mouth.

Hack gave him a few last, lingering licks, then quickly unfastened his pants. He rubbed his hard dick against Leti's soaked hole, moaning. His fingers stretched him, then he positioned himself and pushed deep with one thrust. Leti clenched his tight passage, and Hack seemed to lose control. He hooked Leti's legs over his shoulders and plunged deep and hard into his welcoming body. Leti looked down, watching Hack's cock disappear in his ass over and over.

Leti came with a scream, and Hack followed close behind him. He thrust into him one last time, then emptied deep within him.

Hack pulled out of Leti slowly, rolling to his side, then pulled Leti close, running kisses over his face and neck until Leti finally caught his breath. Leti snuggled up against him, perfectly content in his mate's arms. He rolled his eyes when Hack began to snore. He looked at his mate. Hack's face looked peaceful in the dimmed light, as if he had no cares in the world. Leti knew his mate worried about the upcoming battles, but for this moment at least, he could be at peace.

Leti sighed, then forced himself to get up. His mate

felt good in his arms, even if it was still strange to him. Hack could make him feel weak one moment, then ecstatically happy the next. Of course, being pregnant didn't help his emotional stability.

The one thing he could be absolutely sure of was that, for better or worse, in battle or not, he needed to be at Hack's side. He belonged to Leti now and nothing would take Hack from him. Nothing.

"DADDY LETI, I'M GETTIN' married tomorrow," Rizzie said, biting into her sandwich. "Juny can make cookies, right?" she asked around a mouthful of food.

Leti nodded seriously and moved Pepper to his other arm. She was growing like a weed and getting heavier every day. "Okay, ladybug. Now, who are you marrying?"

He peeked in the corner playpen. Sami was down for the count, surrounded by teething rings. Pax filled up the rest of the pen, curling around Sami protectively. The large cat had already broken the pen once.

"Milo. I love him, and Netsie said folks gets married when they loves each other." Milo, her ragged, purple stuffed wolf, sat in another chair at the table with a sandwich in front of him. One that Leti would eat when Rizzie lay down for her nap.

"Who's going to officiate?" Leti placed the freshly-diapered baby in her bassinet.

"What's of... offi... officiate?"

"That means who's going to do the ceremony, so you can say your vows."

"Oh, Daddy Will is goin' to, right? You'll ask him?"

"Of course, ladybug."

"I needs a dress and flowers too," she said. *Of course, she wants to go all out*, Leti thought, thoroughly amused. "I guess Princess Buttercup can come if he promises not to eat Milo."

"He won't eat your true love." Leti laughed. "We'll talk to Ava and Juniper about a dress and flowers. I'm sure we'll find something. Are you ready for your nap?"

Her little blue nose scrunched up. "Do I have to?"

"Yes. It's good for you, ladybug," Leti said.

"Can I sleep in the big bed?" Without waiting for his answer, she awkwardly climbed into his and Will's bed. Her broken leg was healing nicely, but she still stumbled quite a bit as she moved.

"Of course," he said and tucked her in with Milo.

"Daddy Leti?"

"Yes, ladybug?"

"Are you and Daddy Will goin' to get married too? Since you loves each other?"

Of course, Leti thought with a groan. "Did Nettle say that we ought to?"

"Yep," she answered with a grin. "I wanna be in the wedding too. You can be in mine."

"Thanks, ladybug, and yes, you will be in our wedding when we get married. Now, go to sleep." She giggled, and he left her to nap.

Nettle and the other crew members kept asking him when he was going to marry Hack. Leti knew where his reluctance came from. They'd only known one another for a short time, soulmates or not. He didn't want Hack to marry him tomorrow, then regret it a year later. It would completely break him if Hack decided he didn't love Leti. Leti would have to kidnap the man and keep him chained up, and that just wasn't practical.

Plus, things were just now settling down from the fight on Union Station. Morrick's body in the cryo chamber was a rough reminder that lives were at stake in this game they played with the Concord mercenaries. If Leti was being honest with himself, he wasn't handling Verion's death well, but life moved on, whether he wanted it to or not. It didn't help that he'd heard nothing from Wyatt Morrick. Each morning, Leti scanned and mailed one of Verion's letters to Wyatt's account. So far, he'd gotten no response. Time moved on anyway.

The three ships were set to arrive at Charybdis Station in two days, and Leti wasn't afraid to admit he was more nervous than any of the refugees. It would be home to all of them, and Leti didn't have great experience with a home. At least until now. This room had become special to him. It was crowded, but it was his space.

He sat at his desk and glanced over the mess strewn about. Leti looked again at the message from a colleague at his university on Vextonar.

Dr. Ando,

I'm afraid I don't know of anyone who has specialized in Post-Human Diaspora Crellic history or archeology. To my knowledge, the record of their history is simply not there. I have put out some feelers and will update you if I hear anything. You didn't ask, but I've taken the liberty of requesting all of the books covering this topic from our head librarian. As you well know, most materials, even ancient books, were added to our online system hundreds of years ago. Surprisingly, there were four dealing with Crellic history that were not. They look to be written in ancient Crellic which might explain it. They also have many images, which, while not exact, are similar to the image of the artifact you sent. I'll have my TA scan them all, then send them to you. This looks to be a fascinating topic, and I envy you the chance to delve more into it. Good luck!

Dr. Advaith Chopra

Leti looked at the element, innocuously sitting on the corner of his desk. The small pyramid was covered in markings, but Leti was unfamiliar with the language. He knew it was related to Crellic, but it was not the modern version of the language. He had already requested a translation guide for ancient Crellic, but that would take a few weeks to arrive at Charybdis Station, and there was no guarantee it would be accurate. Maybe Dr. Chopra's books would help shed some light on the purpose of the element.

Morrick's notes were also like a foreign language. While most of it made sense, the scientific jargon completely baffled Leti. Morrick focused on analyzing materials found on and within the element. Without the historical context, Leti couldn't understand the significance of the materials or Morrick's theories.

Well, he told himself that he couldn't. Otherwise, they seemed too far-fetched.

Unfortunately, he knew someone who could help. Someone he absolutely despised. Leti sighed and called Lilah to come watch the kids and locked up the element while he waited. He knew what he needed to do.

THE COMMONS WERE CROWDED TODAY. Juniper ran about as usual, happily handing out food and drinks. Pork Chop followed behind him, the pot-bellied pig content to be near his favorite person. It also didn't hurt that stray food often found its way to his mouth. Ms. Speckles, a black and white hen, sat in her nest and people-watched.

Dr. Olivia Franklin sat at a table alone, reading through a stack of papers. A familiar dark gray bag sat on the floor next to her chair. Leti took a deep breath and told himself not to murder the only person who might be able to help him.

He grabbed the stack of papers out of her hand and stuffed them into the bag.

"How dare you," she screeched.

"Those are Morrick's personal letters," Leti said through clenched teeth. "How dare *you* steal them? I know for a fact they were in my quarters last night."

Franklin gave him a cold look. "Why are you in charge of his belongings? Are you a doctor? Are you a scientist? No, you're a fat little whore taking up space on this alien-infested barge."

"I will pretend you didn't say that Dr. Horrible Person," Leti said firmly. "I'm in charge of his stuff because they are his *personal* belongings, and he did not like you." Her eyes narrowed, full of fury. "Why would you need to read his letters anyway?"

"They were proving to be useless," she admitted. "Just rambles to his son. For such a brilliant man, he truly was weak. If only we still had his mind."

Leti made a concentrated effort to ignore her words and focus on what was important. He sat across from her and put his tablet on the table, bringing up the most troubling of Morrick's notes.

"This is from Morrick's notes. He keeps referencing how the artifact reacts to necrosis. Do you have any idea what that might mean? Dead flesh doesn't react, right? I really don't understand all the jargon he uses, and I don't want to believe his conclusions. I hope I'm just misunderstanding."

Franklin scanned the page, swiping the screen to read ahead and then back. "This is absolutely fascinating," she said. "It appears that he did several experiments with the artifact and dead animals."

"That's not disturbing at all," Leti said, nose wrinkling.

"None of this makes sense though. He claims the dead flesh would react to the artifact, appearing to live, but only temporarily," she said. "That can't be possible."

"That seems too strange to be true. Morrick, though, he wasn't the type to lie or exaggerate."

"I don't understand his conclusion here though," she said and pointed to a passage. One of the passages Leti had read several times.

"I believe he's saying that the more intelligent the animal, the longer it stayed animated."

"Hmm," she said. "You're right. Look here at their behavior though. I'll dumb it down for you," she added.

"Gee, thanks."

"He says the animated animal walks around, following the behaviors of its species. Extraordinary." She shook her head, eyes wide and full of wonder. "I've never heard of such a thing. I don't understand the science behind it at all. It looks like Morrick didn't either. It couldn't really be possible, could it?"

Leti shrugged. "I wouldn't think so, but I've read his notes several times, and his tone is so certain. This just seems like an impossible thing. How could that even work? Why would he even be experimenting with that?"

"In the early history of Old-Earth, experiments with dead bodies and electricity were quite common."

"Yeah. I remember reading about experiments on a dead criminal, Matthew Clydesdale, and of course, I've read the novel *Frankenstein* by Mary Shelley. It was from that same Old-Earth time period. Those were just gruesome experiments done as humans learned they could do more than poke things with sticks," Leti said. "Why would Morrick be studying this?"

Franklin read through the passage again. "It all goes back to the artifact. This isn't electricity, this is something else." She shivered, eyes bright with excitement. "Give me the copies of his notes and the artifact. You shouldn't be reading these anyway. I'll keep them safe."

Leti gave her a hard look. "Forget it. You may be smart as hell, but we don't trust you. I'll keep a hold of them until we get to Charybdis Station. I imagine they'll let you have copies of the notes then."

"What good can it do for you to have them?" she said, sneering. "I can discover the artifact's purpose, maybe even use it. You? You can sit on it and keep it warm."

Leti rolled his eyes. "Just stop talking when you don't have anything intelligent to say, okay? Now, one more question," he said. She reluctantly remained quiet, but Leti could tell it hurt her soul to do so. "What do you know about the early Crellic System?"

She frowned. "Just the normal history of the system, what's in the history books. None of that's important anyway. History's just words. Science is what we need to focus on. That's what Morrick was doing."

"The artifact's from that location and time period, the Post-Human Diaspora, Early-Crellic Period," he said, then rolled his eyes. "And of course the history is important. It might tell us the purpose of the artifact. Why is it called an element? What's it do?"

"Well, bad luck then," she said flatly. "As far as I know, there isn't much known about that period."

Leti sighed. "Humans didn't come back when they entered the Crellic System. Other alien species flat out refused to go there," he said. "It wasn't until the Modern Period that the system opened up, and that was because the Crells were all but extinct. Each planet was uninhabitable and desolate, except one."

"Dargner," Franklin said. "Nothing to trade, so of no interest to anyone."

"But it existed, at least before it was destroyed," Leti said. "It had a history, a language, a culture. The rest of the system? Just a mystery."

"This is pointless," Franklin said, standing. "We should focus on the science." She leaned forward, hands on the table. Her sly eyes met his. "Imagine if we could figure out the element. Imagine if we knew how to bring back the dead. Think about that when you go sit and cry in the cryo chamber tonight." She walked off, smirking over her shoulder.

"Gods, I hate that woman," Leti grumbled. He knew there was no bringing back the dead, but he held Morrick's bag tightly to his chest. The doctor had been so kind, so concerned with helping people. He had wanted to reconnect with his son and live life for the first time.

6

*L*eti walked to the cryo chamber. He knew he shouldn't visit Morrick's body so often. It was just a body. He wasn't there. For some reason though, it comforted him.

Today, like many others, Sebastian sat next to Morrick's closed chamber door. Princess Buttercup lay beside him.

"You're not stealing my Princess," Leti said, sitting next to the young man.

Sebastian smiled. "Trust me, no one wants to steal Princess. He still hisses at me most of the time, but I think Lilah kicked him out of your room." The woman did not like poor Princess. She also wasn't a bit intimidated by him or anything else really.

"Aww, it's your nap time, isn't it, baby boy?" Leti scratched Princess's head as he huffed and rumbled, telling Leti all his troubles. "It's okay. You'll get to sleep tonight."

"Leti, can I ask you something?"

"Of course, Seb," he said.

"Do you think Charybdis Station is as good as it sounds? Everyone makes it sound like a place of tolerance and peace, but it's a mercenary station, right?"

"From what I know, it started out *just* a mercenary station," Leti said. "Well, more like a pirate station, honestly. Then, as the planet governments in the system settled into what they are now, it became a neutral territory. When two planets went to war, they negotiated on Charybdis. The station profited from it, of course. They took jobs from anyone and everyone, did the normal mercenary thing. They just made sure to stay out of their system's politics."

"That's what I mean though. What if someone offered them the right amount of money to hand over the element? To just stay out of it. They're mercenaries, right?"

"Nowadays? I don't know. From my talks with the crew, I get the impression they've evolved from your basic mercenary group. They aren't what they started as, but what are they now? I don't know, but I think they're the good guys, Seb. At least, as good as anyone really is. We're both heading there to make it our home, so I really hope they're the good guys."

"You're probably right," Sebastian said. He still looked worried. Tired, withdrawn, and worried.

"What's going on? I know we met not too long ago, but I can tell you're bothered by something. Really bothered," Leti said.

"I'm pregnant," he said bluntly. Sebastian's eyes

widened, and he put his hand over his mouth. "I can't believe I told you," he said, voice muffled.

"Oh wow, Sebastian," Leti said, smiling. "Congratulations!" He paused, smile disappearing. "Should I congratulate or commiserate?"

"I honestly don't know," he said, looking worn and defeated. "I'm three months along."

"The father?"

"Who knows? My old boss had rights to my body. It was in my contract as an indentured servant. He'd sell me every Wednesday night when the bar was slow." Sebastian looked down, cheeks stained red.

"Hey, now," Leti said. "There's nothing to be ashamed of. You didn't have a choice in the matter. Even if you had a choice, it's no one's business. I'm sorry you had to go through that though."

"I never wanted that. I never really wanted anyone sexually before, and then I had to do *that*. It really sucked. Fuck, I don't even know what species the baby's father is. Nettle says he could tell me a lot, but I just don't want to deal with it."

"I can't fathom the pain and trauma of rape, never have been able to. When Draif came into my care, he was so... It was bad. I can't understand what you're going through, even as much as I can empathize, Seb, but Draif and Lilah both know exactly how you feel. Talk to them. Talk to me. You aren't alone, okay? I'd be happy to go to your appointments with Nettle. He's a good guy, but sometimes, it's nice to have even more support."

The young man looked up, wet eyes shining.

"Thanks, Leti. I guess I'm worried about everything now. If I'm pregnant, they aren't going to let me fight, are they?"

"Probably not, but I know Will, and he'll find something for you to do. Something to contribute to cleaning up this mess with the element."

"Good," Sebastian said. "I owe it to Dr. Morrick, and I owe it to my cousin, Nina. I loved her so much, and she never gave up on me. She was paying toward my contract too, you know? It was my parents' debt, but she didn't care. She just wanted to help me."

"She sounds amazing. I wish she was here now," Leti sighed. "I hate having to work with Franklin to understand Morrick's notes."

Sebastian shrugged. "I can try to help. Nina talked about work all the time. I can't guarantee I'll know anything useful, but I'm a hard worker and good with languages. I'll do anything you need."

Leti wrapped his arm around Sebastian. "Good. We can be research buddies and preggo buddies both."

———

LATER THAT NIGHT, Leti sat with Hack and their kids, talking to Hack's young brother, Mo, and Hack's dad, Fasi, through the vid-screen. Rizzie sat in her Daddy Will's lap, as usual, hugging Milo. Pepper rocked in her carrier between Hack and Leti, and Sami sat in Leti's lap.

"Sami is your brother now, Mo," Rizzie said. "Now I haves two brothers and one sister, and you have one brother and two sisters." She loved a chance to show off her new skills with numbers, but she didn't really understand that Mo was Hack's brother, not his son.

"Good job, Rizzie," Mo said. "Sami is pretty cute. So, when will you guys be home?" Mo was excited, eyes shining. He really had come out of his shell in the past few weeks. Leti and Hack spoke with him every night, and Leti had grown attached to the sweet teenager. Even if he was a teenager.

"Two more days, Mo," Hack said.

"Awesome," he said. "I can't wait to meet Princess Buttercup in person. Oh, and you guys too."

Leti laughed, hands full of Sami. He was feeling wiggly tonight. "Oh, we know who's really important here, Mo." The boy smiled, blushing. Leti wanted to hug Mo so badly right then. Damn ship needed to move faster.

"I think we finally came up with a solution for your living space, son," Fasi said. "I called in Pops, and we got a plan. It'll be ready by the time you get here."

"Who's Pops, Grandpa?" Rizzie asked.

"Pops is Beck's daddy," Hack answered for his father. "He's a big ole green Grell like Beck."

"Is he a marshymellow too?" Rizzie giggled and hugged Milo close.

Fasi snorted. "The biggest marshymellow in all the galaxy, baby girl."

"He really is a nice guy," Mo agreed. "He lets me follow him around after school. He's like the best engineer in the galaxy. I can't wait for you to see the station, Leti. You won't believe it's possible. It's not like a giant ship or anything. That's what I was expecting at first, but there's whole neighborhoods, gardens, parks, and the market. They even have, like, a night time and day time. Somehow, the engineers keep it all running. You're going to love it."

Mo's rabbit, Abbot, sat in his lap, eyeing Princess through the screen. For some reason, the plump jackrabbit didn't look like he trusted the dragon. Imagine that. Pax sat on the bed above the couch, watching the rabbit, tail swaying back and forth. Yeah, Princess wasn't the danger here. That would be fun to deal with.

"Oh yeah, before I forget. Fasi, can you make sure there's space for Sebastian too?" Leti smiled sheepishly. His mate's poor father kept having to extend their living space for their growing family.

Fasi just sighed and went with it. Leti might have only known him a month, but the man could make anything happen. He had the sneaking suspicion that he adored his future father-in-law.

"Does he need to be in with you, or can he be in his own space near you?" Fasi asked. Yep. He adored the wonderful man.

"Near us is fine. He's pregnant too, so we're going to be preggo research buddies. He's nervous about being in a new place though, so I want him near me if possible." Maybe Leti wanted Sebastian near him because Leti was nervous too. Maybe. Leti chose not to think too hard on that.

"Fu… fudge," Hack said, looking at the kids. "Sebastian's pregnant?"

Fasi just shrugged. "What's one more baby? Our station's overrun with families already, and you spoke pretty highly of him, son."

"Yeah. He's a good guy." Hack shook his head and grinned. "So, Mo, how's school going?"

"Pretty great actually. I didn't know what to do at first."

"Yeah. Burnished Outpost doesn't really do education that way," Hack said.

"Definitely," Mo agreed. "There's a group, though, that took me in. Makes sure I don't act too weird."

"You're not weird," Leti said firmly. "You act just like yourself, and if someone doesn't like it, Princess can eat them."

Mo laughed. "Thanks."

Leti leaned back in Hack's arms, happy to watch his family, and the visit sped by too fast.

"Time for bed, boyo," Hack's mom's voice came from outside the view of the vid-screen.

Mo made a face but stood. "Love you guys. See you in a few days."

"Night, Mo," Leti said.

After bath time, Leti tucked Sami and Rizzie in while Hack changed Pepper's diaper one more time. He kissed Rizzie's brow, the little girl already asleep. Sami was almost there. He yawned wide, treating Leti to a look at his baby fangs. He clutched his teething ring and looked for Pax. The large cat curled up with Gravy, between the kids' bed and Pepper's bassinet. Satisfied, Sami fell asleep, curled into his sister's arm.

Arms wrapped around Leti, pulling him away from the kids. "I missed you today."

Leti smiled gently, turning in his mate's arms. "You saw me this morning, at lunch, and spent all evening with us. How'd you have time to miss me?" Leti didn't mention he missed Hack too. They didn't get a lot of alone time anymore.

Hack just shrugged and pulled him to the bed. "I don't need a reason. If I could have you at my side every second of every day, I would." He eyed Princess, already comfortable and sleeping on his side of the bed. "I really need to talk to Dad about a bigger bed. I never thought I'd need to fit three in my bed after I mated."

Leti settled between Princess and Hack. "I refuse to acknowledge the *after I mated* part of that statement." He poked Hack's arm. "I don't like to think of the women who had you before."

"They never had me," Hack said, wrapping Leti in his arms. "You, Leti, have all of me. Every sorry bit. I should pity you, but I'm too selfish."

Leti kissed his mate's lips, lingering at his taste. "I'm not stupid," Leti said. "I know the value of what I've been given. You, my love, are stuck with me. For better or worse."

*H*ack held his little monster on his hip and watched Leti across the med-bay where he sat next to Alois's bed, reading his tablet, completely focused on Dr. Morrick's notes. His nose scrunched up adorably, and he kept muttering to himself. Sebastian sat beside him, a book in his hand, and looked just as focused. The two men were determined to figure out the history of the artifact.

Leti didn't have any scientific training, but Hack had complete faith in him. He knew his mate was intelligent, but he hadn't realized how focused and obsessed he could be when he started a project. Hack shouldn't find it so hot, but it was. His little history nerd was so very fuckable.

"Come on, baby monster," Hack said, bouncing his son. Sami grinned, little fangs gleaming. He shook his teething ring at Hack and giggled. Sami and Gravy would be his sidekicks today. The ships were about a day and a half away from the station. So far, there had been no trouble, but Hack still insisted they stay camouflaged using Beck's shielding prototype. They might be in the Anchor's Rest System, but he wouldn't let his guard down.

Gravy trotted behind him, tongue hanging out, as Hack walked onto the bridge. He passed Finn and Dannol, the pilot, pausing when he realized they were arguing.

"Why would you possibly want to do that?" Finn seemed genuinely puzzled. "You're single and away from home for months on end. Why would you adopt a kid right now? There are plenty of families back at the station or on one of the planets that would be happy to take her."

"Yeah, but I love her," Dannol said. "The captain's probably going to change our routes anyway, so he can be home more with his family. Why can't I have my own family?"

"You're adopting, Dannol?" Hack did plan on changing routes but wanted to okay it with his father before announcing it to the crew.

Dannol looked over his shoulder, smile wide and bright. The little Havenite was always in a good mood. "Yep! I talked to the admiral yesterday, and he approved it. I've become attached to one of the refugees. She's a Wello hybrid, eight years old, and a complete angel. Well, as angelic as an eight-year-old can be anyway."

"That's awesome, Dannol," Hack congratulated. "You'll make a great dad."

"Incoming call from the Green and Yellow Solaces, boss man," Finn said, the light moment gone.

"Hack, we have a problem." Cas's face popped up on the vid-screen. He wore his stern captain face, contrasting with the gold beads in his long hair. "Four large Concord battle cruisers are approaching. They've definitely seen us. Their weapons are out."

"Our priority is to get that artifact to the station," Audre said. The severe woman was in her element, and Hack knew she was a second away from suggesting Hack run while she and Cas stayed behind.

"Shit," Hack said. "Finn, announce it. Dannol, can we outrun them?" He sat, holding Sami in his lap. Gravy sat on his haunches next to the captain's chair. Four battle cruisers against three overloaded, smaller ships weren't good odds.

"No," Dannol said. He ran calculations on his screen. "Our ships are smaller, but their cruisers' weapons have a damn long reach."

"We won't survive a battle though, so it's our only hope," Hack said.

"Cas and I can…"

"Let's run then," Hack said, interrupting Audre. "Charybdis Mercenaries don't leave friends behind, Audre. Forget it. Dannol will lead the flight. You two have your pilots mirror Dannol's movements."

"Got it," Cas said.

"Very well," Audre said, a small smile creeping across her face.

"Beck." Hack called his engineer as Dru and Selene joined him on the bridge, taking their seats.

"Captain?"

"We have four large battle cruisers on our tail. You said you've made more of those net things from that mission last year?"

"We have two, but they're not large. We can probably disable two ships, but the other two… I don't think so."

"Okay, let's do this. Load them up," Hack said. He looked back to Cas and Audre. "We have two nets that can trap and disable two of the ships. The other two will need to be taken out," Hack told them, bouncing Sami on his knee.

"Nets? What's this? Are we fishing?" Cas's sarcasm was strong today.

"They're one of Beck's side projects. We've used them before. They're like little energy nets. You shoot it out, it hits the ship, grows and wraps around it, sending an energy surge through their system. They're dead in the water. If they have back-up systems, their life support stays on."

"Damn, man. And you didn't think to share that?" Cas asked.

"They aren't easy to make, so it didn't seem practical to do them large scale. Now, we're a little busy here, bro," Hack said. "Whine later. When the first ship approaches, Dannol will drop behind you two and shoot a net. Hopefully, the same tactic works for the second."

"What happens if it doesn't hit?" Audre asked.

"It spreads out, like a large sheet. Anything runs into it is affected, including one of us, so be careful."

"Okay." She nodded, determined. "The last two ships?"

"Three of us to two of them. We need to disable them instead of destroying them, if possible."

"Got it."

The ships lined up, the Blue Solace at the front like an arrow. The pilots went all out, moving as fast as possible. Within the hour, the cruisers reached firing range. They fired, aiming straight for Hack's ship.

"They're firing disabling shots, Captain," Selene said. "They shouldn't be able to target us with our shield up. This doesn't make sense."

Dannol and the other pilots dodged shot after shot until the first cruiser reached range. Like Hack planned, the Blue Solace dipped behind the other two and fired the net. It hit spot on, wrapping around the ship and frying its system.

"Damn, that's fucking awesome," Cas said.

"Still need to hit the second ship," Hack said. Gravy woofed softly in agreement.

The three remaining ships zipped around the stranded one and closed in. They flew side to side, not making easy targets.

"Silly cruisers," Dannol said. "Auto target is a thing." He flew out from the other two ships, then sped up to dip between two of the cruisers. He shot the second net, taking another one down.

Cas and Audre's ships pinned the third ship, firing neutralizing missiles from two sides, disabling it. Unfortunately, the last ship proved more difficult. It managed to get a few shots off, missiles aiming to kill, not disable now. The Yellow Solace was hit, shields down, but not broken. The Green Solace flew in front of Audre's ship, shields at full power.

Hack prepared to fire at the ship before it hit Cas, but before he could give an order, a small, dark ship appeared next to the last cruiser. It wasn't a model Hack recognized, and it was tiny, a single passenger ship.

The way it appeared, though, was frightening. It was too sudden. One minute, it wasn't there, and the next, a shield *melted* from around it, and it was perfectly visible. It zipped around the last cruiser, firing shot after shot and the ship was disabled, floating dead in space. As suddenly as it appeared, the mystery ship disappeared, shield wrapping around it again.

"Beck's going to be so pissed," Finn said. "He wanted to invent invisibility shields."

"Did you guys see that too?" Audre asked. "A single passenger ship just took out a battle cruiser."

"Oh yeah," Hack said, whistling low. "Let's focus. Now we have four ships to board and subdue. They likely have prisoners, so we need to get them out fast. We'll divvy them up between us all."

"Then blow their ships the fuck up," Cas said.

"Fuck!" Sami clapped his hands and laughed.

"Oops," Cas said. "To be fair, you're the only one I know who brings his son to a space battle."

"Yeah, well, watch your mouth," Hack said, blushing. "Selene, you gather everyone up. Cas, Audre, we'll do this one at a time. We need to hurry, but you know they're full of mercs."

"Yes," Audre said. "We don't want any more casualties if possible."

Hack carried Sami to their quarters. Leti met him at the door, beautiful face full of worry. Rizzie and Pepper were taking a nap, unaware of what was happening. Maia and Silas were, of course, with Leti, watching the battle out the window.

"Sorry, baby. I didn't have time to bring him back before we were in the thick of things. You hear Finn's updates?"

"Yeah," he said. "I'm worried about that mystery ship. What if it's still here or comes back?"

"We'll leave the ship guarded, but we need to hurry before more Concords come. Finn said none of the ships got a distress call off, but you never know."

"I understand," Leti said. "I need to stay with the kids. Lilah's giving birth. Finally. Bad timing, but it's happening. Princess is here with me. Maia's going to direct the refugees you bring back, and Silas will help guard the ship. Be careful and stay focused. Draif and Cordy will both keep me updated."

Hack kissed his mate deeply, then forced himself to step away. He dropped kisses on each kid's head and left. Gravy and Pax followed him. He stopped, turned around. "Guys, you can't come with. Go back and protect the kids." He tried to push the two back toward the rooms. They didn't budge. "Damn it."

Dru ran past, Monty perched on her head. "Come on, Hack," she said. "We got asses to kick."

The older refugee children herded the rest of the children on the ship the opposite way, toward Leti.

Hack knew his mate would keep them calm and protect them if needed. Gods, he was so lucky to have Leti. He wished he could stay and help him, but he was the fucking captain.

"Damn it," he repeated and followed Dru, Gravy and Pax alongside him.

8

The shuttle flew them to the first disabled ship. The Yellow Solace crew was already there, forcing their way into the docking door.

"Blast it," Audre ordered, and one of her men blew the door in with a pulse cannon. The Concord mercenaries behind it were blown back, dead in an instant.

Hack and his crew pushed through, stepping through debris. Turning the corner, they were instantly met with more Concords. Audre and her lieutenant led them, shooting their way through the first wave, personal shields holding well.

"Audre, take the right passage," Hack said. "Cas, take the left. That should head toward the prison cells. We'll take the bridge."

"Oh, and Cas?" Audre paused, looking over her shoulder. "I love your hair beads."

Cas scowled. "Leti gave them to me."

"Leti is currently wearing a sweater with sheep pirates on it," Hack said. He patted Cas on the shoulder.

"I mean it," Audre said, frowning. "They look good." She sighed when they both looked skeptical. "Men can be so stupid."

The three groups separated, and Hack led his forward, slowly and quietly clearing out each room as they went. Most of the rooms were empty, but a few had groups of two or three. Walking into one, a man screamed, rushing Hack. Pax leapt forward, digging his teeth into the man's throat. Draif shot the second one, and the room was clear.

"Why did we even come?" Morgan asked. "I haven't gotten to shoot anyone."

"Oh, poor baby," Cordelia said, pushing into the next room. Empty.

Finally reaching the bridge, they found the reinforced door welded shut, and Hack knew not a one of them brought a pulse cannon. "On it, Captain," Beck said, pulling out a torch.

"You brought a torch?" Draif's voice was dry, and he watched Beck in amusement.

"Of course," Beck said. "Why wouldn't I?"

In minutes, he had the door open and the battle began. The bridge was flooded with Concords. Apparently, most had decided to hole up here, waiting for power to return.

Selene didn't hesitate, running into the room, dodging fire. She tossed miniature grenades into groups, blasting mercenaries and equipment both.

Morgan and Draif followed her as Dru and Cordelia started working the other side of the room.

Beck dodged shots and settled behind a large chair and pulled out a tiny pyramid-shaped object. He fastened it to his hand and shot it toward a group in the corner. Bright bolts of electricity—it looked like fucking lightning—burst from the object, frying the mercenaries Beck aimed for. Damn, Hack loved his engineer.

Hack called his fire, pushing a large wave of molten heat toward a large group, hidden behind consoles. The metal melted, and the fire hit the mercenaries. Their screams filled the room.

Meanwhile, Pax darted through the room, biting down on legs and jumping toward throats. Cornered by three men, Cordelia planted her foot in one man's gut and pushed him toward the hunting cat. Pax was on him in an instant and the man was dead. She quickly took out the remaining two with her vibro-sword.

Gravy stayed at Hack's back, barking loudly in warning when an enemy approached from behind and tearing into their calves when they got too close. Soon enough, some of Audre's crew joined them, and the bridge was secured. The Concord captain knelt at Hack and Audre's feet.

"Cas has the prisoners secured," Finn said. "He loaded them into his ship since it was the closest."

"Finn, Morgan, take the captain here back to the ship and lock him up. We'll question him later," Hack said.

The three crews moved on to the next ship, then the next. The Concords fought hard, but against the three crews, they didn't stand much chance. The third captain was already dead when they reached him. Poison.

The fourth ship was the hardest. It had the most mercenaries onboard, and they were spread out, ready to ambush the Charybdis mercenaries. The three groups had lightened in numbers too as the wounded returned to their ships. Three of the refugees from Hack's ship stepped in, replacing Dru, Finn, and Ava, and, finally, the Concord ship's crew fell. The captain of the last ship was also already dead by poison.

"That's so weird," Cordelia said. "The Concords aren't known for their loyalty. Why would they kill themselves rather than be taken prisoner?"

"Maybe they're more afraid of their boss than us," Draif said, flipping the dead captain over. All of the Concords were human, and this one was no exception. "Hmm, look at this tattoo. The other dead captain had it too. Right here on the back of their hands."

"Did the two we took alive have that? I haven't seen it on anyone else," Beck said.

"I didn't see it on the one I took back to the ship," Cordelia said.

"Me neither," Morgan said.

Hack took a picture of the tattoo and sent it to Leti. "Come on, let's get these ships blasted." Pax and Gravy followed him and the others back to the shuttle. They arrived back on the Blue Solace to complete chaos. The additional passengers crowded the cargo bay and the hallways, and many of those passengers were in dire need of medical aid. Hack didn't remember the other rescued groups being quite this bad.

Maia, Silas, and Sebastian sorted people, helping them to the med-bay or sending them toward the commons if their injuries could wait. Hack had to admit that the new permanent additions to his crew sure came in handy at times like these. Hack strode past, trying to stay out of the way.

Nettle ran around the med-bay, Juniper and two of the older children assisting him as best they could. Cordelia and Morgan dived in, organizing the crowds.

"I'm going to the commons," Beck said. "I'll get it ready for the newly rescued folks."

Hack found Dru sitting in a chair next to Lucas's bed with her leg in a cast seal. "The fucker ripped my favorite pants," she muttered. She was pale and clearly in pain but managing. Ava was in a similar way with a shot to her arm and a slash on her abdomen. She hurt but was stable.

Finn sat on the edge of Lucas's bed, bandage over his forehead. The tip of one ear was missing. "How can you not be injured," he asked Hack. "You always get injured."

Hack grinned. "Don't jinx it. Your ear going to be okay?"

"Yeah," Finn said, wincing. "Nettle's going to sew the tip back on when he gets time. This is so embarrassing."

"Come on, remember when Morgan took a shot in the ass? Now *that* was embarrassing," Lucas said.

"Lucas," Morgan said from behind Hack. "No one is supposed to ever mention that again, remember?" He growled at the men as he helped an elderly Wello man sit down.

Finn laughed. "Okay, I feel better now. Damn it, Lilah, what are you doing up?"

Lilah held a newborn in her arms, wrapped in a soft green blanket, one of Leti's if Hack wasn't mistaken. She walked slowly around the med-bay, helping people get settled.

"Lilah," Hack said. "You literally just had a baby. Sit down and let Nettle and his sidekicks deal with this."

She gave him a frustrated look. "Nettle said the same thing, but I'm fine."

"Please, Lilah," Ava said weakly. "Come sit with me, so we don't worry about you."

"Very well," Lilah said, huffing and taking a seat. Ava winked at him. Hack grinned. Gods, he loved his crew.

"Permission to blast some ships, Captain?" Dannol's voice was cheery and light through the comm.

"Permission granted. Enjoy the view." Hack wished he was near a window, but he had things to do. "Come on, Dru and Ava," Hack said. "Let's get you two to your quarters, so you're out of the way. Can you help, Lilah?"

"Please," Ava said. "Then you could stay with me tonight as I heal."

"Fine," Lilah said, grumbling. "You probably shouldn't be left alone."

Hack left them in their rooms, heading toward the

cells. Selene and Draif were already there. Selene was keeping each man separate. Hack nodded to her. "I'll take one; you and Draif take the other. Ask about who they're working for and mention that the other two captains killed themselves." They set recorders to pick up the interrogations and split up.

Hack entered the prisoner's cell and stood in front of the seated man. Pax sat on one side of Hack and Gravy on the other. The captain from the first ship they'd boarded looked tired and pissed.

"What the fuck do you want?" the man asked. "The Concords will pay my ransom, man. Just tell them it's Captain Barron."

"Ransom? Who said we're going to ransom you?" Hack crossed his arms and let his fire seep through his eyes, knowing they'd glow a hot white. Gravy growled, low and menacing, while Pax stalked closer to the man, licking his lips. Barron shrunk back.

"Why not? That's normal protocol."

"You attacked my ship, you piece of shit," Hack said, growling. His tattoos turned gold, glowing with his fire. "Why wouldn't I just kill you the fuck now? Give me a reason."

"It was just a job," Barron said, stuttering. "The higher ups took a big contract. All of the Concords are after you. We were to disable your ship, board it, and take back some stolen item."

"Stolen?"

"Yeah. They said you stole some item from an important person. That person's paying to get it back."

"Who's this important person?"

"Don't know, man. I'm just one captain. You want to know more details, ask Captains Teshain or Morral. They're all buddy-buddy with Admiral Sharp."

"Teshain and Morral are dead," Hack said. "They killed themselves."

Barron's eyes widened, and he paled. "Why would they do that? You get caught by another mercenary, you're ransomed. That's just what happens."

Hack shrugged. "You tell me. Why would they be so afraid of failing or being questioned that they kill themselves?"

Barron shook his head, amazed and baffled. "We just got orders. Get back a stolen object. I don't understand."

Hack pulled the picture of the tattoo up on his communicator, the odd image projected from the small device. "Do you recognize these?"

Barron pushed back against the wall, face slack with horror. "They had them? Teshain and Morral had them?"

"Yeah. What are they?"

"A few months ago, the admiral makes this new friend. I don't know who it is, never saw them, but I heard things," Barron said. "Mercs that make the admiral unhappy start disappearing. Supposedly, they go visit the admiral's friend. That's what they say anyway. Never been so happy to *not* be in the inner circle, you know? Anyway, word is, they disappear for a while, then come back with those tats. But they don't really come back, you know what I mean?"

"No. Explain."

"When they come back, they're different, silent and empty. It's not them no more. They still do their job, but they're just shells. Get it?"

"I think so," Hack said, brow furrowed. "You didn't notice Teshain and Morral acting like this?"

"Didn't really talk to them about more than the strategy for our attack. Thinking back, I can see it. Teshain always had a sense of humor, you know? He'd crack a joke, make a sarcastic remark. Barely spoke this time."

"So, you know nothing about the Concords' client?"

"No," Barron said, shaking his head. "You going to ransom me?"

"I'll let our admiral decide," Hack said. "We've taken a dislike to your treatment of your non-human prisoners. Admiral Juren wants to have a little chat with you."

Hack smiled as he left, Barron's protests echoing through the room. Pax snarled at the man, gliding out behind Hack and Gravy.

Draif and Selene entered the conference room right after him. "How'd it go?"

"Idiot didn't know much," Draif said, disgusted. "How can you not care who you're working for?"

"They care about the money," Selene said. "That makes it easier to look the other way."

"He did about piss himself when he saw the tattoos though," Draif said. "He spun some story about a spooky man turning people into mindless servants."

"Mine too," Hack said.

"He did mention something interesting," Selene

said. "Captain Dorcan said that Morral was in contact with someone on the ship. That person plugged them into our location through the camouflage shields."

"Beck," Hack called the Grell.

"Captain?"

"Check our systems and the ship for a signal. Someone was able to connect us to one of the Concords' ships, giving our location away."

"On it," Beck said, then called back seconds later. "Okay, found a bug. Looks like it's in the restroom back toward the cargo bay. Everyone uses it daily. I'll get rid of it and keep a scan going from now on."

"Now, who do you think might be interested in working with the Concords?" Draif asked, his voice a slow drawl. "Maybe someone who's pissed about Leti guarding the element?"

"Dr. Franklin's my first thought too. Keep eyes on her, Selene. Don't tip her off yet that we know anything. Plus, keep in mind that Franklin's not the only new addition on board."

"Do you really think one of the refugees might want to help the Concords?" Draif sounded doubtful.

"No," Hack said. "I think it's Franklin, but I learned a long time ago not to assume shit."

After sending his drooping crew to bed, Hack finally gave in and returned to his quarters with Pax and Gravy. The lights were dimmed, and Leti had just finished tucking Rizzie and Sami into bed. Children lay in little nests all over the room, sleeping or playing quietly. A few slept on the couch, and their bed was completely covered with little bodies. Princess slept in the middle of them all.

Leti looked up from their kids and smiled in relief when he saw the three of them come in. Picking his way across the room, Hack looked over Leti's shoulder. Their little Siren curled around her brother, holding him close from behind. Sami's fist was stuffed in his mouth, and he snored softly.

"They are too cute," he whispered.

Leti turned around, tucking himself against Hack. "I'm glad everyone's okay. I talked to Draif a few minutes ago. He listed out the wounded. Said we have fifty-two more passengers."

"Yes, sorry I didn't update you too."

"You were busy, doofus," he said, hugging Hack tightly. "It's okay. I listened in on the communicator and bugged Draif and Cordy once you guys got back on board."

"Lilah had her baby," Hack said. "Did you know?"

"Yeah, she sent a picture. Oh, that reminds me. That picture you sent me is related to the artifact," Leti said. He pulled a book off his desk and flipped to a page. Holding it up to Hack, he pointed to an image. It was identical to the tattoo the men had. "I have no idea what it means though. It's in ancient Crellic, so I can't read it. I've ordered a language guide that'll be at the station soon. I'll let you know what we discover."

"Thanks, baby," Hack said. He could feel exhaustion pulling at him, but he took a minute to fill Leti in on what the prisoners said. "Weird, right? I'm going to shower, then sleep, okay?"

Leti kissed his cheek. "You got it, Will. Love you."

"Love you too," he said. When he left the bathroom, Leti had a nest ready for him near the door. Gravy and Pax lay on either side of it. The quiet of the room soaked into him, and he happily collapsed in his nest, pulling Leti with him. He didn't even care that Princess crawled over too, settling his scaled head on Hack's pillow.

He did care when he felt Leti get up a few moments later, but he knew his mate. Leti wouldn't rest while there were those that needed help on the ship. Hack knew this would be the pattern of their life. Leti would protect their family while Hack was gone, and Hack would take over when he returned. He would fight the battles, and Leti would deal with the fallout. Hack thought that maybe Leti had the harder job.

9

"I don't want to die," the young man whispered, voice full of pain. Leti held his hand as Nettle worked on putting him back together. He was missing his legs from the knees down and had been stabbed in the stomach multiple times by the time he was rescued.

"It's going to be okay," Leti said. "Just focus on me, alright? We're going to get you better."

The young man's blue eyes slowly drained of life, tension leaving his body slack. "Fuck, fuck, fuck," Nettle said. He tried to resuscitate him, but it was too late. "Oh, Leti," Nettle said.

"Doctor, we need help over here," Julia said. She was thirteen and a complete rock. She helped in the med-bay when needed, and Leti had seen her jump straight in, fighting to save lives. Leti looked at the young man. They hadn't saved this life. Nettle kissed Leti's forehead and hurried to the next patient.

Leti still held the man's hand, looking into his

empty eyes. He could see Morrick that day on the battlefield, plain brown eyes staring at the sky, empty of life. Empty of awareness.

"Leti, can you help me?" Maia asked. She carried a Dedril woman into the room.

Leti gently set the man's hand on the table and moved to the next of the Concords' prisoners. The woman didn't have many noticeable wounds, but she was unresponsive. She breathed in tiny gasps, but her eyes were already dead. Leti helped Maia put her on a bed.

Nettle rushed over and quickly scanned her. After reading his screen, he closed his eyes, face twisted in sorrow. "She was pregnant. The child's dead inside her, and she has so much internal damage I don't know where to start." Nettle tried, but a second later, she was gone, her last breath one of relief. Nettle gently closed her eyes and moved on to the next.

Maia sobbed, trying to hold back her tears. Leti wrapped her in his arms. "Those fucking bastards," she said. "The things they did to us. I don't blame her for not wanting to live." She clutched him close, then took a deep breath, pushing out of his arms. "Come on, Leti. We have people to help."

The next morning, Leti and Sebastian sat beside Alois's bed in the med-bay. The new group of rescued Concord prisoners were finally settled in, but it had been a long night. Altogether, the three ships lost five of the prisoners. Leti's face was red from crying and his heart broken. A pair of blue eyes haunted him, and he didn't even know the man's name.

"We did what we could, Leti," Sebastian said. The young man stroked Alois's hair, seemingly unaware of his actions. Leti noticed Sebastian did that a lot. He'd hold Alois's hand and then startle when he noticed, yanking away. It was odd.

"I know," Leti said, voice hoarse. "It's just hard to lose anyone, especially after they're finally safe." That man deserved to live. He could have a family out there somewhere, wondering where he was, a mate or children, even just friends.

Nettle rushed over, running his scanner over Alois's still form. "What's going on?" Leti asked, sitting up. Sebastian yanked his hand from Alois's head.

Nettle frowned at the scanner, then looked at Sebastian thoughtfully. "Can you put your hand on his head again?"

"Oh, okay," Sebastian said, shrugging. He gently stroked Alois's head again, and Nettle smiled at his scanner. "Keep touching him. The fucker is finally waking up. Gods, we need something good right now, and your touch makes him react."

"Seriously?" Leti jumped up, thinking quickly. "Should Sebastian kiss him?"

"Eww," Sebastian said. "Why would you ask that? I'm not kissing an unconscious guy. That's wrong on so many different levels. Think of consent, man."

Alois's eyes fluttered open, and he looked around him. "What's going on?" he asked, voice rough from disuse.

"Well, Sleeping Beauty," Nettle said, "you're finally

waking up from a month-long coma, and about time, ass-face. We were really worried."

"What?" Alois's eyes were unfocused, and he was clearly still out of it. He grabbed Sebastian's hand, holding it tightly in his own.

Nettle focused on his scanner. "Things look real good, Alois. You were out longer than I thought you'd be, but your body is completely healed, so there's that."

"Out? What happened?" He looked at Sebastian, still clutching his hand. "Who are you?"

Leti wiped the tears from his face and summed up events for Alois.

His friend's eyes started to droop. "I can't believe I missed Yusef the Terrible's debut. You'll stay here, right Sebastian?" Alois's eyes closed and his breaths evened out.

"Uh, what do I do?" Sebastian stood there, holding Alois's hand, puzzled.

Leti smiled softly, pushing a chair closer to the bed. "Have a seat and hold his hand."

"You know," Nettle said. "The Dedril find their mates through a kiss. Next time he's awake, maybe you *should* give him a kiss. See if something happens."

Sebastian looked horrified. "I'm a former Wednesday night whore, three months pregnant, father unknown, and completely penniless. There is no way I'm anyone's mate. Not right now." His eyes grew sad when he looked over to Alois's sleeping face. "Maybe when I get back on my feet. Maybe…"

Nettle snorted. "Like Alois would care about any of that."

Leti understood where Seb was coming from, but Alois really wouldn't care about any of it. He wanted his mate. Sebastian needed time though. He patted Sebastian's shoulder. "You don't mind sitting with him, do you?"

"Of course not," Sebastian replied. "I'll sit here and read over Dr. Morrick's notes. We'll arrive at the station sometime today, right? You and I can meet up again after settling in and talk about the artifact. I have a few ideas I want to run past you."

"That works, Seb. Thanks," Leti said. He bent and kissed Alois's forehead and waved goodbye to Nettle and Sebastian. On the way out, he checked over Nettle's patients. Lucas was the only crew member still there.

He leaned against a mound of pillows, sleepy but awake. Marmalade snoozed on his lap. "Hey, Lucas," Leti said, standing near his bed. "Alois finally woke up."

Lucas grinned. "Finally. I was getting worried, even though Nettle kept saying he was fine."

"Me too," Leti agreed. "So, we'll arrive at the station today. I've talked with Hack's dad about having some space for you to stay with me and Hack while you recover. Do you mind? I didn't really think to ask before I did it, but he said there would be a space for you and Draif right next door to us. Would that work?"

Lucas leaned back, pleased. "Draif and me living together? Definitely okay."

"Um, Lucas, you know Draif is demisexual, right?"

"Yeah, we've talked a lot since you guys got here." He shrugged. "I'm patient."

"You know that he's perfect in every way, and I love him more than anything, right?"

"Um, yeah," Lucas said. "Does Hack know that?"

"You know that Princess Buttercup could eat you, right? Or set you on fire or simply crush you into little pieces, right?"

"Yes, Leti, I know Princess Buttercup is a badass," Lucas said solemnly. "I know you love him, but honestly, I'm close to it too."

"Do Cardinals and Betonize have mates?"

"Yes, we do, even hybrids like me, and Draif's mine. I knew from the moment I scented him."

"Okay," Leti said, thinking. "Is it going to be hard for you? Waiting for him?"

Lucas shrugged. "Honestly, it won't. Part of me wants to mate him now, this very instant, but a larger part of me knows this is the best way. Not a lot of mates take their time and fall in love before they mate. I'm lucky to get that. I'm lucky to get him."

"I'm glad you understand," Leti said. "You should also know that I've been practicing with my phaser. Selene says I'm really good now." Okay, so she said he was as good as the average child, but the word *good* was mentioned.

"Well, at least if you do decide to shoot me, I can't run away right now, right?"

Leti groaned, frustrated. "Can't you just act afraid of me for a minute? I'm threatening your life here."

"Oh, okay. Let's try it," Lucas said, sitting up straight. "Oh gods, please Leti, please don't hurt me! I'll be good, I promise." He cringed and pulled away from Leti, waving his hands in fear.

"Wow, that sounds kind of kinky," Morgan said, falling into the seat next to Lucas's bed. "Captain won't like you playing S and M games with his mate, Lucas. You want to lose your other leg?"

"Fine," Leti said, throwing his hands up. "I'm done with you." He stalked out of the med-bay and headed to the commons. He needed some food.

10

In the commons, the new refugees sat at tables and in armchairs, talking and eating. Pork Chop snored in his bed in the corner, near the kitchen entrance, while Miss Speckles looked content with her life, walking around, pecking at corn on the ground in front of the plant she'd made her nest in.

"I thought she needed some exercise," Juniper said when he noticed Leti's puzzled look. "So I made her work for her corn today. She seems happy."

Leti laughed. "You're right. If she had her way, she'd sit and be pampered all day. Lazy chicken."

Juniper set a steaming cup of hot tea in front of him. "I'm about to start on breakfast. Any cravings today? I have some of your squirrel chocolates left over from yesterday."

"Yum, of course I want those. Maybe some waffles too? With fruit and whipped cream? Do we have any ham?" He looked at Pork Chop, guilt settling in. "Why do pigs taste so good?"

Juniper laughed loudly, startling Pork Chop awake. "He doesn't know he's a pig, Leti. Don't worry."

Leti smiled and sipped his tea. "Thanks, Juniper. I'm really going to miss your cooking when we get to the station. I can't cook anything, and I don't think Hack's going to have time."

"Oh, don't worry about that," Juniper said. "Between me and Beck's Ma, we keep the crew fed back home too. Hell, with you and Sebastian both pregnant, you should be prepared to be stuffed with food at all times. Ma has a serious need to feed her loved ones."

"I will force myself to accept yummy food. For your sake, Juniper, for your sake. Oh, by the way, do you have the cupcakes ready for Rizzie's wedding this morning?"

"Yes, I do. Chocolate and raspberry, her favorite."

"Thanks," Leti said. "Ava dropped off a pretty dress she pulled together somehow, and Beck made a bunch of metal flowers."

"So, what kind of flowers will you have at your wedding?" Juniper asked, all innocence.

"Well, maybe when Hack gets around to asking me, you'll find out, hmm?" After last night, Leti's mind was made up. Anything could happen at any time. That blue-eyed man had been safe. He had been rescued. It didn't matter. Not in the end. Leti was ready to trust Hack, trust the love they shared. He didn't want to wait anymore.

"Maybe I'll ask him instead," Leti mused.

"Do it! Also, record his face when you do. For me?"

Juniper laughed as he left for the kitchen. Breakfast wouldn't cook itself.

* * *

"Do you, Milo the stuffed wolf, take Rizzie as your unlawfully wedded wife?" Hack asked Milo. He stood at the front of the crowd with little Pepper strapped to his chest while she slept.

Morgan stood beside the stuffed animal and whispered out of the side of his mouth. "I do." Rizzie giggled, looking adorable in her white, ruffled dress. She held an elaborate bouquet of gold metal flowers. Leti had to admit he was a little jealous.

"Now, I pronounce you: husband and wife," Hack finished, expression serious and official.

The crew of the Blue Solace clapped while the other refugee children cheered. Rizzie hugged Milo tightly. They needed this moment. The new refugees watched with wonder as the crew pandered to the little girl. The other refugee children knew their time was coming. They knew family awaited them. They all needed a little joy right now.

"Now, if I can have everyone's attention," Leti said, Sami perched on his hip. "Behind you, we have some refreshments to celebrate the union of Rizzie and Milo. Please, help yourselves. Juniper and Cordelia will be around with beverages. Thank you for joining us today."

The crowd surged toward the tableful of cupcakes, fruit, veggie trays, and little sandwiches. Leti should have known Juniper would go all out. Rizzie ran around the room, laughing and playing with the other children. Ava had created a bunch of pretty dresses and dress shirts for the other children too, so they wouldn't feel left out. She even had some things for the new children. How she and Juniper had done all of this in such a short amount of time, Leti truly didn't know.

"So, how does it feel to see our little girl married?" Hack hugged Leti to him, careful not to squash Pepper or Sami.

Leti snorted. "Ha," he said. "Hack, I have to ask you something, something important."

"Do you want to step into the hallway?"

"It might be better." The two stepped out of the commons, the hallway much quieter.

"What's wrong, baby? I know last night was rough. I'm sorry I wasn't there for you."

"Don't be stupid. You were exhausted and needed to rest." Leti took Hack's big hand in his, tracing the markings on his hand. The markings covered his mate, head to toe, begging for Leti's tongue to trace them. Yum. "I know we're mated and that's forever in our eyes, but I'd like to get married too. What do you think?"

The worry on Hack's face disappeared, changing into joy. "Really? You'll take my name and everything?"

"Yes, Will. I'd be honored to take your name," Leti said, smiling.

"Oh, Leti, you have no idea how happy you make me," he said. "Let's go tell everyone!"

"Contain your joy. We can't tell anyone yet. We

shouldn't mess up Rizzie's big day. We'll talk about it with everyone tomorrow, alright? Besides, we're almost to the station. Shouldn't you tell your dad first?"

"Like he's first to hear anything," Hack said. "By the way, you see how Alois watches Sebastian?"

"Like he wants to gobble him up?"

"Exactly," Hack said.

"Sebastian needs time. Do you know Lucas is Draif's mate?"

Hack grinned. "Seriously?"

"Yeah, but don't say anything. Draif also needs time. They'll get there when they're ready… or Princess Buttercup will eat Lucas. I'm not sure yet."

"Lucas is a good guy," Hack said. "Don't worry so much."

"Of course I won't worry. That's just crazy. Why would I worry about my best friend or my new preggo research buddy, or our daughter and her new husband? Crazy."

"Leti?" Julia stood in the doorway. "Can I talk to you for a minute?"

"Sure, sweetie," he said.

Hack smiled at the girl, pulled Sami into his arms, and headed for the door. "I'll make sure Rizzie doesn't eat too many cupcakes."

"How's it going, Julia?" Leti asked.

She bit her lip and looked toward the floor. "Not so good. I think I did something really bad."

"What's wrong?"

"A few days before the attack, I found a note on top of my bag in the bunks." She finally met Leti's eyes, her own rimmed in red and full of worry. "It said that if I didn't do something, the captain would find out about something I didn't want him to know."

"What did it ask you to do, sweetie?"

"There was this little device in with the note. The note said to stick it somewhere where no one would notice. I stuck it in the bathroom near the cargo bay."

"Okay," Leti said. That certainly explained how the Concords found them. "What were you afraid of Will finding out?" She looked down again. "Sweetie, it'll be okay, but whatever it is might help us find the person who blackmailed you."

"I ran away when I was ten," she said. "My dad drank a lot, and sometimes, he'd do mean things. He'd hurt me, so I left. I told the captain, when you all rescued us, that I didn't have a family, that they were dead, but I know my dad is still alive. I looked him up right after we settled in on the ship."

"Okay, Julia. Thank you for telling me, and I'll let Will know. Now, one thing I want you to understand is that we will not send you back to an abusive home, alright? As far as I'm concerned, you're one of ours now. You're a Charybdis Station mercenary. I know Will's dad already has a wonderful family waiting for you and that won't change. There may be some legal questions, but you leave that to us, alright?"

The teenager looked relieved. "Thank you, Leti. Oh, and I fed and brushed Wobble earlier. Do you think us kids can still come by and play with Wobble when we're with our new families?"

"Oh, yes, you certainly can," Leti said, hugging her

gently. "Make sure you tell them all I expect them to visit as often as they can."

She grinned crookedly. "I will." She went back in the commons, much more relaxed than when she came out.

"Shit," Leti said aloud. Someone blackmailed a teenager into doing his or her dirty work. He poked his head in and waved at Selene. Daintily eating her cupcake, she joined him in the hall, and he told her Julia's situation.

"That's not good," she said, voice dry and emotionless. "I'll let the captain and Ava know. Ava can start the legal proceedings, so Julia's parents don't become a problem. You did well, Yusef."

Leti grinned. "Thanks," he said. "Are you looking forward to being home?"

"I am," she said. "My sister and brother flew to the station to meet me. We'll have a few weeks to visit before they go back home."

"That's great," he said. "Do your parents know they're coming? I know you said they didn't want your siblings talking to you."

"They've officially broken from the rest of our family, so they'll be visiting much more often."

Leti smiled, happy for the Siren. He was fortunate in his family and truly wanted the same for her, though she would always have him by her side. Together, they went back into the commons to celebrate Rizzie's marriage.

11

ANCHOR'S REST SYSTEM, CHARYBDIS STATION

Hack watched Leti's face when Charybdis Station came into view. The large station was roughly circular, resembling a planet. It was a massive, fully man-made planet. It had a thick, impenetrable, and clear barrier between the surface and the empty space surrounding it.

Unfortunately, they were too far from the system's suns to have steady days and nights, so while space was always visible, the engineers made sure to mimic day and night lighting. Right now, it was night, and lights were dotted all over the station.

"Oh gods, look at that! It's as big as a small planet, Will. How is that even possible?" Leti held Sami on his hip, Pepper's carrier next to him ready to roll. Princess Buttercup was his normal traveling size, stretched out across Leti's shoulders.

"Daddy Will, it's so pretty," Rizzie said. She held Milo in one hand and pressed the other against the window of the ship.

"It is pretty, ladybug. It takes lots of engineers like Beck and Pops to keep it running."

"Oh, look at that, Draif," Leti said, pointing. He wore his lucky baby bunny sweater. That alone told Hack how nervous Leti was. He didn't seem nervous now though, just fascinated.

Draif's eyes followed obediently. "There's green stuff. What's in there?"

"That's the large gardens. There are several throughout the station. People want to feel dirt and grass under their feet sometimes, right? The station has only one large park, but a lot of smaller ones. People seem to like them. The station also has small farms all over. We try to be as self-sufficient as possible, but we still trade for food and other goods. Benefit of being in an allied system."

"That's just… I've never felt grass before, Will," Leti said, amazement in his voice.

"Really? Oh, yeah. Vextonar. Sometimes I forget you come from a city planet. You'll love it Leti. I promise." Hack enjoyed watching the happiness on his mate's face. He might be nervous, but maybe his joy in the station would make it a little easier. "I can't wait to show you the markets. If you enjoyed Derelict's trade market, you'll love ours."

"Look at all the ships coming and going," Draif said. The young man stood next to Leti, holding Marmalade in his arms. Morgan and Beck stood behind them all, watching the two in amusement.

"Captain." Dannol's voice piped in from the comm. "We've docked."

"Come on, guys," Hack said. "Let's go home."

The group joined the rest of the crew and the refugees as they exited the cargo bay. Draif pushed Pepper's carrier, while Maia had Gravy on a leash, and Silas struggled with Pax. The large hunting cat did *not* like the leash. Sebastian held Alois's arm, walking along behind them and laughing at Pax. The Dedril was still a little weak, but Hack knew he played it up a bit for sympathy from Sebastian.

Medics ran into the ship with stretchers, prepared to bring the wounded to the medical center on the station. Lucas would be brought to his new quarters after being checked over by the station's doctors and measured for a robotic arm and leg. The eye would take longer.

Right outside the ship, the Yellow Solace and the Green Solace's crew and passengers gathered alongside those from the Blue Solace, creating a large, loud crowd. Hack's dad stood at the gate to the station with Hack's mom, Mo, and Xavier, the youngest Juren son. Charybdis Station personnel gathered around, tablets at the ready to sort through the refugees.

Fasi Juren stepped forward, his loud voice projecting into the room and echoing off the walls. As he started to speak, the large crowd grew quiet, fast.

"Welcome to Charybdis Station," he said. "My name is Fasi Juren, and I'm the admiral of the Charybdis mercenaries."

Hack could feel Leti's stare burning into his head. Slowly, he turned to look at his beloved mate. Oh yeah, mean glare coming his way.

"The admiral?" Leti whispered, almost hissing.

"First, I want to thank my mercenaries for their hard work. You each went above and beyond, and I'm proud to call you a Charybdis mercenary. If you'd like, the crews of the three ships are good to enter now. Your family and friends are waiting." No one moved, and the admiral smiled proudly. "I see, I see. You want to get your new friends settled first. Well then, refugees, we welcome you home. Adults, you are welcome to make your home here. We have families willing to sponsor you while you find your place within our station. Children, oh, we have some excited families here. They've been chomping at the bit to meet each of you."

The big, purple Grell grinned, somehow still looking fierce as hell. Hack knew the truth though.

"So, we'll call each refugee up, one by one, and you'll meet your new family or your new sponsor."

One by one, names were called. A child or adult would step forward, and a family would meet them, greeting them and taking them to a new home. Some families were happy to take two or three children, keeping friends and siblings together.

"Julia," a man called.

The girl looked back at Leti, face full of worry and tears in her eyes. Hack's mate smiled and nodded to her, tears of happiness in his own eyes. She walked up front to meet an excited couple and their son. They were a Havenite couple that worked on the station. If Hack remembered correctly, the man worked in the gardens and the woman had a small restaurant that made divine desserts.

The woman pulled her close, hugging the teenager tightly. "We're so happy to meet you, Julia," she said. "We've been looking forward to this all month."

The man grinned and took her bag. "We got you a room set up and a warm meal waiting at home. We're so glad you're joining our family. Come here, sweetie. We're huggers." He pulled her close and squeezed her tightly before releasing her.

The little boy jumped up and down, trying to get Julia's attention. "Hi. Hi. Hi." Finally, she smiled at him, kneeling in front of him. "My name's Jared and I like robots. This one is my favorite, so I wanted you to meet him." He held up his toy. Julia oohed and aahed appropriately, then looked back to Leti. Her smile was radiant and full of wonder. Together, the family slowly walked into the station.

"Nessa," a woman called. A little girl reluctantly stepped forward, on the verge of tears. She pulled Dannol behind her, refusing to let go of Hack's pilot. The woman smiled gently. "You'll be staying with Dannol, sweetie, alright?"

The little girl squealed, spinning around and jumping into the small Havenite's arms. "I knew you'd be my new daddy. I knew it."

"Oh, damn it," Leti said, sniffling. "That's so sweet."

"Xu?"

The boy stood beside Selene. "I'm not going. I'm staying with Selene!"

The woman shrugged. "Okay. That was the plan since she's already agreed."

The young Dedril looked up at Selene. "Really? You'll be my mom?"

"Of course," she said. "I've always wanted children." Her voice had no inflection, and she looked bored, but the boy knew her now. He knew she wasn't what she appeared to be.

Xu hugged her, his head pushing into her stomach. "I love you, Mom. I'll be a good boy, and you won't regret it. I promise."

Selene hugged him back. "I love you too, and all you need to do is be yourself. Mothers love unconditionally, you know."

"Oh gods, Hack," Leti said, sobbing. "So many good feelings!"

Eventually, every child met their family, and, except for a select few, the adults were assigned their sponsors. Dr. Olivia Franklin was one of the remaining adults, and Hack couldn't wait to be done with the woman. Dr. Orsla Manning, accompanied by two very large guards, stopped in front of Franklin.

"Dr. Franklin?"

"Yes," she said, suspiciously. "What do you want?"

"I'm your sponsor. We'll be working together to discover what we can about the element. If you'll come this way, please?"

"Of course," she said, pleased. "I'm so pleased to see you're human. I was starting to worry with all this rubbish running around."

"I suggest you refrain from making such ignorant

remarks, Dr. Franklin," Orsla said, nose wrinkled in disgust. "We pride ourselves on our intelligence and logic in Charybdis Station, not bigotry."

"Sweet Mama," a very large, very ugly man yelled. He ran past Franklin, and the human scientist sneered. One of the guards took her arm and pulled her along.

"Lerais," Dru squealed, jumping and wrapping her legs and arms around her husband. They kissed. A lot. There was also groping. Hack winced and looked away.

"Rizzie, look away, ladybug," Cas said, coming to join them. "Those two are your inappropriate aunt and uncle, okay? Every family has a pair. Just look away."

Ma and Pops Brackenstone, along with Beck's siblings and their families piled in next, making a beeline for Beck. "Oh, my Beckie Boo," Ma said, pulling him into a big hug.

Draif chuckled. "Beckie Boo?"

Ma looked up. "Oh, you must be Draif," she said. "You get on in here too, Draify Loo. I got hugs for all my babies." She pulled Draif to her, holding the two men squished together in her arms.

Hack absolutely adored Beck's Ma. The woman was large and yellow, almost as big as Beck, but she was soft where he was hard. She was also confident where he was a little self-conscious. Ma Brackenstone was easily the backbone of her family and took in strays as easily as Leti.

Maia and Silas looked around, frowning.

"What about us?" Silas asked. They were among the last of the refugees.

"Do you want hugs too? Give it a minute and Ma

will get you." Hack smacked him on the back. "Anyway, you two are staying with us. Might as well since we can't seem to get rid of you."

"Hack," Leti said, struggling to hold back his laughter. "Don't be mean to my guards—I mean, friends."

Maia rolled her eyes. "Someone needs to guard you. You've got important things to get done, Leti."

"Wait," Hack said. "I thought you two guarded him so that I could focus on work."

"Nope," Silas said. "Leti here has to figure out that artifact and then save the galaxy, one adopted kid at a time."

Hack sniffed, frowning. "I see who's important here."

"Yeah, my new son-in-law," his father said. The admiral pulled Leti and Sami into his arms. "Gods, I'm glad to finally get to hold you, son."

"**H**mph, fimphfple," Leti said, face trapped against the Grell's chest.

"Don't smother him, Dad," Xav said, pulling Hack and Rizzie into a hug. "Damn, man, you sure make pretty babies," he said. "Who's this gorgeous little girl?"

"I'm Rizzie," she said. "That's Pepper. She's a gorgeous little girl too."

Mo inched around people, getting closer and closer to Hack's group. Tension pulled his shoulders tight, making him move stiffly. A light blush covered his cheeks, and he kept his eyes on the ground. He carried a large, fat jackrabbit in his arms.

"Too right you are, precious. Come on, let's go meet your grandma," Xav answered Rizzie. The little girl reached out and latched onto Xav, completely trusting.

Arms free, Hack pulled Mo to him. "Hey there, little brother," he said. The boy was a string bean, tall and skinny. Like every Burnished, he was covered in blackened and twisting tattoos. Mo buried his face against Hack and sighed, tension leaving his body.

"I'm glad you guys made it back," he whispered. "Me and Abbot were worried about you."

"We're glad to be home too," he said. "I'm so glad you're here, that we found you. I know it hurts, being left there and abandoned, but gods, I'm glad you're here."

"Mo," Rizzie said. "My turn for huggies."

Mo laughed, then slowly backed out of his brother's arms. "Come here, ladybug," Mo said, and Rizzie jumped into his arms, almost knocking him over.

Renee Juren took her turn and hugged Hack tightly. The small, dainty Havenite was the strongest person Hack knew. Her arms around him were safety and love. They had been since the first day he met her.

"Oh, my handsome boy," she said. "You're finally home." He knew she didn't just mean home from this trip. He'd been gone in more ways than one for a long time.

"Shmple farmkepmfle," Leti said into Fasi's chest. Sami giggled and chewed on his grandpa's arm.

Hack's dad stroked Leti's head. "Oh, I'm glad you're home too, son. We have so much to show you, and I got you a present."

"Prempghe?"

"Of course we got you a present," Fasi said. "It's not every day you get a new son and new grandkids. Definitely present worthy."

"Babe," Renee Juren said to her husband. "Please release that poor man before he suffocates." She reached down and released Pepper from her carrier. "Oh, my little girl," she crooned.

"Oh, fine," Fasi said and loosened his hold. Leti took a deep breath. "We really are happy you all made it home."

Hack shook his head. "Yeah, finally."

"Where's Mo?" Leti asked, looking around. His eyes fell on the boy, freshly released from Rizzie. "Oh, Mo," he squealed, running to the boy and hugging him. "Abbot is so pretty."

"Princess is so tiny! I can't believe he can shrink and grow like that." Mo returned Leti's hug. He stood just a few inches short of Leti. The kid was going to be huge when he finished growing. Hack smiled at the two, taking his little monster from Leti so he could hug Mo properly.

His father held Rizzie now, listening carefully as she regaled him with important information. "Milo doesn't like broccoli. He won't eat it at all," she said. "It's okay though, 'cause Gravy will, but then he poots all night and it's stinky."

Fasi nodded gravely.

Hack shook his head and checked on his crew. Dru and Lerais were still going at it. Beck and Draif were free from Ma now, but Pops had them. Ma was currently crushing Morgan and Cordelia. Biscuit sat waiting for Cordy. Finn and Alois stood nearby, laughing at their crewmates.

Juniper and Ava had corralled the three newest members to his crew, Hazel, Quinn, and Linc. The former refugees already trained with Selene and looked promising. Hazel would likely join Beck in engineering, and Linc would be Dannol's copilot. Quinn followed Cordelia around like a puppy, emulating her in battle and hanging on her every word when not sparring. Hack could practically see hearts filling Quinn's eyes every time she thought Cordy wasn't looking.

"Selene?" Two well-dressed Sirens approached from the gate. Selene nodded to them, Fluffle draped across her shoulders. The young man ran to her and hugged Hack's friend. Selene held still for a minute, then slowly wrapped her arms around him too. He looked to be about eighteen, eager and gangly.

The woman looked a few years older than Selene and was much more composed than her brother. Approaching, she smiled gently and nodded to Selene. "Sister. It's truly good to see you in person after all these years."

"This is Xu," Selene said, pulling the boy to her. "My son." Her brother decided the young Dedril needed a hug too, and her sister nodded politely.

"Aww, look at that. I'm so happy for Selene," Leti said, cuddling into Hack's side. "Oh, what the hell is happening there?"

Hack followed Leti's gaze, and his eyes widened in surprise. Nettle held Lilah's hand as he directed the medics in moving Lucas and the refugees. She held Sophie, her newborn, and met Leti's eyes, smirking.

"That hussy didn't tell me her and Nettle were a thing. *What?*"

"He did follow her around a lot. Plus, she's slept in his quarters for the last three weeks," Hack said.

"Seriously? Why didn't you tell me this? I thought you loved me," Leti said. He sniffed, turning away from Hack.

"I do love you, and I promise to tell you every bit of gossip from now on."

Leti looked over his shoulder, coy eyes flashing. "Good."

Fasi interrupted them, grabbing Leti again, holding him close. "Nettle asked for larger quarters about two weeks ago, so I suspected something was happening," he said. "Now, speaking of quarters..."

"Wait, admiral," Ma said. "I haven't had my hugs yet." She finished with Alois and Finn, then grabbed Hack and Leti. The woman's embrace was almost as familiar to him as his own mother's. Beck's Ma had made him one of her own the day Beck dragged him home from school. Sami squeaked from between them, and she pushed them back.

"Aww, look at this little darling," she said.

"Be careful, he bites," Hack said and handed Sami over.

Ma tossed the giggling boy in the air, then pulled him in close for a snuggle. "He's a little angel."

"Now, as I was saying," Fasi said, giving Ma a wry look. He turned to the crew. "I've arranged a little surprise for Will and Leti after talking with each of you. Thanks for playing along guys," he said. "Pops, you want to explain?"

The massive Grell lumbered over and smiled at

everyone. "The station's been growing kinda crazy for a while now, and us engineers build onto it as needed. Well, we've made a completely new section with homes for you all. If you want them, that is."

"Hell yeah, we do," Dru said. "The admiral showed us pictures. We are so onboard." She cuddled into Lerais's arms, Monty now perched on her husband's head.

"Wait, so you'll all live close by?" Leti asked tentatively. "You'll be right there if we need you?"

"We certainly will, sugarplum," Ava said. "We would be there for you no matter where we lived, but this makes it easier."

"Plus, we get an upgrade on our own homes," Morgan said. "So, we're all kinda selfish too."

"So, Juniper can make me some more chocolate squirrels today? Maybe some corn chowder too?"

"Oh, we see how it is," Cordelia said with a smile. "You just want Juniper around."

"Can you blame him, Cordy?" Juniper smirked.

"Now, now, children," Ma said. "Let's get these kiddos home so they can settle in. Little Nessa is about to drop." They all looked to Dannol. The small man grinned, happy to carry his sleepy little girl.

"Okay, okay," Fasi said. "Xav will get Wobble and the Druffle. We'll come back for the rest of your belongings tomorrow. Let's get you home."

The large group filed through the entrance to the station. The docks were crowded, as usual, but there were some perks to being with the admiral. Hack's dad led them straight to the shuttle tram, and they loaded up without having to wait.

"How big is the station?" Leti asked.

The station was wide open inside, with miles of air between the ground and the barrier. The thick, impenetrable, and clear barrier closed the station in, but left an open view of the star-laced sky. Buildings stretched high and shuttle tram tracks twisted and turned throughout the whole station, connecting everyone together. Small personal shuttles flew above it all.

The higher ups had long ago decided to make it as green as possible, planting trees, bushes, and flowers. Hundreds of years later, they had a thriving ecosystem. There was truly nothing like it in all the galaxy.

"It has a diameter of 1,563 miles, but it's getting larger every day," Pops answered. "We've added two new sections this year alone."

"It really is as big as a real world," Draif said. "Guess it's a good thing this tram goes so fast, huh? Has to travel all over the planet."

"Fitting you should call it that," Renee said with a smirk.

"Not now, sweetheart," Fasi said. "We'll discuss all that tomorrow."

"All what, Dad?" Hack asked.

Fasi smiled sheepishly. "Let's just say, there's a reason Pops and I picked this location for your new quarters. We'll talk about all that in the morning though. Oh, here we are."

The shuttle tram came to a stop, and the group

piled out. They were in the middle of a newly constructed area, materials still stacked in piles, but walkways were built and sod placed alongside them.

"This is your neighborhood," Fasi said. "You'll notice that it's still under construction, but it's livable now." He led them down the walkway, pointing out features. "There's where you'll have a small community garden. I thought I'd leave it to Juniper to decide what goes in it. That's one of ten meeting areas," he said, pointing to a few benches gathered around a small fountain. Trees were planted around it.

"Oh, chocolate squirrels," Leti said. "Is that a goat? That's a goat." He squealed and ran to a fenced-in area between two sleek-walled houses. It was a large, open pen with a small barn in the far corner. A small white goat chewed on the freshly laid grass, ignoring the many piles of hay available to her.

"Chocolate squirrels? Why is he obsessed with chocolate squirrels?" Renee shook her head, amused.

Draif sighed. "He was seventeen and it's... a long story. You really don't want to know."

"Hey there, pretty girl," Leti said, clumsily climbing the gate. He got stuck on the top, and Alois rushed over to help him over. He petted the goat, stroking her soft fur. "You are so cute. Look at that little tail!" Princess Buttercup hissed at the goat from Leti's shoulder. She ignored him, flicking her tail.

"That better be his present, Dad. If not, then I need to know whose goat that is." Hack laughed at his mate.

"Will he even see the house now?" Pops sounded dejected.

"Leti!" Draif yelled. "Leave the goat alone and come on. I want to go to sleep."

Leti glared at his friend. "Can't you see we're having a moment?"

"Have a moment in the morning." Draif tried to keep his face stern.

"Fine," he said, dragging the word out. He again got stuck on top of the fence, but Alois was waiting.

Fasi struggled not to laugh. "Alright then, let's get you all settled," he said. He pointed out houses along the street, assigning each crew member a home. "Hazel, this is yours."

The young woman's mouth dropped open. "Mine?"

The admiral frowned. "Yes, why? Is it not what you wanted? I know we didn't get to talk, but I modeled it off what Dru and Cordelia requested. Yours too, Quin and Linc," he said, nodding to the other two.

"We get a house? Each? A whole house?" Linc looked amazed. "We just joined though."

"You've fought with us in two battles now," Hack said. "I've seen you each training hard with Selene. You're part of my crew now. No different than any of the others."

"Seriously," Dru said. "Don't be drama queens, guys. You're ours now, and there's no getting rid of us."

"Draif, this is your house," the admiral said. "Lucas will stay with you for a little while as he recovers. You okay with that? Leti seemed to think it would be okay."

"Thanks for throwing me under the bus there, Dad," Leti said.

The admiral teared up at Leti's words, and Cas and Hack laughed. Their dad was such a softie.

"No, that's perfect," Draif said, eyes wet and shining. "Gods, my own house. I'm really free, aren't I?"

Leti tackled him, hugging him tightly. "You are the freest freeman in all the galaxy."

"Hack, Leti and you go here," Renee pointed, sniffling just a little and pointing at a three-story house. "Maia, Silas, you two have apartments on the third floor since you insist on staying close. If you want to move out, just let us know. You're part of the crew now too."

"That's our home, Will," Leti said, dazed and in awe. "Our *home*."

Hack wrapped an arm around his mate and the other around Mo. "Yeah, baby. We're home now."

"It has seven bedrooms on the first two floors and four suites on the third floor," Pops said. "I made sure you have plenty of space since you'll probably have a bunch more kids in time."

"I can share my room, Daddy Leti, if you wants to have more babies," Rizzie said. "Just makes sure they're girls like me and Pepper."

"Oh, ladybug, you're a very good sister," Hack said.

"Thanks, Pops," Leti said, pulling the man into a hug. "I'm so happy to have a home, and you've completely spoiled me."

Pops hugged him back, a big grin on his face.

"Sebastian, you're on the other side, there," Renee continued, smiling gently at the man.

He looked completely overwhelmed. His hand

settled on his stomach as he took in the small two-story house. Someone had planted a few flower beds in the front yard that looked beautiful, even in the evening light.

"I had best stay with Sebastian, since I just came out of a coma," Alois said, coughing weakly.

"Oh, don't worry, big guy," Dannol said, hugging his friend. "You can stay with me and Nessa. We'll take care of you."

Leti and Draif snickered.

Hack shouldn't be surprised that Leti had told his friend about the possibility of Lucas and Sebastian being mates. If they talked about his penis, they talked about everything.

"We'll leave you all to rest tonight," Renee continued. "Tomorrow evening, we'll meet with everyone. There are some things we need to discuss with you."

"Nothing alarming," Fasi added. "Just important. Oh, and we're taking Pepper with us tonight, son. You need some sleep, and your mom wants some baby time."

With that, they hugged Hack and his family one more time, then left them to rest. Ma and Pops also got in more hugs.

"I left some food in the fridge with you, dearie," Ma whispered, hugging Leti. "I'll bring more tomorrow."

"Thanks, Ma," Leti said, grinning. "Juniper was right. I won't starve."

Hack carried an exhausted Rizzie into their new quarters... er... house. He was so used to being on a ship. The place was large, even larger than his parents' house. It was warmly decorated, with creamy-brown walls, warm wooden floors, and multiple rugs. There wasn't a lot of furniture, but Hack imagined they wanted to leave it to them to pick what they wanted. There was, however, a lot of space.

Gravy made his way to a large pet bed and plopped down, huffing. Seconds later, he was snoring. Princess Buttercup, now eight feet long, sniffed Gravy's head, then followed Hack. He walked down the hall, peeking into rooms.

"This is Rizzie's room," Mo said, pointing to a door. "I helped decorate it." The boy had lost his rabbit somewhere. Hack looked at Princess.

"Where's Abbot?" Hack asked, opening the door. Rizzie's room was decorated for a little princess, all ruffles and daintiness. He laid her on her bed, removed her shoes, then covered her up. She burrowed into the bed, sighing happily.

"Abbot's visiting with Leti now," Mo whispered. "Want to see my room?"

Hack grinned. "Show me, little brother."

After following Mo all through the house, getting the personal tour, Hack found Leti, Maia, Silas, and Sami eating in the kitchen. Abbot sat in Leti's lap.

"Is it bad that I already miss Pepper?" Hack asked.

"Your mom stole her," Leti said, stuffing a large spoonful of stew in his mouth. He didn't seem very concerned though, despite his words.

"Do you think she'll return her?"

"Tomorrow," Leti said. "Maybe. Depends on how much sleep she loses tonight."

"Grandma wanted you guys to get some sleep tonight," Mo said, yawning. "I think I'm going to go to bed now too. You need anything before I go?"

Hack grabbed his brother, crushing him in a big hug. "Nope. We have you with us now, and that's just about all we needed."

Mo blushed, a wide smile covering his face. He grabbed Abbot and left at a run.

"That boy is the sweetest thing ever," Leti said. "Where did Princess go?"

"Lost him in our bedroom. He's already enjoying our bed."

"Figures," Leti said, laughing. "We need to get this one to bed."

Hack grabbed a sleepy Sami, tickling his tummy. "I'll put him down, baby. Meet you in our room."

"I meant Maia. She's about to fall asleep in her plate," Leti said.

Hack rolled his eyes as the others laughed.

Entering his son's room, Hack cuddled a freshly diapered Sami, then laid him down in his crib. It was low to the ground, so Pax could easily jump in. Once Hack had settled his son, the large cat curled around Sami, purring. Hack watched Sami smile. His eyes fluttered, then closed, his snores soft and adorable.

His room was decorated for a wild boy. Brown and green walls and decorations. Nothing to chew on within reach, and cute little stuffed animals on shelves up high. He needed to let his parents know how much he loved them. They'd put a lot of thought into his home.

Finally reaching the master bedroom, he found Leti curled around Princess. His beautiful green eyes watched Hack sleepily.

"Will, I love you. You know, right?"

"Yeah, baby. I know."

"We haven't gotten a lot of time to talk lately," Leti said. "Everything's moved so fast, from the moment we snuck on your ship."

"We have time," Hack said. "We have our whole lives, and I, for one, plan on learning all your secrets." He undressed and climbed in behind Leti, pulling him close. He nuzzled his neck and wished he had the energy to make love to his mate. "What do you think of Charybdis Station so far, baby?"

"I think I'm home," Leti said. "For the first time in my life."

13

"Help me." Blue eyes filled with pain wouldn't let Leti go. "Why won't you help me?"

Leti couldn't move, couldn't breathe. All he saw was a pale face, accusing blue eyes, and blood, so much blood.

"It hurts," the man said. "Help me!"

"I'm sorry," Leti said, sobbing. "I'm so sorry."

Blue eyes turned into lifeless, brown eyes in the plain face of Dr. Morrick. They stared up at the sky one second, then looked straight at him the next. "Wyatt." Morrick's pale lips didn't move, but his voice filled Leti's head. "Where's Wyatt?"

A baby's cries filled the air, and a young woman sat in a rocking chair, cuddling an infant. She tried to quiet its cries, but they got louder and louder. Leti walked closer. "Do you need help? I have a little girl of my own and singing always works with her."

The woman looked up, eyes dead inside. The baby in her arms crumbled into dust while she stared at him.

"Let me help you," Leti said, trying to move closer to the woman. Something pushed back against him the closer he got, and it was like walking through quicksand. The woman slowly disappeared, a piece at a time.

Maia's voice filled his head. "The things they did to us. I don't blame her for not wanting to live."

Franklin's voice took over. "Imagine if we knew how to bring back the dead. Think about that when you go sit and cry in the cryo chamber tonight."

"*HELP ME!!!*"

"Leti!" Hack's voice cut through Leti's dream, his hands shaking Leti awake. "Baby, wake up."

Leti came awake, drawing in deep breaths. "I'm sorry. I'm sorry." Tears covered his face, sobs wracking his body.

Hack held him as he cried, rocking him. Princess Buttercup curled his massive, scaly body around Leti's back, rumbling deep in his chest.

"Why can't I forget them?" Leti buried his face in Hack's chest. "I keep seeing them everywhere."

"Them? I get Morrick, but who else?"

"One of the refugees that died, a man with blue eyes, sticks with me the most. I don't even know his name, but I can't get him out of my head. The other was a woman. She was pregnant."

"Oh Leti," Hack said. "I forget you aren't used to seeing death."

"I don't know, Will," Leti said. "I'm your mate, so I need to be stronger than this. You aren't having nightmares, and you were in the thick of things."

"I wasn't holding that man's hand, Leti. I didn't watch them die."

"No," Leti said in a small voice.

"There are different kinds of strength, Leti. Your strength lies in your ability to care, your ability to love. I can distance myself from things in battle, but aiding the wounded, helping the abused and traumatized? Unless they're my crew, people I know and love, I struggle with it. I intimidate people. Comforting them isn't my strength."

"I can't even help people without having nightmares, Will. What good am I to you?"

"You don't know your value, baby," Hack said. "I'm sorry you're hurting, and I don't know how to make this better. I know you grew close to Morrick."

"I don't like losing people," Leti said. "Then reading Morrick's notes, learning about the artifact, all that doesn't help, I guess."

"Maybe you need to take a break from it," Hack said.

"No! I handed it over to your father, but I still have answers to find. I have to, Will."

"Okay, okay," he said. "Sebastian will help you too, but try to take it easy, baby. Your life has turned upside down in the last month, you've lost a friend, and you're pregnant. I could go on and on. Point is, you need a little time. Also, it's not like you have to be in around the wounded. You have no responsibilities as my mate, Leti. All you need to do is be happy."

"Yeah, but I'm home now. It'll get better, right?"

"It will," Will said, squeezing him tightly.

"Will, you know I can't just stand aside while people are hurt. If they need comfort or help, I'm going to be there, nightmares or no nightmares." He had held that man's hand as he died. He couldn't save him, but the man didn't die alone.

"Oh, I know, Leti. Doesn't mean I like it, but I know you. I love you." Hack kissed his head. "Go back to sleep, baby. I'm going to get the kids up and fed. Get some rest."

"Okay," Leti said softly, already falling back to sleep. "Love you." Princess's warm body snuggled close, easing him to calmness.

A few hours later, he stumbled into the kitchen, yawning, Abbot in his arms. The rabbit really was a handful. He'd been waiting outside the door when Leti finally got out of bed. Light streamed through the windows all throughout the house, giving Leti a better look at his new home.

Leti loved his house. The floors were real wood. Everything was so warm and comfy, even with the bare walls. He'd have to move some of their stuff from the ship into the house. *Oh, bacon!*

Juniper stood in the kitchen, scrambling eggs. "Hi Leti," he said, smiling. "Hope you don't mind me visiting. I wanted to make sure you guys got a good breakfast."

"Anytime, Juniper," Leti said. "Anytime you want to cook for me, you just do it. Don't even ask. If you want to move in, I'm good with that."

The golden Fallon smiled brightly, happily flipping bacon. "I love that you love my food. Oh, by the way, take a look out the back. I think you'll be happy."

Leti shuffled to the back windows and moved the white curtain aside. Wobble's fuzzy face pressed up against the window. "Wobble!" Leti yelled, laughing. Setting Abbot down, he opened the window, and the llama pushed his head through. Leti scratched his ears. "Silly boy," he said, giggling.

A soft bleat came from below, and Leti saw his goat standing close to Wobble. "Wobble, is she your new best friend?" Leti asked. "Let's get some snacks and think of some names."

Leti turned around, and Juniper handed him a bowl of cut apples. "You're the best, Juniper," Leti said, smiling. He turned back and fed Wobble a few slices, then leaned out the window, and fed the goat some. "Trixie," Leti said. "Your name is Trixie."

"That's a cute name," Juniper said. He moved on to mixing up some waffles. If Leti wasn't already mated…

"How are Pork Chop and Miss Speckles?"

"Pork Chop is with your daughter, visiting, and Miss Speckles is enjoying her new roost. It's in my backyard, and I decorated it with plenty of straw this morning. I think she misses people-watching though."

"She can come visit. I have a feeling our house won't be short of people to watch," Leti said, nibbling his lip. He watched Juniper move around the kitchen, mysteriously not burning it down as he made yumminess. "Can I ask you a favor? It's kind of embarrassing."

"Of course, Leti."

"Do you think you could teach me to cook? At least the basics? People are harder to take care of than animals."

"I would love to teach you, Leti. Ma taught me, you know? When I came here as a kid, my parents worked constantly, so I spent a lot of time by myself. Beck took me home after school one day, and Ma adopted me. She taught me to cook, and Beck's sister got me hooked on plants."

"Were your parents jealous? I think I'd be."

"Honestly? They were more concerned with rising in rank. My mom was a diplomat, still is. My dad captains his own ship. At the time, he took the long routes, but now he sticks closer to the station."

"That had to hurt when you were a kid," Leti said. He could definitely sympathize.

"It did. They aren't bad people, but I'm glad I didn't have any siblings. They didn't have time for me, let alone another. Ma, though, she knows how to make time. Even if it's just a few minutes a week, she makes me feel special and cared for, not like I'm an inconvenience."

"Daddy Leti." Rizzie's voice came from down the hall.

"You've been summoned," Juniper said.

"Coming, ladybug!" He surprised Juniper with a hug from behind. The man froze, then leaned back into Leti. "You're a great friend, Juniper. I can't wait to learn some cooking stuff. Just don't tell Draif. Ever since I burned the kitchen down in Vextonar, he won't let me try again."

"*What?*"

Leti ran to the door, ignoring Juniper's questions and picked up Abbot. Rizzie stood outside her bedroom door with Milo. She was freshly bathed and dressed, curly hair in a loose bun at the top of her head.

"You awake now, Daddy Leti?"

"Sure am." Leti smiled at his daughter, leaning down to kiss her cheek. "What are you doing?"

"Playing," she said. "We having a tea party."

"We *are* having a tea party, ladybug," he corrected.

"Yes! Yes! Come on for tea before breakfast."

Leti laughed and walked into her room, Abbot in his arms. It was decorated for a little princess. The floor had warm white, purple, and pink fuzzy rugs covering it. The walls were a swirl of light blue, gray, and a dark purple that Leti thought was beautiful. She had a bookshelf, dresser, and a small, child-sized white and purple couch.

In the corner was a small table with four tiny chairs. Sami sat in one, chewing on his teacup. Pax sat behind him with a furry, long-suffering expression. Mo folded into his seat, holding a small, dainty teacup in his hand. His knees just about touched his chin and his golden skin was flushed with embarrassment, but he stayed put. Pork Chop sat next to him, looking around hopefully, sure someone would drop food soon.

Hack sat cross-legged on one side of the table, Gravy by his side, furry head against Hack's shoulder.

Leti's mate cheerfully fake-sipped his tea, pinky finger sticking out properly.

"Hey, baby," he said. "Joining us for tea?"

Leti couldn't keep the grin off his face, looking at his big, bad mercenary captain. "Yes, thank you," he answered. "Where can I sit, Rizzie?"

"Right here, Daddy Leti," she said, pointing between Mo and Sami. "Here, I'll pour you tea." They sipped tea, made casual conversation, and ate fake biscuits… Well, Sami really ate one, but Leti managed to pull it out of his mouth before he swallowed it.

Juniper came in, snickering at the sight. "Breakfast is ready," he said. "You all hungry?"

Sami clapped and giggled. "Fuck," he said, nodding.

Leti glared at Hack and picked up his son. His stomach growled loudly, ruining his punishing look, so he sighed in disappointment instead.

"Leti is definitely hungry," Mo said with a laugh as Leti's belly growled again. He was eating for two, so he couldn't help it, damn it!

Hack stood, grabbed Sami from his arms, then kissed Leti's cheek and ran. "Love you, baby," he said over his shoulder. Gravy whined, following on his heels. Damn troublemakers. Mo just grinned and ran after his brother. Leti shared a commiserating look with Pax.

"Will is going to corrupt Mo," Leti told Abbot. Pax leaned over, sniffing the rabbit. "You know you can't eat him, right?" Pax looked disappointed but nuzzled Abbot, accepting his prey as family.

Maia and Silas were already at the table, waiting on them. Plates of steaming hot food made Leti's belly rumble again. Juniper sat and they ate breakfast with Pork Chop and Gravy sitting under the table, keeping the floor clean.

"When does school start, Mo?" Juniper asked.

"We'll need to be there in about an hour," he said. "I ride the tram for about five minutes, then I'm there. It's not too bad. Usually, we'll go in earlier, but today they let us come late."

"Are you going to come home or go follow Pops around after school?" Leti asked.

Mo smiled shyly. "Can I come home and stay with you a while? I thought we could spend some time with Abbot and the others."

"Of course," Leti said, excited. "I would love that. We need to introduce everyone to Trixie."

"I'm going to school too, Daddy Leti," Rizzie said. "Mo says he'll take me in."

"What? But you're too little," Leti said, tears filling his eyes. "You're my baby girl, you can't possibly start school." Tears poured down his cheeks, and everyone looked at him in horror.

"It's okay, Daddy Leti," Rizzie said quickly. "I'll stay with you."

"You can't," Leti wailed. "You have to grow up, learn new things, experience life." He grabbed Abbot from below his chair and buried his face in the rabbit's fur. He sobbed and stuffed bites of waffle in his mouth. He could see her now, going off to university, getting married, having kids of her own.

"Okay, I think hormones are at play here," Juniper said.

"Ladybug," Hack said. "I think Daddy Leti's feelings are really strong now because of the baby in his belly, alright? You're starting school, and it'll be fine."

"It will, Rizzie," Leti said, tears still pouring. "I'm sorry."

Rizzie giggled, worry disappearing. "It's like when Daddy Will ate the last chocolate squirrelly, right? Then you threw the pillow and then a shoe at him. The baby makes you feel too much?"

Leti nodded. His girl was so smart and his mate so stupid. Why would he eat the last chocolate? It was Leti's. "You'll like school, and Mo will take good care of you."

She ignored his tears now, but Mo still looked anxious. He hadn't been privy to the spontaneous crying of the last two weeks.

"I'm gonna makes so many friends, and I'll bring 'em home to play in my room with Milo. Milo can come with me, right?"

"Are you sure you want to bring him? You'll have to keep up with him," Hack said.

"Well, he cans stay here with Daddy Leti," she said. "He might need him."

"Thanks, Rizzie," Leti said, smiling wryly. "Mo, will you keep an eye out for a girl about your age? Julia? She's one of the new adopted kids, and I know she's going to be really nervous today."

Mo smiled, lopsided and sweet. "Of course. My

friends are really pretty great. We'll take care of Julia and the other refugee kids."

Leti breathed a sigh of relief. They might be home, but that didn't mean he could stop taking care of the refugees.

14

They all walked Mo and Rizzie to the shuttle tram, waving them off. Mo held tightly to Rizzie's hand, leaning down so he could hear her rambles. Leti could feel the tears coming again. Damn hormones.

Leti adjusted Sami on his hip. "I can't believe she's already in school."

Hack stood from petting Gravy. "Charybdis starts kids in school at four, then training in a specialty at sixteen. When they're eighteen, they can go to university or start with a crew."

"What do you think Mo will train in? Engineering?"

"I think so. He told me all about his trips with Pops this morning. He's really excited about it."

"What about Rizzie?"

"No clue," Hack said. He looked thoughtful. "She's confident, a leader, but I don't know." His sad eyes met Leti's. "She's just a baby, right? We have time with her."

"We do," Leti agreed. "She's her Daddy Will's little girl though. She'll captain a ship."

Juniper and Leti laughed at Hack's look of terror.

"Leti," Sebastian said excitedly. The young man jogged toward Leti's group. "The translation guide came today," he said. "I found it on your porch." He panted. "I really need to exercise more." He leaned over, sniffing at Leti. "You smell like bacon. Do you have bacon?"

Juniper rolled his eyes. "I cooked bacon and eggs for you earlier this morning. Are you hungry again?"

"It's been three hours, Juniper," Sebastian said, sulking.

"We have leftovers," Leti said. "No bacon, but some waffles and some of Ma's stew. Come on, we'll polish them off and look over the guide."

"I'm going to check in with the rest of the crew," Hack said. He leaned down and kissed Leti, who savored the taste of his mate, but reluctantly pulled away so Hack could take Sami.

Leti really needed to spend some time with his mate. Alone time. He wiggled his eyebrows at his mate's back as the man walked away.

"Why are you doing that?" Sebastian watched him, trying to suppress his smile.

"He's thinking naughty thoughts," Juniper said, chuckling.

The three men watched Hack's firm, fine ass. Leti sighed happily, then smacked Juniper and Sebastian's arms. "Keep your eyes off my man."

Juniper smirked, then walked toward his house. "See you guys later."

"In a few hours, right?" Leti tried to keep the concern out of his voice. "For lunch?" He really needed to learn to cook. Juniper just shook his head and continued on his way.

"I hope he comes back," Sebastian said. "Though in a few hours, it'll be dinner, not lunch. You slept late."

"I did and it was wonderful," Leti said. "Let's tackle the guide while I have an empty house."

The two men spent the next few hours munching on leftovers and studying the guide. "Why are you so good at this?" Leti asked. "Ugh, I know twenty-seven languages, but this one is really annoying. It's hardly like modern Crellic at all."

Sebastian blushed, smiling softly. "I've always been really good at languages."

Leti stood, stretching his back and shoulders. He looked around his little office. Pops had designed him a small private room with bookshelves on one of the walls and a comfy window seat on another.

Another wall housed his Druffle and their mansion. Pops had gone all out, creating a huge home for them and multiple tunnels branching all over the wall. He could imagine many comfortable days of research and writing.

Right now, images of the artifact were projected from his tablet on the desk. Morrick's notes were pulled up on his vid-screen. Books and printed pages were scattered across his desk. Despite the mess, he finally felt like they were making some progress.

"Oh, listen to this," Sebastian said. "I think the book you bought at the trade market is a book of myths or fairy tales."

"Hmm, that's kind of neat."

"Yeah, but look here," Sebastian said, holding up the book. On the page was a circle connecting six pyramids, one of which looked familiar. "The page is titled *The Six Elements of Rising*. Well, I think it is."

"That's our artifact," Leti said. "What's the story about?"

"I need to spend more time with it," Sebastian said. "It's about a queen, maybe? I'm not sure."

"That's great, Seb," Leti said. "Keep with it and let me know. I'll keep looking too."

"It may take a while, but I'll do my best," Sebastian said, then pored back over the book, excitement in his eyes. Leti reached for his tablet, noticing he had two messages from this morning.

Dr. Ando,

I hope you are doing well and your research into the artifact is progressing. As you know, I have been making inquiries into experts on Crellic history, and I have some exciting news. I was referred to a university in the Boral System, and the Dean of Archaeology there would like to speak with you. He didn't tell me much, but he said he had some information that you might find interesting. It all sounds very mysterious, and I admit the man seemed quite nervous. On another note, my TA has finished scanning the four Crellic books, and I've attached those here. I will keep my eyes open and let you know if I find anything else. I wish you the best!

Dr. Advaith Chopra

Leti downloaded the attachments and sent them straight to Sebastian. Dr. Chopra had proven to be a better resource than he could have hoped for. Leti knew firsthand how historians could get stuck in their own research, seldom having any extra time. He'd send Advaith the Pre-Human Diaspora Wello mating cup he had bought on Derelict. Dr. Chopra's own research projects were into Wello history. Making a note in his tablet, Leti pulled up his second message, frowning as he read through it.

Mr. Ando,

I'm sorry to bother you, but you've been trying to contact my son, Wyatt Morrick, for over a month now. I don't know how well you know him, but I'm his mother, Sandra Adaden. He works for a nonprofit organization called the Galactic Association of Compassionate Professionals. They send aid to planets in need. He's been in the Sugarworm System for the past six months. Usually, he calls or messages me at least once a week for an update. A month and a half ago, he stopped contacting me. I've called the GACP several times, and they've refused to tell me his status. They say he's fine and I'm overreacting, but I know my son. I signed into his account, and he hasn't read any messages during that timeframe. I've not read Wyatt's messages—I'm trying to respect his privacy—but I did look to see who he's been in contact with. If you know anything about Wyatt, please let me know. I'm remarried now, with two younger children, so I can't go after him.

Please help me.

Sandra Adaden

"Help me," he said softly.

"What? Do you need something, Leti?" Sebastian left the window seat and sat beside him.

"Wyatt Morrick is missing," he said. He had to find him. He had to bring him to Verion. It might be too late for them to reconnect, but he could do this much.

"For how long? Where was he last? Do you think the Concords took him?" Sebastian's questions were very good ones.

"I don't know," Leti said, brow furrowed. "We need to do something though. We have to…" The beep from an incoming call startled him. It was from Vextonar. "Hello?" Leti said, pleased to see Dottie's worn face on his tablet screen. Her eyes were worried, and she looked tense enough to snap.

"Leti, you're okay," she said, relief in her voice.

"Yeah," he said, smiling briefly. "You put me on the right ship."

"I wasn't worried about that," she said, pausing, clearly reluctant to speak.

"What's wrong, Dottie? I've never see you so worried."

"Sweetie, your parents have gone bonkers," she finally said.

"Uh, they were always bonkers. Were they horribly upset that I left? I knew they'd be mad, but it's not like they were happy about my existence anyway."

"It's not public knowledge, and I just found out, but as soon as you left, they put a contract on your life," she said. She ran her gnarled hands through her wild grey hair. "They've hired the Half-Moon Assassin's Guild to kill you."

"They want me dead?" Leti struggled to breathe. He knew they didn't like him, but they wanted him dead? They wanted someone to kill him?

"Leti!" Sebastian yelled as Leti fell to the floor, heart pounding and vision blackening. "I'm calling Nettle."

He heard Seb speaking to Dottie but couldn't make out his words. His parents wanted him dead.

"Leti." Hack's voice wrapped around him, familiar and beloved. He opened his eyes and there was his mate. Hack sat on the side of their bed, concern and worry haunting his eyes.

"Will, my parents—"

"Sebastian told me. He heard what Dottie said."

"They hate me, Will. They want me dead," Leti said, panic rising again.

"Hey now, Leti," Nettle said, coming around to the other side of his bed. "Try to stay calm. You know we've got your back."

"We'll be with you all the time now, Leti," Silas said from a chair in the corner. "Even at home, someone will be here with you."

Leti crawled into Hack's lap, needing his mate. He shook as Hack hugged him tightly, but his mate's warmth slowly soaked into him.

Nettle sat on the bed. "Now, you're going to be fine. You had a shock, which is why you passed out. The baby is just fine, but you need more rest. Today, you just play with your pets, eat lots of food, and get a good night's sleep. Okay?"

"My parents hate me, Nettle," Leti said. He couldn't move past that thought. He knew they wished he was different, but wanting him dead was mindboggling.

Nettle sighed, looking unbearably sad for a moment. "Hate is… difficult to understand, Leti. The Concords and your parents both have a lot in common. They let their belief in their own superiority control their actions, then they take it too far. Listen to me though, Leti. Everyone has that darkness in them. They can let their own desires twist them into something wrong. We have to search for the light in people. We have to search for our own light."

"I have to accept them as they are," Leti whispered. "No rose-colored glasses. They aren't like Fasi and Renee, or Ma and Pops. They never will be, and I have to let that go."

Hack held Leti tightly, curving around him, as if he could protect his mate from everything in the world.

"It's not easy," Nettle said. "My own parents are a lot like yours, and, well honestly, no one can hurt you more than family."

"Your parents stink like Wobble poo?" Leti watched Nettle smile, even as his eyes remained sad.

"Yeah. They're human purists. I was for a long time. It was all I knew."

"You aren't anymore." Maia watched them curiously. "What changed?"

"I went to a school that had non-human species. I had never met a single person who wasn't at least seventy-five percent human. Then I suddenly met hundreds." He laughed sheepishly. "I was used to being the smartest kid, and then suddenly, I'm competing for top of the class with a Fallon woman. She kicked my ass, took a lot of joy in it."

"You probably deserved it," Leti said, nudging Nettle with his foot.

"Hell yeah, I did." Nettle's laugh filled the room. "Then, she cornered me and asked what the hell was wrong with me. I told her that she wasn't human, and she was a woman. I didn't understand how she could score better than me. I was honestly baffled."

"Did she cut your penis into little pieces?" Maia asked. "Because I would have."

"She wanted to, but I was told we have to find our own light."

"Yeah," Leti said softly.

"She shoved down her own anger and decided she was going to be my best friend. I tried to avoid her. I insulted her, yelled at her, but she kept coming back. She said she was my friend, and I just needed to get used to it."

"That's what I did with Draif," Leti said. "Love a person until they can't take it anymore. Then they're yours."

"That's what happened. I went home on break, and suddenly, my family's words just hit me. They were wrong. Becca was smart, she was beautiful, and she damn well deserved my respect. I never went home again. I knew my parents and siblings were never going to change. They were never going to leave our home world."

"You must have been lonely," Silas said. The large

Betonize man looked adorable with Sami sleeping in his lap.

Nettle snorted. "The first thing I did when I got back was apologize to Becca. From then on, she took me home with her during breaks. Her family somehow accepted me and became my own. The point is, though, that everyone can hate, everyone has that darkness. But you, Leti. You have to keep your light shining. Okay? Promise me you won't let their hate twist you."

"I promise," Leti said. "I don't want to hate people, and I won't let them change me."

15

*L*ater that evening, Hack and his friends stood waiting for the shuttle tram to arrive. Leti, Lilah, and Sebastian kept the kids at home, and Maia and Hazel stayed behind to guard them. Pax and Gravy had insisted on coming with Hack. The two seemed to know they were part of the crew.

Hack had to admit he had an amazing crew. Right before he left the house, Lerais had casually stopped by, joining Leti for dinner. The large engineer thought he was sneaky, but Hack knew he was really there to add more protection for Leti. When Selene's siblings walked into the kitchen, Hack just grinned and silently thanked his friends.

The crew of the Blue Solace was collectively pissed about Leti's parents, and there had been no less than three adults, besides Hack, at the house today, keeping an eye on Leti. Hack didn't think his mate realized how loved he was. He hadn't told Draif yet though. He knew the man would lose it.

Silas pulled on Pax's leash when the hunting cat wouldn't move. "Why do I have to be in charge of Pax?"

"Because we love you," Hack said, smiling and rubbing Gravy's ears.

"I feel it," he said.

Minutes later, they unloaded at the hectic center of the station. The building was large, with plain, pale gray walls and hallways. Smaller buildings were built onto the original, with other buildings connecting to them. Overall, it looked like a great big hive, swarming with busy bees. Hack held tight to Gravy's leash.

Eventually, they reached his dad's largest conference room. All the Solaces' crews were there, along with Cas, Xav, Audre, and Pops. Sheiria, a young Cardinal woman and captain of the Red Solace, sat between Xav and Audre.

"Have a seat if you can everyone," Renee said. Each and every person hopped to it. Nobody liked to anger the station's Security Chief.

Hack sat between Dru and Selene. His mom and dad stood at the front of the large, oblong table.

"As many of you know, Charybdis Station will be declaring war on the Concord Mercenaries due to their attacks on our ships and their inhumane treatment of non-human species." The admiral surveyed the gathered people. "Most of you have lived on the station long enough to know we've always prided ourselves on treating species with equality, so this is seen as an injustice by both the Council and myself."

He pushed a button and a live image of the station

projected in the middle of the table. It was split into five sections, color coded purple, green, blue, yellow, and red.

"After speaking with the Council about what I wanted to do, we had a long discussion on the possible consequences. As a mercenary group, declaring war against another group isn't easily done. To be honest, it would never be done simply because one group sees the other as morally wrong. In the past, financial deals going wrong have been at the core of mercenary wars."

"A few of the other groups would stand with us on this," Audre said. "The Concords haven't endeared themselves to many."

"Very true, Audre," the admiral said. "That is something we will be looking into in the future in fact." He smiled brightly at the young captain before he grew solemn. "The Council has long wished for a change within the station, a natural evolution really. This situation brings forward the need for that change." He looked to his wife.

"Charybdis Station's history shows our progression from an early pirate-like station to one of diplomatic neutrality," Renee said. "We've called ourselves mercenaries for a very long time now, but it has been ages since we've fit that term."

"The Council and I both agree that now is the time to initiate a change that's been long in the making," Fasi said. "Charybdis Station is declaring itself a self-governing territory, a world of its own."

Silence filled the room as Fasi looked around. Hack

was shocked. Essentially becoming a planet in the system was... Damn, it was big.

"Holy shit," Dru said, finally breaking the silence.

"What do the other planets in the system think?" Ava looked excited, golden eyes shining with interest. Hack thought, as a diplomat, she would find this fascinating.

"We have full support and the expectation of acknowledgment from all planets in the system except Burnished Outpost. However, they haven't responded to communications from anyone in years," Fasi said.

"Holy shit," Dru said again. "This is big, Admiral. Really big."

"Yes, it is," Fasi agreed. "Truthfully, we've already been acting as our own territory for centuries. We have trade agreements, allies, known boundaries. Things will change, but not as much as you might think. The Council is still voted in, and they still choose the station's leader."

"What's our role in this?" Draif asked. Leti's best friend had stayed quiet throughout the announcement. Now, he looked intrigued.

"Good question, Draif," Renee said, smiling. "Will, Audre, Cas, and Sheiria, you four have been captains of our best ships, the Solaces. Each of you have also expressed an interest in advancement. This is your chance."

"We want to separate our station into four sectors and have each of you directly lead them, just like you captain your own ships," Fasi said. "Each sector is evenly proportioned with mercen—soldiers, engineers, medics, and civilians. We want you four to be Charybdis Station's generals, reporting to me, the Lord Admiral of the Station. I would like it noted, I did not choose the title."

He pointed to the projected image. Hack noticed his neighborhood was in the blue sector. The colors started to make sense—blue for Hack, green for Cas, red for Sheiria, and yellow for Audre. The small purple spot covered the center of the station. Purple for royalty.

"Holy shit," Dru said.

"Dru, will you stop saying that?" Cordelia said, elbowing the woman.

"With a war in the works, this will also mean leading your own ships into battle with the Concords," the Lord Admiral said.

Oh, Hack was going to have fun with that title. He would be a general though. It would be a tough position, but he could help a lot of people. It'd also be good for his family, more stable. "I'm in," Hack said.

"Of course you are," Dru grumbled. She fought her smile, but he could see the intrigue in her eyes. She'd be a captain.

"Hell, why not?" Audre shrugged. "I'm in too." Her crew cheered from the back.

Sheiria grinned. "Hell yeah. I'm in too." Most of Red Solace hollered in support of their captain.

"Cas?" Renee asked.

"Won't people get pissy if two of your kids are in positions of power?" Cas asked their father.

Sheiria snorted. "Yeah, until they get to know you

and Hack," she said, leaning across the table to meet Cas's eyes. "The two of you earned your positions as captains of the Blue and Green Solaces. Blood doesn't matter. That's one thing Charybdis Station knows well."

"The Council agrees," Renee said, smirking. "What will it be, son?"

Cas nodded, a cocky grin on his face. "I'm in."

"That settles it then. I'll e-mail you your new titles, rosters, and first set of orders," Fasi said. "Also, please remember that we're a team. Help one another; I'm here to help too."

"Now, the first thing we will be dealing with is the Concords," Renee said. "Beck and Pops came up with some ideas to disable the ships, so you can board them, hopefully saving as many prisoners as possible."

Pops stood and pulled up some images. He smiled proudly. "A while back, Beck created some fun little nets that can disable a ship." He showed the energy nets and a recording of Dannol using them during the recent attack.

"Oh my," Sheiria said. "I want some. Please."

"They seriously kick ass," Cas said.

"The problem is that they're hard to make," Pops said. The large, gruff man frowned thoughtfully. "Engineering can probably put together about six a week. That means it ain't too smart to only use them. Selene and Beck, though, have come up with an alternative." He pointed toward the image of a long, shimmering missile.

Selene stood, looking around the room. "Beck and I

took the technology behind his nets and applied it to a standard missile. These are easy to adapt because the engineers won't be making them from scratch. They'll modify the current missiles we have."

"The missiles we chose to change up are our weakest missiles too," Beck added. "An enemy ship will see them as a smack on the hand. They're likely to rely on their shields to deflect them."

"Hack, I want your engineer and weapons masters," Audre said.

Each person in the room looked damned impressed.

"Wow, Captain, we feel really loved." Audre's engineer grinned, not at all upset. "Okay, okay, I'd trade us too."

Hack just sat back in his chair and smirked. As if he had anything to do with their genius or where they served. He'd just lucked out in befriending the two as a kid. They insisted on staying with him when they could have easily advanced.

Beck blushed. "A-anyway," he stuttered. "Each ship will get a slew of these, plus some of the nets. Hopefully, this will help us stay alive and keep their prisoners safe until we can rescue them." He quickly sat beside Selene.

Hack's dad watched the gentle man fondly, then pulled his attention back to the room. "Our first action will be to increase patrols and look for solitary Concord ships. We want to pick them off as much as we can before we move to larger battles. Our contacts in individual spaceports have already begun to track sightings of the Concords. My next step is to, as Audre suggested, reach out to the other mercenary groups."

"We will also increase the medical presence on each ship. As we take in Concord prisoners, we'll need to be able to help them," Hack's mom said. "For the larger battles, we'll have a full ship equipped with medical equipment that will take in all wounded and rescued prisoners."

Fasi gave the room one last tired smile. "I think that update is enough for one day. You are all on leave for the rest of the week, so please, go home and process everything. Send Renee and me questions..." He paused a moment. "I would like my new generals to remain behind for a few more minutes."

Dru patted Hack on the shoulder. "I'll stay with Leti until you get home, boss." She ignored his glare and headed for the door. The rest of his crew nodded or waved before they left. Once the room was emptied of all but the six of them, Fasi sat heavily in his seat.

"Cas, Audre, Hack, I've updated Sheiria on the situation with Morrick and his artifact," Fasi said. "Unfortunately, we've come to a bit of a standstill. The three bodies we unloaded from your ship, Hack, disappeared. They belonged to two unnamed, rescued Concord prisoners and Dr. Morrick himself."

"Franklin," Hack said angrily. "Leti said she's obsessed with Morrick." Fuck, this was going to upset Leti.

"That was our first thought too," Renee said. "She has two guards with her at all times, and we've assigned her an 'assistant' who will also keep track of the work she's doing. Dr. Manning refuses to work directly with her. Apparently, Franklin isn't a very likable person."

"Why not just toss her off the station?" Sheiria asked.

"Next to Morrick, she's the best in her field," Hack said. No matter how despicable the woman was, they could use her knowledge.

"Yes," Fasi agreed. "Orsla knows she's necessary but says they'll work separately and consult when they have to."

"Have they made any progress yet? I know it's just been a day," Cas said.

"Leti sent Morrick's notes to Orsla right after he died, and she's been working her way through his theories. She's skeptical of his conclusions, and I can't say I blame her, but she said he wasn't one to exaggerate, so I don't know. Right now, she's just settling in and drawing her own conclusions," Fasi said.

"What's it supposed to do?" Audre sprawled out in her chair, exhaustion making her paler than usual. They all really needed a break.

"That's what's up for debate," Fasi said. "Morrick's notes suggest it can reanimate the dead. Of course, Orsla was rather doubtful of that conclusion."

"Fuck, I don't blame her," Sheiria said. "Morrick was a legit scientist? Why would he think that?"

"Leti said he did experiments on dead animals. He reported that they actually appeared to reanimate for a short length of time," Hack said. "He has recordings to back up his conclusions."

"That's just crazy," Sheiria said. "I don't think I believe it."

"That's why Orsla is having such a hard time with this," Fasi said. "She trusts Morrick and knows he wouldn't have fudged the results."

"Has Leti made any more progress in his own research?" Cas asked.

"Today, actually, he got a lead from a colleague of his. They also got the translation guide they were waiting on. Leti says Sebastian's picking up the language pretty fast. They have some old books and articles to read once they can translate them."

"Think he can figure out its purpose?" Renee looked both worried and hopeful. They badly needed a break in this mystery.

"If anyone can, he will," Audre said confidently. "I've only spoken with him a few times, but that man is determined and smart."

"That he is," Renee said proudly. "Another concern we have is this mystery ship that stepped into your last battle. The ship's technology doesn't match anything we have on record." She paused, thinking hard. "The closest I can think of is the Half-Moon…" Horror flashed in her eyes. "Leti."

Hack paled. "You think it was the assassin Leti's parents sent?"

"An assassin is after Leti?" Audre stood, pissed. "Why the fuck would someone want to hurt him?"

"His parents?" Sheiria's voice was full of sympathy.

"Yeah. His fucked-up parents put a contract out on him," Cas said, scowling.

"Why would an assassin help though? Why reveal their ship or location?" Renee mused. "I'll reach out to a few of my own contacts in the Half-Moon Guild. They're located in Union Station, and we need to get that contract voided anyway."

"I planned to send someone to have a talk with his parents once you all got home," Fasi said. "I'll pick a team and send them."

"Oh, I'm leading that team, babe," Renee said. "I want to have a few words with his mother."

Hack couldn't stop his grin. His mom already considered Leti hers.

"We'll all keep an eye on him, Hack," Cas said. "We won't let anyone hurt our Leti."

16

Arriving home to an empty house, Hack followed the noise out his back door and was greeted by complete chaos. Pops and Beck were in their shifted forms and played in the corner of the yard with all the kids and Trixie. Pax and Gravy quickly joined in.

Dru and Lerais made out in a patio chair, completely unconcerned with public decency. Poor Monty sat on the back of their chair, a little dejected.

A hiss drew his attention. Princess Buttercup was sprawled in a hammock with Marmalade, Biscuit, and Abbot cuddled close to him. He watched Hack in amusement. Damn it! Now Hack was thinking of the giant lizard as a person.

Wobble was currently being pampered by Nessa and Dannol, while Miss Speckles and Hector were wandering around, pecking at the grass. Ma and Juniper carried platters of food to the patio table, Pork Chop following close behind.

Finally spotting Leti, he couldn't help but laugh at the sight of his precious mate sitting on Alois while most of his crew surrounded them, cheering.

"That's not fair," Alois whined. "I'm still recovering."

Leti looked smug. He bounced a bit, Alois groaning beneath him. "I kicked your butt! That's what you get for staying unconscious for so long. Better not worry me again."

Mo sidled up to Hack. "Leti caught Alois off guard. He was staring at Sebastian's butt."

Hack grinned. "What's going on here?"

"Impromptu dinner gathering. Then, Selene said Leti missed too many training sessions, so everyone thought they'd give him pointers. Honestly, Lerais's advice is best. He said grab whatever you can and hit the hell out of the person attacking. If there's nothing to grab, bite and kick."

Hack shook his head and threw an arm around Mo. "How was school?"

"Surprisingly good. Julia and the others fit right in," Mo said. Hack's brother watched him for a minute, biting his lip.

Hack waited patiently while the boy thought. Nodding, Mo pulled him to the chairs next to the hammock. They settled down, Mo pulling his legs to his chin and watching Princess laze about.

"Is it bad that I don't miss my mom and dad?" His sad, worried eyes finally met Hack's.

"No," Hack said firmly.

"How did you feel right after?"

"When our mom left me, I was mad. Really, really

mad. At the same time though, I still loved her. It took a long time to come to terms with what happened. Did I miss her, though? Hell no!"

"I don't even miss the planet," Mo said sadly. "Shouldn't I miss the place that created me?"

Hack was quiet for a minute, remembering how he felt in his first few years here. "When I first came here, I missed the heat, the sand. It seems stupid now, but that's what I knew. Even then, I absolutely loved it here. My new mom and dad loved me, focused on me. I wasn't a burden to them. The station itself is so different from Burnished Outpost, and to be honest, our home world is really backwards. Every kid learns the same traditions, the same way of doing things every single generation. There's nothing new."

"Definitely no engineers back home," Mo said and smiled softly. "Uncle Bowan told me and Alex that we used to fly through space, traveling the stars. He was always drunk though, so we didn't believe him. It's kind of sad because he's going to be chieftain one day. Probably not too far away actually. I do miss him, though, and my brothers and sisters."

"Is Alex one of them?"

"Yeah. He's the oldest of us. He's going to be so pissed when he finds out what she did to me. He's seventeen and would have taken either me or the new baby in. Rosie is the next eldest. She'll raise hell for sure. The other three are too little to know what's going on, I think."

"She didn't try to find someone to take you in?"

"No," Mo said, shrugging. "It would have looked

really bad for our dad if people found out he couldn't support his family. Alex would have taken me, but so would have Uncle Bowan and Grandpa Moses."

"Grandpa would have? I'm surprised he's still alive," Hack said, chest hurting. He'd loved Grandpa Moses so much, thought he'd loved him back.

Mo watched him carefully. "That's something I wanted to talk to you about. Privately."

"Yeah?"

"When Alex, Rosie, and I were kids, we went on a lot of hunting trips with Grandpa Moses. My dad's father is the chieftain, so he never had time with us. Right after Alex found out about you, I think he was ten or so, he told us what happened. How Mom abandoned you. So when we went out, he asked Grandpa Moses about it."

Hack's eyes burned, and he watched Princess. "What did he say?"

"He started crying," Mo said.

"What?" Hack sat up, looking back at Mo. Crying was taboo on Burnished Outpost. Most people saw it as a weakness.

"Yeah," he said with a shaky laugh. "Shocked us too. He told us about your dad and what your former tribe did. He told us that he refused you, disowned you. Once you were gone though, he realized what he'd done. He said that it broke him, and he was never the same. He doesn't know you're alive, Will. None of them do."

"Would it make a difference?" Hack's eyes were wet, and he hid his face. The next instance, Leti was there, burying Hack's face against his stomach. His baby was in there. A little peanut growing bigger and bigger.

Hack let his tears come. He cried for Grandpa Moses, for his dad, for Mo. He cried for his fucking mother.

Mo wrapped skinny arms around him, surprisingly strong. His own face was wet with tears. "It would matter, Will. I know it would. Even Uncle Bowan would care."

"We'll let them know then," Leti said. "They may or may not check their messages, but we can at least send it to them."

"I think Uncle Bowan checks them sometimes," Mo said. "He's the only one in the ruling family who's interested."

"It's a plan," Hack said, pulling his head from Leti's belly when it grumbled loudly. "Now we'd better feed Leti before the baby revolts."

He looked around and noticed everyone was already gathered at the four tables spread throughout the yard. His dad and mom had arrived while he talked to Mo, and he spotted Pepper in his mom's arms. It was time to steal back his baby girl. Leti pulled Mo behind him, lost to the call of food.

"Give me my baby, Mom," Hack said, reaching for Pepper.

"Fine," she said, pouting. "But either me or Ma gets the kids once a week. I think that's more than fair, son."

"Take it up with Leti," Hack said, cuddling his little girl. He checked her over. Yep, all her toes and fingers were still there.

"As long as you visit during the week too," Leti said.

"Of course, Leti darling," Ma said, putting a small plate of chocolate squirrels in front of him. She kissed Leti's head, chuckling as he attacked the plate.

"So, I'm going to be a captain, right, General Hackett?" Dru smirked at his growl and fed a baby carrot to Lerais. "Lerais has agreed to be my engineer."

"Yes, Dru," Hack said drily. "You'll be a captain. Morgan, you want to be her weapons specialist? You need some experience in leadership."

"If she'll have me," Morgan said, cutting up Rizzie's chicken for her.

"I guess so," Dru said. "If I have to." She couldn't hold in her laugh when Morgan flipped her off. The two would complement one another well.

"Finn, you mind being my lieutenant?" Hack asked. "It'll be a harder job if I'm a general."

Finn looked up from his plate. "Seriously? Me?"

"Of course," Hack said. "You have the necessary communication skills, and you're a damn good fighter. Selene and the others will have larger roles too with this new position."

Finn blinked, the news sinking in. He grinned and leaned back, smug and happy. "I'm a lieutenant," he said. "Damn."

Dru smacked him. "Get over it, weirdo," she said. "So, Leti told us Dr. Morrick's son is missing." She grabbed another scoop of potatoes. "Want me to take a small ship out to look? It'd be a good first mission, I think."

Hack shared a grateful look with his friend. It

would be a relief to Leti to have her in charge of finding Morrick's son. He trusted her, and he was worried to death about Wyatt Morrick. Dru would miss out on some of the fighting though, so he knew it wasn't her first choice. She wanted to do it for Leti.

"If you're sure, that'd be perfect," Hack said. "Dad, what's the fastest ship in my new fleet?"

Fasi looked up from hugging Leti for the fifth time since he'd arrived. Leti didn't seem to mind. Just kept eating. "The Blue Sparrow," Fasi answered. "You'll love it, Dru. It's small, just a passenger ship, but it's damn fast."

"Damn fast," Sami repeated from Beck's lap.

Fasi looked at Leti, his furry purple face as innocent as could be. "Did you hear anything? I didn't hear anything."

"Sure, Dad, sure," Leti said, rolling his eyes. "Hmm, I love your baked ham, Ma." He helped himself to a third piece. Meanwhile, Fasi looked on the verge of tears. He loved it when Leti called him Dad.

Hack hid his smile and turned back to Dru. "You'll need a smaller crew than Blue Solace has. Take Quinn, Hazel, and Linc with you. Hazel can continue training with Lerais. Dannol said Linc was ready for solo flying, so there's your pilot."

"Alois, you up to be my lieutenant?" Dru eyed Sebastian with interest.

"I'd love to," Alois said. "You'll need one, and I didn't do much more than get shot and sleep for the last mission."

"You're still recovering though," Sebastian said. "Do you really think you're ready?"

Alois gave him a gentle look, smiling softly. "It'll probably be a short mission, and I think it would be for the best."

Hack noted that Sebastian didn't seem to think so. He frowned at Alois, holding his hand and stroking his thumb across the Dedril's palm. Hack didn't think he even noticed he did it.

"Well, that's a crew of six for you, Dru," Hack said. "We'll contact the GACP and get what information we can from them first."

"Oh, I called them already," Leti said, then took another bite of rice. He slowly chewed and swallowed as everyone watched, waiting for him to continue. "I called the CEO's assistant, and she did some digging. Wyatt's supervisor hadn't reported him missing, but she couldn't reach his team. Apparently, that's really unusual. She talked with her boss and they investigated. Wyatt's team went missing a month and a half ago on the planet Tammol in the Sugarworm System. The planet's been a warzone for the past twenty years, and the GACP sent doctors and supplies to help the displaced. According to Gina—she's the assistant—the CEO was really concerned. They're hiring us to find them."

"I thought you were ordered to rest today," Hack said.

"I sat in a chair and made a call, Will. It was hardly work." Leti turned his big green eyes on Fasi. "You don't mind them hiring us, do you? I'm just really worried about Wyatt."

The soft-hearted Grell melted. "Of course not, Leti. Dru's already agreed to go, so we ought to get paid for it, right?"

"We need to discuss something else too," Renee said in a no-nonsense voice. Everyone sat up straight, ready for orders. "Leti and Hack need to have their wedding before Dru and I leave the Station."

"Wait, where are you going?" Leti asked.

"Making a trip to Vextonar, dear one," she said. "Enough of that though. How fast can we make this happen?"

Juniper and Ava exchanged looks.

"Give us two days," Ava said.

$\mathscr{L}$eti looked at himself in the bathroom mirror. His hair lay neatly and gold glinted at his throat and wrists. He wore a loose pair of rich brown trousers and a floaty, shimmery gold shirt. He had to admit he looked nice. It was missing something though.

"Ava," he called, leaving the master bathroom, then stopped, startled. On his bed lay the perfect addition for his wedding outfit: a lovely green silk robe with golden roses. It looked familiar, but Leti knew it wasn't his. Ava must have put it out for him. He put it on, then looked in the mirror over the dresser. Oh yeah. It was perfect.

"Did you call, sugarplum?" Ava waltzed in, dressed beautifully in a red dress and heels. "You are going to love the setup outside. Juniper and I are geniuses, I swear. Oh, Leti, you look gorgeous."

Leti spun around happily. "I feel gorgeous," he said, truly meaning it. Today, he would become Hack's husband. It shouldn't matter so much since they were already mates, but it did. The ceremony and legalities mattered more to Leti than he thought they would. Hack wanted him, wanted to be his husband. He really did love Leti.

"Damn, Leti," Draif said, shutting the door behind him and Fasi. "You look beautiful. Well, even more beautiful than usual."

"Oh, my beautiful boy," Fasi said, pulling him into a hug. Leti loved the man's hugs. They were love—pure, unabashed love.

"Are they ready for us?" Ava asked.

"Yeah. Selene's brother and sister will start singing when we enter," Draif said

"Their names are Shae and Sabina," Leti said.

"They're both so shy I keep forgetting," Draif said, wincing.

"They'll get used to us," Fasi said. "I think Shae's going to stay on the station instead of leaving. He's going to start training with Selene. Now, Leti, are you ready?"

"I am," Leti said simply. He was beyond ready for Hack to belong to him. "Princess, you ready?"

Leti's dragon was feeling a little larger than usual. He was fifteen feet today, but luckily, the big gold bow around his neck stretched. Leti left the bedroom and followed Renee to the back door. They'd decided to have the wedding in the backyard so Lucas wouldn't feel too self-conscious, and really, because Leti adored his new home. It was his.

Draif, Rizzie, Alois, Sebastian, Selene, and Cordelia

waited for him at the door. He had asked them to stand with him during the ceremony, and he was glad they'd agreed. Each of them wore dark green clothes, his favorite color.

"You look really nice, Leti," Cordelia said, hugging him. "Are you ready?"

"Oh yeah," he said. "Let's get moving. I'm starting to get hungry, and I know Juniper made me a big cake."

"Here's your bouquet," Sebastian said, handing him an intricately designed bouquet of metal flowers.

He recognized Beck and Pops's work. "Oh good. I don't need to steal Rizzie's now."

The little girl giggled, holding her basket of white flower petals. "I'd let you borrow it, Daddy Leti.".

"Come on, everyone," Fasi said happily. "Ladybug, you go first, just like we practiced."

"I will, Grandpa." Rizzie stepped out, and Sabina and Shae began to sing. Leti had never heard anything more beautiful in all his life. There were no words, only emotion and the images they recalled.

Joy was the moment he first laid eyes on Will, dumbfounded and clumsy. Passion was their first real kiss, right after Will told him about his mother's abandonment. Peace was holding Will close when he came back from battle, feeling him alive beneath him. Happiness was sitting on the couch, watching the vid-screen with Will and the kids, knowing they were right where they needed to be. Love, oh so much love. Every minute he'd spent with Will was full of love.

"Cordelia, you're next," Ava said. "Selene. Sebastian. Alois." One by one, they walked out the door.

"Leti," Draif said. "You're sure about this, right? This is what you want?"

"More than anything in the galaxy, Draify-love."

Draif looked close to tears and set his hands on Leti's shoulders. "Look at you, Leti. Look at that smile."

"I have Will, you, the kids, tons of new friends, new parents," Leti said. "I never knew that I could be loved so much. I never knew I could feel this much happiness, Draif."

"Draif," Fasi said softly, watching them with a smile. "It's your turn, son."

Draif blushed at the word son but nodded and walked out the door.

"So, how do I get Princess to go? Oh, well, would you look at that," Fasi said, as the dragon followed the others a few seconds after Draif. "You ready, Leti?" He held his arm out.

"Thank you, Dad, for walking beside me."

"Oh, it's an honor, Leti. The way you make my boy feel and your own loving self… Well, I'm a lucky dad. Now, let's do this."

Together, they walked outside, and Leti gasped as he saw Juniper and Ava's hard work. Their backyard was transformed into a tranquil paradise. Arbors decorated with plants and shiny bits of glass were nestled in each corner. Fairy lights hung all over the yard from tall, thin wooden columns encircled with climbing flowers. White petals dotted the path, courtesy of Rizzie.

Ma and Pops were in their shifted forms, sitting with the kids and the rest of the crew. Sami and Rizzie both sat on Silas's lap, and Pepper rocked in her carrier between Finn and Morgan. Lucas was propped up against Maia, and Pax and the other pets surrounded them, sprawled out comfortably.

Around fifty guests sat on pillows all throughout the yard, all friends and colleagues of the Juren family. Leti knew the whole Council was mixed in there somewhere as well as other leaders of the worlds in the Anchor's Rest System. Leti could feel nervousness start to rise, but Shae and Sabina's song pushed it down, reminding him why he was here.

In the middle of everything stood the wedding party, arranged in a circle. Hack was dressed in a flowing, sleeveless black tunic and tight pants. His tattoos glowed golden, and white fire filled his eyes. To his left stood his friends, dressed in black. Mo stood next to his brother, followed by Cas, Xav, and Beck, all three in their shifted forms. Dru and Nettle finished Hack's side. To the right of Leti's spot stood Princess on his hind legs, followed by Draif, Alois, Sebastian, Selene, and Cordelia.

Fasi walked Leti to his spot and then entered the circle with Renee. Hack grabbed his hand, winking, so Leti bumped him with his hip, his smile wide and joyous. Sabina and Shae lowered their voices to a hum and the ceremony began.

"Today we gather to join two people in heart, body, and soul," Fasi began. Neither Leti nor Hack were religious people, so they had chosen to follow the ceremony of Fasi's people, the Grell. Fasi spoke of Leti, of his strengths, his weaknesses. Renee then spoke for her son. She listed his strengths and weaknesses as well, holding nothing back. It was hard, to hear his less than wonderful traits, but the Grell believed that no one could be a true partner to their beloved until they knew themselves well.

"Where Will is stubborn and cantankerous, Leti is empathetic and loving. Where Leti is naïve and a bit gullible, Will is realistic and practical. Every person has darkness and light inside them. Every person has good and bad. Together, these two beautiful people call to the light in one another," Fasi said.

"Join us," Renee said, "in welcoming this uniting of soulmates."

Every shifted Grell in the circle and audience roared, while those who couldn't cheered. Gravy and Biscuit joined by howling, and Pax, Marmalade, and Fluffle yowled. Wobble and Trixie ignored everyone and chewed on one of the arbors.

The audience jumped, startled when Princess Buttercup roared his own welcome, loud and quaking. Small puffs of smoke came from his snout. Leti and Hack didn't hear anything, too wrapped up in each other. Hack's mouth was on Leti's, the kiss deepening quickly. Leti pressed against his body. His mate, his husband, his home.

***

"OUR WEDDING CAKE was so good, Will," Leti said as Hack carried him into the house. Ma and Pops were taking the kids, Maia and Silas were staying in their suites upstairs, and Xav and Finn were patrolling the neighborhood. Hack and Leti were finally alone. *Finally*. That cake, though, it might actually be his real soulmate.

"It was squirrel-shaped, baby," Hack said. "Juniper knew exactly what he was doing."

"The chocolate was so… Oh gods, Will, I can't even describe it."

Hack settled him on the bed. "Mhmm," he crooned and started pulling off Leti's shoes.

Leti watched his mate from the bed, full and happy. Hack wore a soft, dreamy expression as he removed his own clothes, then started on Leti's. Leti shrugged his robe off and pulled his shirt over his head, eager for his mate.

Finally, Hack crawled onto the bed, stretching out beside Leti. "Leti Hackett," Hack said. "I love saying that. I love you." He buried his face in Leti's neck, breathing in deeply.

Leti pulled Hack close and shut his eyes, reveling in the moment. "I love you so much, Will. Our life… It's not perfect, but it's ours. Meeting you, being with you, I'm such a better person. Stronger."

"You make me better too," Hack said. "I'm happier and lighter. I never thought I'd mate and marry. I didn't think anyone could stand being with me that long."

"Idiot," Leti said, kissing his mate's head.

"You are so romantic." Hack laughed and started kissing his way down Leti's body. "We're completely alone for the first time in weeks. What should we do?"

Leti smiled wickedly. He had some ideas.

A few minutes later, Leti sank onto Hack's dick, sweat trickling down his back. His mate watched him from below, eyes glowing with fire. The look on Hack's face just about made Leti come then and there. He had never felt more loved or more beautiful.

Leti moaned as Hack slid inside him, stretching him so fucking good. He sank deeper and deeper until fully seated, completely full. Leti still couldn't believe how good it felt to have his mate inside him. Every single time, he marveled at it.

He lifted up, then pushed roughly back onto Hack's hard dick, setting a steady pace. Hack's moans urged him on, and it wasn't long before Leti was there. He came, shooting across Hack's chest. The tight contractions of his body squeezed Hack's cock, and he knew Hack wouldn't last long. His husband's hands tightened on Leti's ass as he came with a shout.

Hack rolled them, settling them on their sides. "Damn," he finally said, chest rising and falling with his pants. "Every single time gets better and better. It doesn't last longer though."

Leti snorted, then started laughing. "We've become experts at quickies."

"Hmm," Hack said, nuzzling Leti's neck. "We have all night, husband. Let's work on our expertise."

"It's sent," Hack said. Leti leaned back against his mate and kissed the bottom of Hack's chin. "Mo said his uncle doesn't check it every day or even every week, but it's there. Now we wait."

"How do you feel?"

Hack dropped his head to the top of Leti's. "I think I'm okay," he said. "I'd like to talk to Alex and the others, but honestly, I really want to talk to Grandpa Moses. I don't want him to hurt anymore. He needs to know I'm okay, that the best thing that could happen, did happen." Hack started nuzzling the back of his neck.

"Nope, not happening," Leti said, pushing up. "My ass still aches from last night, Will. I came so much my dick even hurts. Plus, I'm hungry."

Hack fell back in the chair, laughing. He looked like a kid, so light and joyful. "Are you really complaining? If I remember right, you're the one who kept waking me up and begging for more."

"Oh yeah," Leti said, smiling sheepishly. He pulled his wedding robe on; it was officially his favorite piece of clothing ever. "I'm not the one to blame though. It's your fault for looking so good. Plus, your dick's almost always hard. I wrote an ode to it. Draif liked it, said it had potential."

"Do you really need to discuss my dick with Draif?"

"Of course," Leti said, puzzled. "Who else would I discuss it with?"

"No one?"

"Will, do you even understand best friends?" Leti shook his head. His silly husband needed to get out more. A beep from the vid-screen drew his attention to an incoming call.

Leti looked down. He looked proper enough, and Hack wore pants and a shirt. He pushed Hack back in the chair and sat in his lap.

"Hello?" Leti said.

An older, unfamiliar man appeared on the vid-screen. He was a Silet and wore a dress shirt and sweater vest, reminding Leti of many of the people he worked with back on Vextonar. The man's hair was tousled, like he'd been running his hands through it, and his face was creased in worry.

"Dr. Ando?"

"Dr. Hackett as of yesterday, but yes, that's me," Leti said.

Hack grunted in approval behind him.

"I'm Dr. Ernest Webber, the Dean of Archaeology at the University of Siletus in the Boral System."

"Oh, it's nice to hear from you, Dr. Webber. My friend, Dr. Chopra, told me you would call."

"Yes. I'm sorry for the inconvenience, but a message wouldn't do. Is that your husband with you?"

"He is. This is General Hackett of Charybdis Station."

"I must admit, it is a relief to know you have military support. What I have to tell you is quite disturbing, Dr. Hackett."

"I assume Dr. Chopra's told you what I'm looking for? Did he show you the pictures of the artifact?"

"He did. The topic is a familiar one. The Crellic System is not at all my specialty, but one of my former faculty members was obsessed with it. Dr. Linda Belcort and her husband, Dr. Windell Belcort, both specialized in the Crellic System. Linda worked for me in the archaeology department, and Windell worked in the history department."

"Do you think they'd mind speaking with me?"

"I don't think you'd want that," Dr. Webber said. He sank back in his chair, face gray with stress. "Six months ago, the university funded a research trip for the Belcorts. They only took their two children, Melinda and Roger. Both of them were students here, so they would get some class credit for it. No one else went with them except the pilot that flew their ship."

Leti had a feeling this story didn't have a happy ending.

"The first month was extraordinary," Dr. Webber said. "They landed on Dargner and began excavating the remains of the largest city on the planet. It was slow going with just four of them, but the pilot shuttled back and forth, bringing us the most wondrous artifacts. We documented everything. I'll send what we have to you immediately after our call."

"That sounds amazing, Dr. Webber," Leti said. "Why do you look so unhappy? That kind of discovery can make the reputation of a university."

"It can," he said. "Which is why I dismissed the early warnings that something wasn't quite right. The calls from the Belcorts came less and less, but I justified it by telling myself they were just so busy. Then, the pilot started acting strange. When I met with him, he wouldn't meet my eyes. He was more reluctant to part with his packages."

"Do you think he was selling things on the side?" Hack asked.

"That was my first thought, but I doublechecked the list Linda sent me and everything matched," he answered. "Then we were brought the element, the artifact you now have. I sent it to Dr. Morrick in the hopes of understanding what was in it. Our own research picked up some type of organism in it, and I was afraid it was an ancient virus. He seemed our best bet."

"He was the best," Leti said softly.

"He was." Dr. Webber nodded sadly. "Right after we sent off the element, communication with the Belcorts stopped completely. The pilot never came back to Siletus. Of course, we were afraid something had happened, so we sent a rescue team. They never came back. We sent another with the same results."

"Something happened to the Belcorts? Were they Silet or Human?" Leti curled into Hack. Definitely not a happy ending here.

"They're Silet, and yes, I believe something did happen. We sent another team, but they were instructed not to land. Instead, they just scanned the planet. There was nothing living there. They could see the camp and see where the Belorts had dug. They could even see pieces of the two previous rescue ships, but there was no sign of anyone. Then, they saw Roger's body. From the pictures, he'd been dead a while. He'd been ripped to pieces."

"By what?" Hack asked.

"That's what we wanted to know. I asked them to

fly farther into the system," he said, then paused, closing his eyes. "I wish I hadn't. They never made it home either. Before they died, they found movement on a planet that is not supposed to even exist."

"The Crellic System has one habitable planet, Dargner," Leti said. "All the others were destroyed or made uninhabitable when the ancient Crells drove themselves to the brink of extinction."

"That's what I thought," Dr. Webber said. "However, the third ship found another habitable planet, directly in the middle of the system, where an uninhabitable one was supposed to be. They recorded what they could see and sent it to me immediately. Then they died."

"What did they see?" Hack asked.

"Hundreds of people rebuilding a broken temple. The pilot was among them, as well as some of the men and women we sent to rescue them. They were also able to identify Melinda. She was… in charge of the workers. I knew the girl; she was a complete idiot. There's no way she would be able to instruct someone to rebuild an ancient temple. The way she stood, the way she acted… It wasn't like her."

"Do you think she learned while she was there?"

"She was there because her mother made her come, not because she had any intention of really helping," Dr. Webber said, shaking his head. "Then… I was speaking with the pilot when they were attacked. We were arguing. I wanted him to go down there, and he wanted to come home. Out of nowhere, a Concord Mercenary ship fired on them with no warning. We lost communication with them, and I fear they're dead."

"I'm so sorry," Leti said. The man looked defeated. He'd lost three rescue teams on top of everything else.

"Another month passed, then Windell arrived at the university along with several Concord mercenaries. He wasn't… himself. He demanded all of the artifacts they had sent. He said Linda wanted them back."

"That's strange," Leti said. "No university would willingly part with artifacts found on a funded dig. Did he really expect you to turn things over?"

"He did," Dr. Webber said. "I gave him about a third of them, the artifacts that weren't of much worth. The mercenaries were terrifying, and the university president completely understood. Windell took them and left. He didn't ask about the others. He didn't even seem to remember them, and he didn't ask about the pictures or any of our documentation. Then, on the way out, his cousin saw him. We all thought Linda and Windell were dead along with Roger. He was so happy to see him and tried to hug him."

"What happened?"

"Windell didn't even recognize him. He stared at the man with nothing in his eyes. Nothing. Then they left. I haven't heard or seen from them since."

"Dr. Webber," Hack said. "What do you think happened?"

"I don't think that was Windell Belcort. I don't think that was Melinda Belcort. I don't think they are working *for* the Concords. They were giving the orders.

Other than that, I don't know. No one at the university can read ancient Crellic, and honestly, I don't want to risk anyone else on this. I'll ship everything we have, every last artifact to you at Charybdis Station, Dr. Hackett. The university can fire me for all I care. You are better equipped to handle this, I think."

"We would be grateful, Dr. Webber," Leti said. "I'll do my best and let you know if we find anything."

"Thank you, and please, be careful. Don't go to the Crellic System. I don't know what's happening there, but nothing good can come of it."

LETI WATCHED Dru and the others shut the cargo bay door to their new ship. He stood curled into Hack's side. He hadn't wanted to leave his side since talking with Dr. Webber. Something horrible was happening in the Crellic System, and it was spilling out into the rest of the galaxy. He waved for maybe the hundredth time, watching his friends' faces disappear.

Sebastian stood beside him, completely forlorn. "I know it's for the best," Sebastian said. "I need time to adapt to the idea of being with Alois, but I wish he had kissed me before going. Then I'd know."

"Maybe so, but then you could easily dismiss him if you wanted, even if he was your mate. You could tell yourself it wasn't real," Silas said. "Sometimes having a fated soulmate makes people forget that they still need to fall in love with that soulmate. With Alois at a physical distance, you can talk and get to know one another. You can fall in love."

"Plus, they won't be gone long," Beck said. "Just get to the planet, pick up Wyatt, and come back. It'll take a month at the most."

"Yeah," Leti said. "They'll be back before we know it."

18

"It's been five months, Dru," Leti whined. "When are you getting back?"

"We'll be there in another month," Dru said. She looked rough. Their easy trip had turned into a nightmare, but they'd survived, found Wyatt, and were finally coming home. "How's the war going from your end? I've talked with Hack, but you've been stationed on the medical ship. You've seen the Concords' prisoners first hand."

"So far, so good. Each outgoing Charybdis ship usually comes back with refugees after isolating and taking out a Concord ship. There have been four bigger battles at Anchor's Rest, but the missiles work well. Beck, Selene, and Pops are coming up with new weapons all the time. It's kind of cute the way they work together. Unfortunately, the state of the prisoners is getting worse and worse. It's like the fuckers take out every little frustration on them."

"Charybdis Station is keeping them pretty

frustrated," Dru said. "Hack and the others are good leaders. They'll finish this up as fast as possible."

"Hack won't let me go with him on his ship though. It's rude." Leti pouted, crossing his arms over his chest. His arms rested perfectly on top of his belly. It really wasn't fair though. He needed to be at Hack's side.

"Yeah, so I'm not going to bother explaining how having the general's pregnant husband on a battleship is a bad idea. Anyway, how is Sebastian doing? Alois spends a lot of time in his quarters on the vid-screen, but he's still going crazy."

Leti looked to his right. Sebastian lay on a blanket on the floor of Leti's office, a pillow under his head. He held a book up, reading, while Sami rolled a toy shuttle over his belly.

"Vroom, vroom," Sami said. "Shut go vroom o'er hilly."

"Sami's using his belly as a mountain road for his toys."

Dru sniggered. "Stand up again. I want to see the belly."

"No! You can see the belly when you get home. Anyway, Sebastian's is way bigger." Stupid Sebastian's belly wasn't bigger. It was the same damn size as Leti's, and he was eight and a half months pregnant.

"Wow, Leti," Sebastian said drily. "I'm right here and you're a liar."

"Oh hush. You know you're about to pop."

"Doesn't mean you have to point it out," Shae said. "Also, his belly is so not bigger. Tsk." The young Siren had become a permanent fixture on the station and one of Leti's best friends. He was so young but had a wild sense of humor.

Currently, he sat in the window seat, playing patty-cake with Pepper. Leti's little sister had grown like a weed. She was just over eight months old and was sitting up, crawling everywhere, and generally just being adorable.

"Anyway," Dru said, clearing her throat. "What's the news on your parents?"

"Renee still can't find them. She's talked to Half-Moon, and they've cancelled the contract, but she can't find my parents or the assassin that was assigned to kill me. Half-Moon is going a little crazy because the guy is the Guild Master's little brother."

"That's so fucking annoying. Where would your parents go? Renee was looking forward to a little smack down."

"Nowhere. That's what's really worrying me. They disappeared a week before Renee got there. Just gone. The servants are still there, all their belongings are there, and they haven't touched their money. Another two months and the government will assume they're dead. Apparently, I inherit everything."

"Do you think they're dead?"

Leti shrugged, trying not to care. He shouldn't care. "I don't think they would willingly leave the comfort of Vextonar."

"Who would kill them? Well, besides us."

"I don't know. Renee broke in and searched both offices. My father's was clean, but my mother's had more contracts. She hired four other assassin guilds to kill me."

"Holy shit."

"Yeah. Renee talked with them, and they've suspended the contracts. All four said they've lost assassins on the job so far."

"Hack didn't say they'd caught anyone. Fucker," Dru said, growling.

"That's because they didn't. No one knows where these supposed assassins have gone. I figure if I do end up inheriting my parents' money, I'll give some to the guilds to help their losses."

"Leti. Oh, sweet, dear Leti," Dru said. "You will not pay the guilds for losing people who were sent to kill you. Do you hear me?"

"They lost people, Dru," Leti said. "That's bad enough, but they might lose business too."

"Paid to kill you, Leti. Paid to kill you," Shae said.

"Oh no, Leti," Dru said. "So unfortunate, but I'm going to have to let you go. Got another call to make."

"Don't you tell Hack my plan, Dru," Leti said.

Dru make crackling noises. "Sorry, Leti. You're breaking up. Must be a bad signal." The screen went dark.

"Damn it," he said, slumping. "I had a plan."

"A very stupid plan," Sebastian said. He sat up, dislodging Sami's shuttles.

"Oh no," Sami said. "Shut crash. Fuck."

Leti sighed. At least Sami was using the word in the right context.

"Are we going to go to Dr. Manning with what we

discovered? You haven't told Hack yet either," Sebastian said. The young man had translated everything they had. All the books, articles, and writing on the artifacts Dr. Webber had sent. Leti had read every bit, and it painted a terrible picture, one that Leti found himself believing more and more every day.

"Her assistant told us the doctor didn't want our *rubbish*," Shae said, sneering. "I can't believe that woman."

"I'll try for an appointment one more time," Leti said. "Then we'll go down there." He set the call up, and Monica Ewing's face popped up. The human wasn't too fond of Leti.

"What do you want?"

"Hi, Ms. Ewing. I hoped to see if Dr. Manning had room for me today. I want to talk over a few things with her."

"For the last time, the doctor doesn't have time for your nonsense. She's read through everything you sent, wasting her time, and doesn't want to hear more. Just because you're a general's whore, doesn't mean we have to treat you specially. Don't call again."

The screen went dark for the second time that day.

"Wow, that woman really is a bitch," Sebastian said. "Tram trip?"

"Guess so," Leti said. "I'll go tell Silas and Maia." He tried to get to his feet, but his butt was wedged into the chair too tightly. "Uh, Shae?"

"I'll help you, Leti," Sebastian said. "I just hope my *much bigger* belly doesn't prevent me from being able to pull you out of your chair, where you are stuck like a turtle on its back."

Leti glared at him as he pulled Leti up. "Thanks," he hissed.

Sebastian started giggling, and Leti couldn't help it. He started too. Soon the two of them were laughing and hugging each other.

"You two are so weird," Shae said, picking up Pepper. "I hope the kids don't catch it."

"EXPLAIN IT AGAIN. This trip is necessary because…" Silas held Pax's leash and kept an eye on the crowded tram.

"We need to talk to Dr. Manning about the artifact," Leti said. "We haven't had luck with making an appointment, and it can't go on much longer. We need her honest thoughts on our theories."

He bent down, as much as he could bend anyway, and checked Sami and Pepper. The double stroller was very useful, but Sami had taken to stealing Pepper's stuffies to chew on. In return, she'd grab his hair. Aww, his two angels were behaving—for once. Princess Buttercup was at his traveling size and snuggled in the space between the two of them.

"Why couldn't you just call?" Maia kept Leti, Shae, and Sebastian between her and Silas. The two still took their supposed duties way too seriously.

"We tried, and Ms. Ewing, queen of all bitchiness, won't let us talk to her," Sebastian said, waddling beside Leti. It was nice to have a waddle friend. He didn't feel so alone.

"They can check in with Nettle while they're there," Shae added. "It's about time for both of them to have a check-up."

"No," Leti said, shaking his head. "Check-ups are at home with Will present."

"Nettle will be right there though," Shae said. "Don't you want to see your son again?"

Damn Siren knew Leti's weaknesses. "Maybe," he said reluctantly.

"Alright then, here we are," Maia said, stepping off the tram first. Silas herded the rest of them out, and they started toward the medical research buildings.

"Uh oh," Leti said. "I have to pee, guys."

"Me too," Sebastian said.

"Didn't you two go before we left? It's been fifteen minutes," Shae said.

"Can't argue with pregnant bladders, Shae," Silas said.

"Okay, here's the bathroom," Maia said, leading them to the public restrooms.

"I'll go in with them," Silas said. "You mind waiting here with Shae and the kids, Maia?"

"Not a problem. Be careful in there," she tried to say without laughing. It didn't work. Silas glared and handed over Pax's leash.

The three went in. The room was empty and Leti chose a stall. He didn't like the urinals. He was pee shy, and, embarrassingly enough, he had to sit to pee now. Sebastian followed suit, and Silas leaned against the wall next to the sinks. Leti shut his door and tried to pee.

Leti heard Silas moving around the room. "Can you run some water, Silas?" He waited for a reply or the sound of water. Then he waited some more. "Silas?"

"Come on, Silas," Sebastian said. "Water would help."

Leti's door ripped open and he screamed. He heard Sebastian's echoed scream. A man stood in front of him with a phaser. He aimed it at Leti's head, smiling coldly. Before he could react, the air shimmered behind Leti's attacker, revealing a small, familiar looking man. The small man reached around, grabbing the phaser with one hand and slitting the attacker's neck with a blade in the other.

Leti watched as the body slumped to the floor, the man's head leaning against the stall's wall. The small man spun around, and Leti heard another body hit the floor. Leti jumped up, pulling up his pants and struggled over the dead attacker.

Maia fought with two more men at the entrance to the bathroom while Pax took down one near the sinks. The stranger quickly dispatched the three remaining in the room. Sebastian poked his head out of the stall, and they both saw Silas at the same time.

"Silas!" Leti and Sebastian waddled as fast as they could to their fallen friend. He was unconscious and blood poured from his chest. There were several stab wounds, and the Betonize man was pale, too pale.

Leti pulled his sweater off and tried to stop the

bleeding. Sebastian checked his pulse and whispered encouragement to the sweet man.

"Help!" Leti yelled. "Help!"

The stranger finished helping Maia dispatch the last of the attackers and rushed over. He pulled Leti's sweater from Silas' chest and ripped open the man's shirt, revealing the gaping wounds. He pulled a tube of antibacterial healer out of his pocket and quickly spread it across each wound. The bleeding started to slow, the wounds healing a bit, but his chest was still a mess.

"Leti," Maia said. "You and Sebastian alright? The kids are with Shae. He ran to get help."

"We're okay, but Silas is hurt." Leti looked around. There were eight dead bodies on the ground. "Not to be critical, Maia, but how did they get in here?"

"I have no idea," she said. "I stood right there at the door, and I promise, no one passed me." The stranger pointed up. Leti looked up and noticed the ceiling tiles were a little off right above Silas.

"They came through the ceiling?" Maia shook her head in disbelief. "How did they know you'd stop here? It was completely random, but this attack wasn't."

"Damn," Sebastian said. "This whole area is connected. They could have been traveling above, following us as soon as we entered the medical area."

Leti looked closely at the stranger. "By the way, thank you for your help," he said. "Have I seen you before? You look familiar." The man shrugged, turning away, but the angle of his chin, the predatory eyes. "Wait, I saw you on Derelict, at the trade market. I thought you were watching our group, but then you stopped to buy… my wedding robe! You were looking at my wedding robe."

"Back on Derelict?" Maia looked him over. "This guy was there? Why didn't you mention someone watching us?"

"I didn't think anything about it. Did you leave the robe out for me when Will and I got married?"

The man blushed, then nodded. He hadn't said a word, hadn't made a single noise.

"I don't mean to offend, but can you speak?" Sebastian had noticed exactly what Leti had.

The man shook his head and pulled down his collar. His neck was one big scar.

"Ouch," Maia said. "That had to have hurt."

"So you followed us from Derelict," Leti mused. "You had some kind of camouflage on that looked a lot like the shield on the mystery ship. Remember it, Maia?"

"Yeah," she said. "Coupled with the way you fight, you're the missing assassin from Half-Moon, aren't you?"

The man nodded again. He looked back to Silas, avoiding their eyes.

"Have you been with us this whole time?" Leti asked.

He shook his head. So he'd gone somewhere else at some point.

"Do you know what happened to my parents?" Leti had a half-formed theory, and he wasn't sure how he felt about it. He knew how he *should* feel about it.

The man looked at him, eyes hard. He nodded.

"Are they dead?"

He nodded again.

"Did they deserve it?" Sebastian asked. He put a hand on the man's shoulder, squeezing gently.

The man nodded again. He looked at Leti, eyes imploring. Leti didn't know what for though. Forgiveness maybe.

"Did you kill them?" Maia asked.

He nodded, then stood as enforcers poured into the room.

Leti stood too, pulling on the man to get to his feet. Then he moved in front of him, blocking him from the guards.

"We need to get Silas to the medic," Leti said. "These dead men attacked us all and Silas was wounded."

"You alright, Leti? Sebastian?" Finn pushed his way through the enforcers. "Hack's in a meeting with the Lord Admiral. I just saw Shae running this way with the kids and followed."

"We're fine," Sebastian said. Medics entered behind Finn and quickly loaded Silas up. "Finn and I will go with them, Leti. You get our new friend home. He deserves a beer at the very least."

Leti and Maia explained what happened to the enforcers, then met up with Shae and the kids. Leti pulled his tablet out of the stroller's storage area. "Here," he said, handing it to the stranger, screen blank. "Use this to answer. First, what's your name?"

He typed quickly. *Wolfe.*

"Thank you, Wolfe, for saving us," Leti said.

"Seriously, man, thanks," Maia added. "Now, why didn't you kill Leti on Derelict? You couldn't have known he was pregnant then. I know Half-Moon refuses contracts on pregnant people, but how could you tell?"

I didn't know he was pregnant until we got to Charybdis Station. I saw what he did for Sami. I saw how he treated you two. Cas was his family, but you two were servants. At least I thought you were servants. He treated you like friends. I know now. You're all family.

"Was it really that shocking?" Leti asked. "I didn't do anything special."

"Yeah, you did, Leti," Maia said. "You love Silas and I, and most would see us as servants. Not a lot of people are like you."

"Really," Shae added. "Look at your family. You're a good guy, Waddler."

"Stop calling me that," Leti said, poking his friend. "Okay, Wolfe, why did you kill my parents?" It felt odd to say it aloud.

My brother called me, and I told him you were pregnant. He ordered me to come back home, but I didn't want to. I stayed for a while, saw you get married. Finally, I made myself go home to Union Station. Before I checked in with Half-Moon, I found out your parents hired more guilds. I knew that the others wouldn't hesitate to kill you. I intercepted most of them on the way to Vextonar, then talked with your parents. They didn't care that you were pregnant. They wanted you dead no matter what. There was no way they would stop, Leti. So I killed them. Got rid of the bodies.

Came back here and hunted down the two remaining assassins. They hadn't gotten onto the station yet.

"Why would you do all that for me?"

The same reason Silas and Maia guard you. You have important things to do. I've seen you with the incoming refugees. You comfort them and offer hope to the broken and traumatized. I'm seen you with your kids and with General Hackett. A cold and calculated death is not something you deserve.

"Come on," Maia said. "Let's get home. You know Hack's going to be breathing fire by the time Finn tells him what happened."

"I want to check on Silas," Leti said.

"We'll call Seb when we get home," Shae said. "Leti, I know you're worried about him, but if these guys were waiting on you, then there's no telling what we might run into. Our neighborhood is a controlled area. The rest of the station isn't."

Leti took Wolfe's hand and Pax's leash. "Okay, let's go."

The assassin shifted his eyes between their joined hands and Leti's face. Again and again. The poor guy didn't realize he'd just become family.

19

ack stared at his dad in disbelief. "They replied back?"

After five months, Hack had given up hope of a reply from Burnished Outpost. Beck patted his back, the man's thumps a bit too hard but comforting all the same.

Fasi grinned. "They certainly did. The old chieftain died, which is one reason Bowan took so long to get back to us. There's been some problems, but he seems to have things settled now. You ready for the call? We can get Leti or Mo here first if you want."

"I don't think I can wait," Hack said numbly. "I can't believe they replied."

"I think Bowan will bring that planet out of the past," Renee said. "At least I hope he does."

"Let's do this, Dad," Xav said. He pulled up the vidscreen and connected to the ancient console on Burnished Outpost. All five of them watched the screen in anticipation.

A face appeared, standing too close to the screen. The Burnished man was in his forties, healthy and handsome. His grin was contagious.

"Hi," he said, too loud.

"Chieftain Bowan," Fasi said. "You don't need to speak quite so loud, and if you don't mind, stand back just a bit."

The man made the adjustments. "I can't believe I'm seeing otherworlders. This is amazing!"

"It's nice to finally meet a leader of Burnished Outpost," Renee said. "This is Charybdis Station's Lord Admiral, Fasi Juren. I'm his wife and the security chief here, Renee Juren."

"That man beside you, could that be Will Hackett? You're the right age, and there's no arguing you're Burnished."

"I am," Hack said, clearing his throat. "Mo's at school right now, but he's missed you."

Tears filled the man's eyes. "You have no idea what your message meant to me and the others. We didn't know what that stupid bitch was planning. She told us the two of them were going on a hunting trip. When she returned alone, she said he went out hunting alone and never came back to their camp. We searched for months."

"Our patrols found him the same day he was left. He's doing well now," Renee said.

"Thank you," Bowan said. "Thank you so much. I'm not telling my people about your patrols. Some of the more backward tribes still abandon the weak, and I'm afraid they'll just pick a new area. I did tell the rest of Mo's family."

"How did our mother take it?" Hack didn't think she'd like being found out.

"I hope this doesn't upset you too much, but your mother is dead," Bowan said.

Hack felt a punch to his gut. He shouldn't be sad, and he wasn't, not exactly. Could he mourn someone he'd grown to hate?

"How'd it happen?" Beck asked gently.

"When my father died, as the eldest, I became chieftain. Most folks were fine with it. We've been ready for a change for a while. Some, though, were not. On top of that, I met my mate, a man. If you remember anything about the planet, you might recall they aren't fond of same-sex couples. Laurie has Havenite blood in his ancestry and can carry on our line, but to many, that didn't matter."

"I think I was too young to have picked up on that. I'm sorry to hear you had trouble, but congratulations on mating." Hack wondered how this all ended in his mother's death.

"Thank you, Will. Because of these changes, your mother and my brother planned a revolt. Their two oldest, Alex and Rosie, came to me and told me of the plans. Their followers were too few and their plan was doomed to fail, but my brother had it in his head that he should be chieftain. Both were killed in the fight."

"Are Alex and Rosie alright?" Fasi asked.

"Yes. They're fine. Well, Alex is. Rosie took her parents' deaths hard. She feels responsible, but I've tried to make her see that she did what was right. It's been hard on her, and she's just fifteen. The other four are too young. They know their parents are gone, but Laurie and I took them in, and they've gotten used to us."

"Thank you," Hack said. "For letting me know. If you need any help with them at all, my mate and I would be happy to help. I know Mo wants to talk to you all too."

"Now that things have settled down, I don't have to sneak here, so it'll be easier. I told Alex, Rosie, Moses, and my other brothers about Mo's survival. It's helped things quite a bit. Rosie was the one to kill her mother. She was protecting Laurie's back during the fight. Now knowing what she did, Rosie doesn't feel so bad."

"That poor girl," Beck said.

"My plan now is to set Burnished up to be spacefaring. We have old ships down here, but I have no idea of what shape they're in. I've settled my tribe here. We're doing what your father first suggested, raising our food instead of relying on hunting."

"We can help," Fasi said. "Not just Charybdis, but all the planets."

"We'll take that help," Bowan said, unashamed. "I know what I want my people to be, but it's a long road to get there."

"Hack, you mind if I go and look over their ships," Beck asked. "I can check up on your brothers and sisters too."

"I want to go too," Xav said. "You can't because of the Concords, but I captain a ship. Technically, I'm

Audre's captain, but she won't mind sparing me. Well, probably not."

Hack felt tears fill his eyes. They were right, he couldn't go. To have Beck and his brother do this for him meant a lot. "If Audre doesn't mind me borrowing you, I'd really appreciate it. I trust the two of you and they're my family."

"You realize some of that family will be returning with them, right?" Bowan looked a bit nervous. "I have a feeling Alex and Rosie will insist on going. Alex is an adult now, but he's already set on being just like you. He wants to join Charybdis. Rosie? I think Rosie just wants to get away. She's fifteen, almost sixteen. Would you mind if she came to you?"

"Of course not," Hack said. What was one more kid?

"What about your grandfather?" Bowan asked. "He's been a nervous wreck and doesn't want to ask you, but I know he wants to see you. He wants to go to you."

Hack squeezed his eyes shut, and then his mom was there. Renee wrapped him in her arms. He leaned into her and answered Bowan. "I'd like that. I want him here, if he wants to be."

Fasi kissed his son's head. "We'll send Xav with his ship as soon as they can get aboard. Beck will go along and stay behind to work on your ships. He'll still be in range, so we can ask our little engineering genius questions if we need too. Xav can bring back whoever wants to come. Once we have a status report on your ships, we can help train your people to fly too. I'll reach out to the other planets, and we'll set up a conference call between all of us. We're happy to have Burnished Outpost in the system again, Chieftain."

Hack didn't notice when the call ended. He was still curled into his mom, processing all he heard. His mother was dead, his siblings wanted to come here, and Grandpa Moses wanted to see him again. How could things change so fast from a fifteen-minute conversation?

Finn poked his head in nervously. "Um, Hack. I don't want to alarm you, and everyone is just fine, but there was an attack on Leti."

Hack jerked out of his mom's arms. "What? What the fuck happened?"

Fasi roared. "Is my boy okay? The kids? Sebastian and the others? Where are they?"

"Who the fuck did it? Are they dead yet?" Renee headed for the door.

Finn stepped all the way in, closing the door and leaning against it. "Okay, guys, you need to calm down. Everyone is just fine, and you don't want to give yourselves heart attacks. Okay?"

Hack took a deep breath, knowing his fucking lieutenant was right. Gods, why did he have to choose the calm and collected crewmember to be his lieutenant? "What happened?"

"Leti, Sebastian, and Shae wanted to go talk to Dr. Manning. She's refused to even talk to them on the vid-screen, so they wanted to go in person."

"That doesn't sound like Orsla," Fasi said. "She's been asking about Leti and his discoveries."

"Well, her assistant's been a real bitch," Beck said. "I

was there the other day when Leti asked for an appointment. She flat-out refused."

"That's why they headed out to see her in person," Finn said. "Leti and Sebastian had to pee, so they went to the public restroom right before getting to Manning's building. Maia and Shae stayed outside with the kids, and Silas went in with our two preggo boys. Almost immediately, eight people came out of the ceiling and attacked. They wounded Silas badly. He'll be alright and recover, but he'll be out of commission for a bit."

"Damn, poor Silas," Renee said. "He's at medical now?"

"Yeah, and so are the bodies of the attackers."

"Did Princess and Maia take them out?" Hack asked.

"No," Finn said. "Apparently, Leti made a good impression on the missing Half-Moon assassin. They're friends now, and he's going to live on the third floor with Maia and Silas. Hope you don't mind."

"What? Leti is *not* friends with an assassin. That's not happening."

"You keep telling yourself that," Finn said, shrugging. "So, Wolfe rescued them all and killed the attackers. I just checked in with them, and Ma and Pops came over to help Leti throw him a welcome to the neighborhood party. Juniper's been stuffing food in the poor guy since he arrived, and Ava's been fitting him for clothes. Says he needs a proper Charybdis uniform."

Hack banged his head on the table. Now Leti had a

pet assassin. Nothing good could come from this. Princess was bad enough, but most of the time, the dragon just slept, ate, and hissed at people. Maybe the assassin would do the same? Maybe?

THE PARTY WAS in full swing by the time Hack and his parents arrived home. Ma and Juniper were in the kitchen, preparing a feast with the help of Pork Chop and Biscuit.

"Hey, sweetheart," Ma said, stopping long enough to kiss Hack's cheek. "Beck called to say goodbye. Leti hasn't stopped smiling since I told him about the call." She patted his chest. "Now, you go easy on your mate. I know he drags home his strays, but he has a good heart and a good sense about people. This boy is a good one."

"He's an assassin," Hack said petulantly. "Who's apparently been spying on us."

"You say spying, I say watching us with a longing in him," Ma said. "He needs loving, that boy does. Your Leti has enough love to fuel the galaxy."

Hack sighed. If Ma had already accepted him, it'd do no good to fight it. "How's Silas?"

"He's settled in his room upstairs. It's a good thing my cutie patootie put that little lift in the back. He won't be doing stairs for a while. Leti just finished checking on him and he's resting. Nettle prescribed lots of pain meds and sleep."

"I'll go check again, just to make sure," Hack said.

He ran up the stairs, passing Lilah and Sophie on the way.

The women smirked, knowing where he was headed.

"I just checked on him. He'll be fine," Lilah said.

"Got to check," Hack said. "Just in case."

They rolled their eyes and continued down the stairs. Hack reached Silas's suite. The whole third floor was separated into four apartments. Pops for sure knew what he was doing when he built Leti's house. Plenty of room for strays.

Hack peeked in Silas's bedroom. The man was pale but resting peacefully. He was propped up in bed with a million pillows, and Gravy lay on the rug beside his bed. Hack went in and knelt beside Gravy, playing with his dog's ears and stroking his back.

"Keep an eye on him, boy," he whispered, dropping a kiss on Gravy's furry head.

On the way out, he checked to make sure Silas's fridge was full and the kitchen and living room looked clear of clutter. He noticed a stack of Leti's favorite blankets on the end of Silas's couch. He smiled reluctantly. His mate was an amazing man, a frustrating man, but also an amazing man.

In the backyard, Leti and Sebastian had the stranger between them on the patio couch. Leti looked up, his arm around the young man's shoulders. Hack's mate was a little worried, nibbling his lip.

"Wolfe is it?" Hack crouched in front of the man. He was small, about nineteen, with a pointed little chin and long, pointed ears. He reminded Hack a bit of Draif with his dark, assessing eyes.

The man nodded and held up a tablet with words typed out. *I swear I'm not a threat. I wouldn't hurt Leti for anything in the galaxy. Your mate is a great person. If you want me to go, I will. My brother is throwing a hissy fit anyway.*

"Why is your brother upset? He seemed worried you disappeared," Hack said.

He's way too overprotective. He just came into leadership of Half-Moon, and he's making a lot of changes. He's worried someone will try to hurt me to retaliate.

"Will they? We're a ways away from Union Station, but we'll watch your back," Hack said.

They won't. Anyone who has issues with the changes has already left for another guild. They also know I'm no lightweight. My brother's just my brother.

Hack laughed. "Is it sad that I know what you mean by that? Sometimes I almost feel bad for Mo. Big brothers can be a pain in the ass."

"That's so true," Mo agreed, sitting cross-legged beside him. "They're worth it though." The boy had grown in the last five months. He was at least four inches taller and had bulked up a bit. He was still Hack's string bean though. "You aren't mad at Leti, are you? Wolfe can just be your oldest child."

Hack met Leti's worried green eyes. "I'm not mad. Leti just found me a new friend. He's good at that."

"Why can't we stay up with Grandma and Grandpa?" Rizzie lay in her bed, wrapped in blankets. Hack kissed her forehead one more time.

"Because it's bedtime and you have school tomorrow. I thought you liked school?"

She sighed. "I do. I just don't wanna sleep."

"Well, you need to sleep, or you won't be able to play tomorrow."

"Yeah. I guess. Xu, Nessa, and Roz are still coming over tomorrow for a sleepover. We can stay up late then, right?"

"Of course," Hack said, hoping that he wasn't contradicting Leti. Rizzie had discovered Hack was a weakling parent and had played her hand at manipulation. Leti and Hack put a swift end to that, but now Hack second-guessed himself a lot. "Love you, ladybug," he said and shut her door.

He peeked in on Sami, laughing under his breath at his son's snores. Pax curled around his boy, guarding him as he slept. Pepper's crib was in Sami's room now. She slept more soundly with her brother nearby. The two were trouble together, and Hack knew they'd only get worse as they grew. He couldn't wait to see what they got up to.

Leaving the kids to their rest, he met everyone in the living room. The station's lighting was set to evening, so the backyard was left to Wobble and Trixie. His dad sat in a chair near the fireplace, Hack's mom curled up on his lap. The rest of Hack's crew spread out all around the room, some in chairs, on the couches, or on fluffy pillows on the floor. Ma and Pops sat together on a small couch, arms around one another. Sheiria had joined them too, sprawled out with Princess in front of the fireplace.

Sebastian and Shae shared a couch with Mo and Lucas. Hack's friend had his new leg, arm, and eye. He'd been training non-stop since he got them and was now battle-ready again. Leti stood at the front of the room and pointed to an empty chair. Hack sat and smiled encouragingly. His mate's finger trembled, and Hack knew he was afraid people would laugh at his hard work.

"Okay," Leti said. "Thanks for staying, guys. Sebastian, Shae, and I have been working on discovering as much as we can about the artifact Morrick studied. We've come to some conclusions, but could use some fresh input."

"We'd hoped Dr. Manning would help, but she

thinks our research is rubbish," Sebastian said. "That's a direct quote via her assistant."

"I swear she's not usually like that," Fasi said. "I'm sorry she's been so condescending."

"In any case, as you all know, we have every bit of written work on the ancient Crells along with several artifacts found by the Belcorts. Then we have the whole fucked-up situation with the Belcorts and the element itself," Shae said.

Leti turned on the large vid-screen the family used for movie time. He pulled up an image from one of his books. It showed two pictures. On one was a female figure, dressed in elaborate clothing and jewels. Her white hair hung in thick coils, and she wore a crown with six points. She was Crell, with light green skin, small tusks in the corner of her mouth, and a large frame. Around her swirled symbols and lettering that Hack couldn't understand.

The second page looked almost like a flow chart. Six small pyramids were linked together in a circle. In the center of the circle was the six-pointed crown from the previous page.

"Is that the element?" Cordelia pointed to one of the pyramids.

"Yes," Leti answered. "This is from a book of ancient Crellic myths. Surprisingly, this has been one of the most helpful books, linking our more factual ideas together. So, this woman is called the Rising Queen. According to the myth, when the Crellic race was threatened or weakened, the Rising Queen and her Weapons would awaken to rule the Crells and lead them in a golden age of war and expansion. The Queen always awakens in the center planet of the system, Genarg."

"Weapons?" Renee asked.

"The elements house her six most loyal and powerful servants. Fire, Air, Earth, Water, Life, and Death." Leti paused with a thoughtful look. "Every species whose history I've studied has had some similar myth. The ancient humans had the myth of King Arthur. He was said to defeat his people's enemies and rule them well. He had his Knights of the Round Table. His people believed he would one day come again."

"So, this story is just pretend then?" Finn looked confused. He wasn't the only one. Hack didn't understand why Leti would start with a myth.

"That is a very good question, Finn," Leti said, sighing. "When we began, Sebastian and I were convinced it wasn't factual at all. However, as most historians know, many myths are based on a kernel of truth. I thought this one might have that truth hidden within. After all, we have the element. We know it exists, and according to my date test, it's also over two hundred thousand years old."

"Holy shit," Mo said.

Leti looked at Hack, brow raised. Okay, so he still needed to work on watching his language around the kids. Mo was too mature, and Hack forgot he was just thirteen.

"What led us to think it was more was the historical evidence we gathered from everything else," Sebastian said.

Leti brought up another image. It was one drawing, fractured. It looked like a body lying flat with two people standing on either side of it. The body looked normal, but the eyes were pure black. The two standing raised their hands, looking up at the sky. The element lay on the prone figure's chest.

"We retrieved this from a data cube the Belcorts found on Dargner," Shae said. "It belonged to a priestess/witch."

"Priestess/witch?" Lucas said. "Which one is it?"

"The translation's not clear," Sebastian said. "The word has connotations of both. The data cube contains directions and explanations for different ceremonies, and this picture was the oldest on it."

"We'll come back to this one," Leti said. "It's an explanation of what the element is meant to do. To understand it, though, you need to know what we've pieced together about the history of the ancient Crells." His pregnant mate began pacing, or really waddling, back and forth. "From what I can tell, there were three cycles of Crellic history, about four thousand years each. The last cycle ended right after the Human-Diaspora. About a hundred years before each cycle ends, something similar happens. According to the records, the kid-friendly version is that the Rising Queen is awakened. She leads the Crells to greatness, then falls asleep again, awaiting her next awakening. Then a new cycle begins. That's the myth."

"What's the not kid-friendly version?" Draif asked.

"The Crells are led by a queen, but she doesn't lead them to greatness. She leads them to a bloodbath. She brings the Crells close to ruin every single cycle. Those that are too young or weak to fight are made slaves. Those that are able-bodied are added to her army. Her only desire is to kill or control all things in her path." Leti pulled up another fractured drawing. "The first cycle." A blurred woman stood on a battle field of conquered, six black-eyed figures behind her. Leti clicked again. "The second cycle." This picture was better and clearer. The woman stood on a large pile of dead. She looked like she was laughing joyously, and she raised her arms to the air. Birds dipped low to pick at the bones beneath her. Again, six figures stood with her.

Leti clicked again, and this one was not a drawing but a far more modern photograph. A Crellic woman, the Rising Queen, was bathed in wet blood, large eyes almost manic. Dead bodies circled around her, people of all ages. She carried a severed head in one hand. Behind her stood five blurry figures.

"Fuck," Nettle said. "That's disgusting."

"This was the last Rising Queen. At the end of the last cycle, there were only a few Crells left and only one habitable world. They settled on Dargner, but they were destroyed, driven to extinction, from wars spilling over from the Boral System," Sebastian said.

"It's not unknown to have cruel leaders in a species' history," Leti said. "These events occurred. We have a few records of the earlier cycles and pictures and videos for the most recent. The hard part to explain and believe is that this is the same woman each time." He pulled up the three separate pictures—

the modern gory one and the two more primitive ones.

"That's impossible," Nettle said. "She'd have to be over… Gods, over fourteen thousand years old."

"No person of any species lives that long," Dannol said. "Why do you think it's the same woman? Couldn't it just be someone posing as her? The three women are similar but not exactly like each other."

"That's because it's not the same body," Sebastian said.

"Huh?" Cordelia said, articulate as always.

Leti pulled up the picture of the six pyramids again. "I'll get there. This page is titled *The Six Elements of Rising*. Each pyramid has what they call an element, which are her Weapons. Fire, Air, Earth, Water, Life, and Death."

"Which one's our element?" Lilah asked.

"Death," Selene said. "That's what Morrick's experiments would suggest."

"Yes, Selene," Sebastian said. "It translates as death."

Leti pulled up the picture of the prone body with the death element on his chest. "Which brings us back to the priestess/witch's data cube. This is a ceremony to bring forth one of the Queen's Weapons—Death."

"Oh dear," Ava said.

"These Weapons are six people who have special gifts and are completely and utterly subservient to the Rising Queen. She can conquer and kill as much as she does because she controls them. The only way she is stopped is when enough of the Weapons fall. It weakens her enough that she sleeps again," Leti said.

"This ceremony awakens Death," Sebastian repeated. "It all starts with a dead body."

"Oh fuck," Lucas said. "It's zombies, isn't it? I've seen way too many movies about zombies to deal with that shit."

Leti giggled. "It's not zombies, Lucas. The ceremony needs one dead body. Only one. This person volunteers or it won't work. It must be a person who wants to live. Who wants to serve Death. The body is a vessel for the Weapon, not a reanimated corpse bent on eating brains."

"The sacrifice dies, and his body is used to summon Death," Sebastian said.

"Morrick's experiments were on animals," Selene said. "They weren't worthy vessels."

"No," Leti agreed. "It must be a sentient being, and it must be one that *wants* to live. In one of the books, it told of a man who volunteered because his family was killed. People thought he wanted vengeance. Really, he wanted to stop his pain by dying. It didn't say what happened exactly, but it said the ceremony had to be done again."

"So, it's not a virus or some gaseous mixture in the element," Fasi said. "It's a being looking for a host."

"That's what we think," Leti said. "If it is a being inside the element, that explains some things."

"What do you mean?" Renee asked.

"It explains why the animals were animated. Why it only worked on one animal at a time. It would also explain why Dr. Morrick couldn't figure it out. The man knew viruses. He couldn't figure out what it was because it was an alien being," Sebastian said.

"We also think it explains the Concord admiral's mysterious friend," Shae said.

"Will, you said that the captains you spoke with claimed that some of their fellow people were sent away when they displeased the admiral. Then they came back, with tattoos and completely different personalities," Leti said. He pulled up the image Hack had sent him. The two dead men's tattoos. "This is the symbol for Life."

"Life can't be bad, right?" Cordelia looked hopeful. "Obviously Death is, but Life is living."

"Oh, I think Life is far worse than Death," Shae said. "Death can instantly kill any living thing. Life, though, controls the living. He twists people, their personalities, their memories. He even commands them. When they become his, they *are* his."

"In the stories, he's why the army fights for the Queen. At first, the Crell want her, they awaken her. Then, when they realize what they've done, Life steps in. All he needs is a very half-way, minor agreement from a person, then with a touch, they're his," Sebastian said.

"What do you mean by 'half-way, minor agreement'?" Dannol asked.

Leti winced. "When I learned my parents wanted me dead, that they hated me, a part of me wanted to return that hatred. I fought it, still fight it, and won't let it win, but it's there. All Life needs is a verbal acknowledgement of that little part. Like Nettle once told me, there's darkness in everyone."

"The Concord mercenaries he changes are likely given a talking to. They're given a chance to get back in the admiral's good graces. That small desire is all he would need," Shae said.

"So, you think Life has been awakened?" Lucas asked.

"Each element has a unique ceremony for awakening the Rising Queen's Weapon," Leti said. "I think the Belcorts, at the very least, awoke the Queen and Life."

"Why those two?" Hack asked.

"Life because of what's happening within the Concords and because of Windell Belcort's behavior. Dr. Webber said he was *leading* the Concords. I talked to his friends and family. That man was a lump. He wasn't some charismatic artifact smuggler or anything like that," Leti said. "Plus, remember what he told Dr. Webber when he requested the artifacts?"

"He said Linda wanted them," Hack said. Oh fuck. "The Rising Queen."

"Yes," Leti said. "Except for Death, the others are awakened into living vessels. They don't have to be willing. I don't know how it happened, but I think Linda is now the Rising Queen, Windell is Life, and Melinda is Earth."

"Melinda is Earth? What makes you think that?" Hack asked.

"She was instructing the builders. Earth is the

builder. He, or she in this case, controls the slaves and leads the development of the Rising Queen's kingdom."

"This is crazy," Cordelia said. "It makes sense, but it's crazy."

"Oh, we know," Shae said. "When these two pulled me into the research, I was definitely a sceptic, but with what we've found, it all fits."

"So how big a threat is she? We have Death's element, so he can't be raised," Fasi said.

"Right now, I think they're focused on Genarg and the rest of the Crellic System, but she has the Concords now. She has the ability to travel all over the galaxy."

"We cut them off at the knees," Renee said. "Keep the Concords occupied and wipe them out."

"Yes," Leti agreed. "We need to keep the Death element from them too. I don't think it can be destroyed, but we can sure try."

"Why were there only five Weapons in the last picture of her?" Selene's question startled everyone.

"Um," Leti flipped back to the gory, modern picture of the Rising Queen. "Oh, we're working on that. We have a half document that explains how she was defeated last time. Right now, we're unable to figure it out. It has something to do with Death though. He's the one missing."

"Someone killed him first?" Finn sounded hopeful. "You said she loses strength as her Weapons are killed, right?"

"That might be it," Leti said. "Right now, we don't know." He looked at Fasi. "I know this all sounds crazy, but it explains Morrick's experiments, the Concord captain's story, and what's happened with the Belcorts. It doesn't explain Roger Belcort's death or the science behind it all. However, keep in mind, right after the Human-Diaspora, humans were overwhelmed with the species they came across. People like you who look so different from humans and shift into an animal were unbelievable to the humans. Is it really so unfathomable that an unknown species exists?"

"Oh Leti," Fasi said. "Don't doubt your own instincts. We trust you."

"We believe you," Renee said. "We may not want to, but we do."

21

"Dad said Dr. Manning is meeting with the Council tomorrow to discuss the artifact. He's going to try to get her thoughts on the artifact housing a being instead of a substance," Leti said over the running water in the shower.

"That's good. I don't remember her being so close-minded either, so something is definitely up."

Hack waited, towel in hand, and watched Leti climb out of the shower. His mate watched him sleepily as he dried him off. He ran the towel over Leti's hair, scrunching just the way he knew his mate liked. When he was dry, Hack grabbed the lotion and started rubbing it onto Leti's belly. This was his absolute favorite thing to do in all the galaxy.

Hack spoke softly to his son. "Hi there, itty-bitty. Daddy and Papa can't wait to see you, and neither can your brothers and sisters. You're going to be the most loved person in all the galaxy. I know it."

Leti laughed when their son kicked his daddy's hand. "He says he'd better be the most loved boy in the galaxy. He hasn't even been born and he's already spoiled rotten. Every night, Rizzie sings to him, Mo and Abbot give him kisses, and you talk to him and tell him his bedtime story. Rotten!"

"Ah, there's worse things to be," Hack said. He watched his mate get ready for bed. Damn, he was a lucky man. The emergency alert buzzed from his communicator. Hack picked it up and saw the alert. "Fuck. There's an incoming Concord fleet. They're almost past Fallow now and headed this way." He rushed to the dresser and pulled on his uniform.

Leti pulled his robe off and went to the closet for his own.

"Baby, maybe you should stay home for this one," Hack said. He knew it wouldn't do any use, but he needed to try.

Leti pulled on the stretchy black shirt with Charybdis Station's logo on the left shoulder. It showed off his pregnant belly perfectly. Hack shouldn't find his mate's uniform so sexy. When Leti had complained about all the black, Ava sewed little warrior bunnies on the bottom halves of his sleeves. They wore armor and carried swords. Not a single person in Hack's fleet dared to laugh at Leti's bunnies. Mostly because Princess was always perched on his shoulder, but it didn't hurt that he was their general's husband.

Leti buttoned his pants and rolled his eyes. "Yeah, until I'm about to pop like Sebastian, I'm doing my part. I'm on the medical ship, so I'm not out in the thick of things. Plus, Maia will be there too."

"Yeah, yeah. You've said it all before," Hack muttered, dropping a kiss on his mate's forehead.

"Yet you still argue."

They checked on the kids, then met Sebastian and a sleepy Nessa at the door. It'd become routine for all the neighborhood kids that needed a sitter to pack in Hack and Leti's house with Sebastian and Lilah. So far, it had worked well, leaving the parents with one less thing to worry about as they headed out to battle.

Wolfe, Juniper, and Maia waited outside.

"Wolfe, you sure you want to come?" Hack asked.

The small man smiled and nodded, placing his hands on the blade at his back and the phaser at his hip.

"Yeah, okay, so you can protect yourself," Hack said. He held Pax and Gravy's leashes in one hand. The two insisted on coming with Hack to every single fight, and he had to admit they were good battle companions.

A short tram ride later and Hack kissed Leti goodbye, watching him waddle toward the medical ship. Hack reminded himself there were some soldiers onboard, Nettle was there, and the captain was a good and experienced man. He forced himself to go to the bridge of the Blue Solace. Dannol was in the pilot's seat, Finn sat in the lieutenant's chair, and Ava sat at communications. Selene stood at the window, fully armed and ready.

"Let's do this," Hack said. "Ava, pull up all fleet communications. Dannol get us in the sky."

Each of Hack's captains popped up on the large vid-screen. Hack couldn't help but smile at Draif. In the past five months, Draif had taken the station by storm. It hadn't been hard to get him approved as a captain, especially when Lucas insisted on being his lieutenant. His ship was just a little smaller than the Blue Solace.

"Ava, how many ships are in the Concord fleet and what type are they?"

"They have twenty battle cruisers, eleven mid-grade ships like ours, and thirty-five smaller vessels."

"Draif, lay out some nets right out of range. We'll try to lure some of the smaller ones in. Corbin, lead our battle cruisers against the mid-grade ships. We have about the same number, but don't forget they are smaller with more maneuverability. Try to make a spectacle of it and make sure your shields stay strong. You're going to take most of the hits."

"Shouldn't our battle cruisers counter the Concord's?" Captain Corbin was an experienced captain, and Hack welcomed his thoughts. Even when he disagreed with them.

"We only have twelve. The Yellow General is out hunting in the Boral System, and the Green General is hunting in the Silverlight System. The Red General needs to prepare to defend the station. No help is coming, and our twelve Cruisers couldn't hope to take all thirty of the Concord battle cruisers. Besides, we have over sixty small ships. They can dodge, hide, and fire our special missiles."

Corbin grinned. "Damn. That's a good idea. They won't expect it either."

"D'Sol, you lead our small fighter vessels. Stay

camouflaged and take out the cruisers. Draif, you have those nets laid?"

"Yes, General. I've sent every pilot the coordinates."

"Good. All mid-grade ships, do your best to lure the smaller ships into the nets. We need to take them out as fast as possible. The medical ship will stay on the edge of the battle. Once as many ships as possible are disabled, we'll board them. Questions or suggestions?"

"No, sir," Corbin and D'Sol answered.

The other captains nodded or agreed.

"Let's do this."

Dannol burst to the front of Hack's fleet, leading them to the battle. Corbin's cruisers broke off, isolating and taking out the Concord's mid-grade ships in rapid succession. The Concord cruisers turned and fired toward the Charybdis cruisers, but they didn't last long. D'Sol's whoops echoed through the open communicator as his small fighter vessels took out each and every cruiser.

While his men took care of the other ships, Dannol turned on Hack's insignia. His colors and rank lit up the side of the ship, making Dannol giggle. "Gods, it's like offering steak to Gravy. They come right after us."

Gravy woofed at the insult. He was *not* at all like the Concords.

Over ten ships chased the Blue Solace. Dannol dipped and weaved, dodging shot after shot. The ships followed Dannol straight to one of the larger nets. Dannol slowed, making sure they were close behind, then at the last instant, he shot up, missing the net, but leaving all ten ships trapped.

Soon enough, the Concord fleet was still in the air. Now came the hard part.

"Finn, you and Selene take one team, Cordelia and I will take the other. Ava, please stay on communications. D'Sol, take your wounded to medical and get ready to ferry across the newest rescued prisoners. All cruisers and mid-grade ships, Ava has assigned you vessels to board. Good luck and keep Ava updated."

Hack, Gravy, and Pax met Cordelia and the rest of Hack's team at the cargo bay. They quickly shuttled across to the first ship. Time to get to work.

***

"ALL SHIPS ARE DISABLED," Captain Ryne said. "Damn, General Hackett makes an old man proud."

Leti smiled at the older captain. Hack had served on his ship right out of training. He'd learned a lot from Ryne and said there was no one better to take care of the medical ship.

The first load of wounded came in, only a few. The space battle had gone well, but Leti knew from experience the worst of the injured came from the on-ship battles. It would be easier to blow them out of the sky, but they had yet to find a Concord ship without at least a few non-human prisoners.

"Mayday, mayday." A voice crackled through the communicator. It barely reached. "Help us!"

Leti looked around quickly and breathed a sigh of

relief when the others came to attention. They heard it too.

"This is Captain Ryne of Charybdis Station. Who's on the line?"

"My name's Stepha. My family and I are prisoners onboard a Concord ship. There was a battle, and the ship is at a standstill."

"It's okay, Stepha. Charybdis Station has disabled all ships and is boarding them now."

"You don't understand," she said, hysteria clear in her voice. Voices yelled in the background, and Leti could hear children crying. "The Concords aren't waiting to be boarded. They came straight to our cells. My husband and another managed to kill our guard and seal the door, but they're coming."

The signal crackled again, and Leti could hear loud bangs.

"Oh gods, please help us. They're going to kill us all."

"Sir, their signal's coming from an isolated ship. It's too far away from our fleet. They can't hear them. Should I send the message on to Ava?"

"They won't get there in time," Captain Ryne said. "They are all boarding ships right now, and they're too far out to get there."

"We're here," Leti said. "There are a few soldiers onboard. I can take Princess, Maia, and Wolfe with me."

"No way," Ryne said. "Hack would kill me."

"Captain," Leti said. "Princess is a soldier too, but I need to be with him. Maia and Wolfe won't leave me behind. There's no choice."

"Captain Ryne," Nettle said. "Every medic and doctor is trained to fight. We take an oath to help people." The children still cried in the background, and Leti could hear the panic in the adults' voices even if he couldn't make out their words.

"Fuck," Ryne said. "Okay. Nettle, gather every volunteer you can and meet us at the shuttle. Leti, get your damned dragon and make sure to take multiple shields with you. You *cannot* get hurt."

"Yes, sir," Leti said, grinning. He waddled to the shuttle, taking a minute for a pee break. When his group arrived, he noticed Shae. "Um, Shae, didn't Selene say you were hopeless with a phaser, then banned you from being a soldier?"

"Those may have been her words, yes. However, I have another weapon."

"Your sarcasm?"

"No, my voice."

Leti grinned and grabbed Captain Ryne's arm. "I have an idea."

"Fuck me," Maia said.

Wolfe nodded in agreement, frowning.

"Princess and I can go directly to the cells. He's our heavy fighter here. Shae can go with you to the bridge. He's a Siren. Can you put them to sleep, Shae?"

"Yes, but I have to be able to see them," he said. "Also, I could make them kill themselves, but I really don't want to do that."

"Sleep is good enough, son," Ryne said. He split the volunteers into three teams and passed out shields and weapons. "Stay in contact, and as soon as you finish your portion of the ship, meet at the bridge."

Seconds later, they were at the ship, and it was time to get to work.

2 2

*L*eti activated the two shields covering Princess Buttercup. The dragon had decided fifteen feet long and five feet wide was big enough for his second mission as a Charybdis soldier.

Ryne reached over and pushed Leti's shield button, activating it. Oops. Leti winced, then smiled sheepishly.

"Stay behind your dragon and don't get hurt. That's your only job, understand?" Ryne asked.

"Got it," Leti said.

It wasn't like he *wanted* to join the fight, but everyone thought he'd try something heroic. He knew better. *Though, I am a wildcard*, he thought with a smirk. He could swoop in, roll to cover, firing a phaser from each hand. The bad guys would fall before him. Hack would be so impressed.

"No," Maia said. "Bad Leti. Whatever you're thinking can't be good. Just stay behind Princess."

"Fine," he snapped. "I would have been amazing."

Ryne's team forced open the door. It banged against the ground, echoing off the empty entrance. If their scanners were right, all the Concords were at the cells and in the bridge. Leti hoped they were right.

"Nettle, take your team to the left. The scanners don't show much, but don't let your guard down. When you're done, split the team. One half heads for the bridge, the other half heads for the cells," Ryne ordered.

"Yes, sir."

"Leti, your team goes right. Scanners show twenty-three Concords at the cell doors. Let Princess do his thing. Once you have the doors cleared, get those prisoners out of here. No need for you to come to the bridge. With a ship this size, there shouldn't be more than fifty holed up."

"Yes, sir," Leti said.

"Shae, stay behind me. When you see a large group, sing your song."

"Okay."

Leti's team went right, Princess running ahead. Leti could hear Princess's roars, and the stench of burning flesh filled the hallway.

"That is so disgusting," Maia said, gagging.

By the time they reached Princess, the Concord mercenaries lay in pieces—mostly melted pieces. The dragon banged on the door to the cells, trying to open it.

"Damn it, Princess," Leti said. "I wanted to shoot someone."

"Yeah, that was probably never going to happen," Maia said.

"Princess, back up. We'll get it, baby boy," Leti said. Maia placed her charges, and Leti spoke into his communicator. "Stepha?"

"Yes," the woman said. "Was that roaring? What's going on?"

"That was my pet, Princess Buttercup. The Concords here are dead, and we're about to blow the door, okay?" Princess spit out a leg and started to shrink. Leti tried to bend over to pick him up but couldn't get past his belly. Princess scrambled up his body and made it to his shoulder.

"You're here? Oh thank you, thank you! We'll back away from the door."

Maia waited two minutes, then blew the door. It fell flat, dust rising. The prison was a large open space with several barred cells and an open area where the mercenaries had their *fun*. A dead Concord man lay close to the door, and the prisoners gathered together in the corner. There were about twenty of them, ranging from infants to the elderly.

"Alright, everyone," Leti said. "We're from Charybdis Station and have a shuttle waiting to take you to safety. You all did amazing, and we're so glad you're alive. We need to get the wounded out first."

The medics with Leti's team holstered their phasers and pulled the gurneys from their backs, quickly unfolding them. As they assessed the prisoners, a Grell couple with three small children approached Leti. Two of the children were obviously theirs, but the little boy tugged a little Silet girl behind him. The two clutched at one another's hands.

"Stepha?"

The woman handed the baby she carried to her husband and threw her arms around Leti. "Thank you so much," she said, tears pouring down her cheeks. "My family was captured early this morning. I've talked to the other prisoners and know what these horrible people do. That would have been us."

Leti squeezed her tightly. "I'm glad you're okay. Let's get these people to safety."

"Yes," she said enthusiastically. "I'll help direct. Just tell me what to do."

It didn't take long to get the wounded loaded up and the prisoners back to the medical ship. By the time the shuttle returned, Ryne and Nettle's groups met them at the door. Shae and Nettle instantly started checking Leti over.

"Guys, he's fine," Maia said. "Princess did all the hard work. No one else even got to fire a shot."

Ryne clapped Shae on the back, knocking the young man forward a bit. "That's what happened with us. Shae here put the whole damn bridge to sleep. All we had to do was tie them up."

Shae looked pale.

"You okay, Shae?" Leti pulled him to a seat and pushed him in it.

"The captain of that ship," Shae said. "He belongs to Life. His mind was so… wrong, Leti. It was horrible."

"You didn't hurt yourself peeking in, did you?" Maia asked, crouching in front of the Siren.

"No, it was a little harder to manipulate than the others, but I managed easily enough. Life was in him though. He's not happy someone messed with his work. I could feel him in there, lurking and waiting to pounce as soon as the man awoke."

"So the captain isn't free of Life's influence now?" Leti knew they weren't great people to start with, but he felt bad for anyone Life was using.

"No," Shae said sadly. "I couldn't fix him, not by myself."

"This confirms your theories," Maia said. "It's one more thing to add to your pile of evidence."

Wolfe gently pushed Leti into a seat, and Leti groaned in pleasure. His body didn't like being kept on its feet for so long. Thirty minutes was a long time to a pregnant man.

"General Hackett has been updated on our actions," Ryne said. He grinned at Leti. "I expected him to yell at me for endangering his mate. He just asked if you were alright, then said good job with the quick thinking. Surprised the shit out of me."

Leti traced the bunnies on his sleeve, hiding his smile. His mate understood. He'd be worried and want to see Leti with his own eyes, but he knew their role together. It was hard on Hack to let Leti help people, but Hack knew Leti. He loved and accepted him. They were mates, husbands, and partners.

HACK LIMPED onto the medical ship, Gravy and Pax

following behind him. Cordelia leaned into him, holding the wound on her side. His eyes searched the busy waiting room and landed on a tuckered-out mate. Leti and his group took up the whole corner of the room.

He sat in a wide chair, surrounded by over thirty children. He was busy distracting them with a story from his tablet—one of the more peaceful Crellic myths, if Hack wasn't mistaken. Wolfe stood behind him, and Princess stretched out on the top of his belly.

Shae sat on the floor with the children, two in his lap and a few leaning into his sides. The poor Siren looked like he'd been put through the wringer, but they all watched Leti, hanging onto his every word. Gravy wandered over and plopped onto two of the older kids. They giggled and gave the dog what he wanted, loving pats and scratches.

Maia ran up with a medic. "Cordelia, where are you hurt?"

"Just a jab in the side," she answered, wincing. "Fucker snuck up on me."

"They like to do that." Maia winked at Cordy, then eyed Hack. "You injured, General? You better not be or Leti will be pissed."

Cordelia started giggling, wincing at the pain it caused. "He sprained his ankle, tripping over a dead merc. Gods, it was the funniest thing I've seen in ages."

"So glad I could amuse you," Hack said drily. He rolled his eyes and handed Cordy over to the medic.

Maia helped him to a chair, pulled off his boot, and

placed an ice wrap around his ankle. She patted his head. "Stay in your seat like a good general."

He grabbed her wrist before she could take off. "Leti did okay? Didn't get scared?"

She rolled her eyes. "Princess Buttercup did all our work for us. I didn't even get to fire my phaser. Shae went with Captain Ryne and probably had the hardest time of it. He put a large portion of the mercenaries to sleep. It wore him out."

"Thanks for taking care of Leti, Maia," he said. "He's my mate and I'll always worry."

"Hey, he takes care of everyone. It's only fair." She left to go help the other injured waiting to be processed.

A Grell couple sat nearby, but the woman pulled the man behind her, moving to sit next to Hack. "You're mated to Leti?"

"Yes," Hack answered. He tried to smile but exhaustion pulled at him.

"I'm Stepha and this is my husband, Orvell. Your mate is amazing," she said. "You should be so proud."

"Oh, I am," Hack said, grinning. "He drives me crazy, but I'm definitely proud of him."

Orvell snorted, watching his wife fondly. "I understand the feeling."

His wife elbowed him and glared. "Anyway, my family and I were captured this morning. Of course, we'd heard about Charybdis Station's war on the Concords, but Grellweir has stayed out of it."

"It's a position we understand and respect. Declaring war on anyone is a big step and when that group is as expansive as the Concords, it's a lot of trouble."

"Well, it's not a position that will last," Stepha said. "My father is the King of Grellweir." She pointed to one of the children on Shae's lap. The little boy cuddled with a small Silet girl, both as comfortable as could be in Shae's arms. "That is the Crown Prince."

"Fuck. Your dad is going to be pissed. My dad knows him, says he has a temper."

"That he does," Orvell said. "He's generally a fair man and tries to be cautious in making decisions. When it comes to his family though, fairness and caution disappear."

"I've already called him, and he's meeting us on Charybdis Station," Stepha said. "I've spoken with Leti too, and we'll be adopting my son's new friend. The poor girl's parents were killed, and she has no other relatives."

"It's one thing to hear about the cruelties of the Concords, but quite another to see it up close and personal," Orvell said.

"It's not like father didn't want to help the Lord Admiral anyway," Stepha said. "Those two are like two peas in a pod."

Hack chuckled. "I know. Dad has told me some crazy stories of them as kids."

"Dad? Oh, are you Will Hackett then?" Stepha was delighted.

"Yeah. Sorry, forgot to introduce myself," he said.

"Well, I would imagine you're exhausted," Orvell said.

Hack felt his communicator buzz. "Excuse me," he said, nodding to the couple. "That would be my dad." Stepha and Orvell moved away to give him privacy.

"Hack, we have a problem," Fasi said as soon as his face popped up on the small screen.

"What's wrong?"

"Orsla presented her knowledge on the artifact to the Council about fifteen minutes ago. She said she thought it was an inert virus, a parlor trick from an older civilization. She replicated Morrick's experiments but, understandably, refused to try it on human bodies."

"Did she mention Leti's research at all? It's not a virus and it's certainly not harmless."

"That's the problem," Fasi said. "She didn't receive any of Leti's messages or reports. She knew nothing about his findings. When I told her, she was completely surprised."

"Ewing," Hack said, growling.

"Yeah. She's disappeared with the artifact. We're tracing her now, but she's gone to ground. The only thing we can say with certainty is that she's still on the station."

"Damn it."

"I told Orsla and the Council what Leti found. Showed them the pictures and gave them his report. They're going to read over it tonight and we'll conference tomorrow."

"We'll find Ewing," Hack said. "Are eyes still on Franklin?"

"Yeah, but all she does is travel between her lab and

her rooms. We still suspect she somehow stole those three bodies, but we have no idea how or where she's stored them. Plus, she's had minimal contact with Ewing."

"Ewing can't be doing this alone."

"That brings me to more news. The bodies of the men that attacked Leti have been identified. They were all members of the Concord. We've traced how they got on board the station. Ewing's husband worked in the docks. He helped smuggle them in."

"Is he missing too?"

"No," Fasi said. "We have him and he sure is talking. Unfortunately, he doesn't know much. Good news is he only smuggled in five other Concords."

"Fuck. This isn't going to go well. I can feel it."

2 3

*L*eti lay on his side and leaned back into Hack as his mate pushed inside him, filling him. Hack lifted Leti's leg, leisurely stroking in and out. He moved at a slow, deliberate pace that was so different from their usual hurried moments.

Hack nuzzled Leti's neck, kissing and sucking his sweat-drenched skin. "You feel so fucking good," Hack said, voice guttural.

Leti cupped his mate's head, stroking his hair. His beard tickled Leti's sensitive skin. "Love you, Will," he said, panting.

Hack sped up and the pressure built. Every sensation trickled to his gut, readying his release. Hack's hard body against his back, his strong arms holding him, the length of steel pummeling his ass. All of it quickened, and Leti couldn't hold on anymore.

"Fuck, Will," he said, groaning and coming.

Hack didn't last much longer, filling Leti with warmth.

They stayed wrapped in each other for a long moment, Hack's arms tight around Leti and his face buried against Leti's neck.

"I'm proud of you, Leti," Hack said. "I worry and I always will, but I'm proud of you."

"For having sex with you? You're only just now proud of me?"

Hack laughed and bit Leti's neck. "No, baby. I'm proud of what you did today. It scared the shit out of me, but it needed to be done. If Ryne and you hadn't gone in, those people would have died."

"Thank you," Leti said gruffly, tears pricking his eyes. "I know I won't be able to do things like that much longer because of the baby, but I couldn't hear their screams and cries for help and do nothing."

"Ryne sent the message with the explanation of what you all were doing. I knew right after hearing it that you would go. I understand, because it's exactly what I would have done. I wish you didn't feel that way, but to be honest, I'm also happy that there are people in this galaxy that do care. Charybdis Station is full of brave soldiers, but to give as much of yourself as you do is extraordinarily brave."

"Thank you, Will," Leti said. "I enjoy your caveman moments, but you don't know how happy it makes me that you accept me as I am. I don't have to pretend to be something else. I don't have to hold back. You even eat my cooking."

"We do, baby," Hack said sadly. "We all do."

"Juniper and Ma are still teaching me, but since

Juniper started running the sector's farms, he doesn't have as much time."

"The spaghetti is good," Hack said.

"Anyone can make spaghetti," Leti said, grumbling. He wanted to feed his family, not heat Ma and Juniper's frozen pity dinners. Pity tasted so good though.

Hack laughed, rolling out of bed. "I'm going to check on the kids and take a shower."

Leti burrowed into his blankets. He needed to shower too, but he was so sleepy. A little nap wouldn't hurt anything.

LETI'S COMMUNICATOR BUZZED, waking him. He looked around his bedroom, groggy. He'd slept later than he'd meant to. He picked up the comm and answered it. The caller popped up, and Leti sat up straight, heart beating fast.

The dead, blue-eyed prisoner sat on the floor against a grey wall. Leti didn't know where he was, but he knew this was a dream. Blue Eyes was alive, looking right at Leti. He was naked, and, from the angle of the screen, Leti could see all of him. His legs were healed over stumps, and the stab wounds that had covered his chest were scars.

He was a hybrid with the telltale pointed ears, but where he had been tan with brown hair in life, the man now had bone-white skin and hair. His eyes were still blue, still painful to look at, and had dark circles beneath them. He looked tired and hungry.

"I tried to help you," Leti said.

"I know, Leti," he said. "That's why I called you. I don't know anyone else here. Fuck, I don't even know where here is."

"What are you talking about?" Leti was confused. He'd been dreaming of this man for months. This wasn't how the dreams went.

"Something happened to me. I think it's just been a few hours," he said. "I heard them saying that you cried over me. That's how I knew your name, knew who to call."

"I'm confused," Leti said. "My dreams of you don't usually go this way."

The man looked pained. "I'm sorry you dream of me, but I'm not sorry you were there when I died. I needed someone. I didn't want to die alone."

"You didn't want to die," Leti said. "That's what you told me."

"I did die though," he said. "I don't remember it now, but I remember seeing your tears, feeling your hand on mine. I remember all the pain, then nothing, nothing at all."

"What can I do? This dream's so strange."

"It's not a dream, Leti. Two people named Franklin and Ewing did something to me. I was dead, then I wasn't. Right after, there was something else in my head, but it left really quickly. I wasn't *worthy*," he said.

Leti pinched himself. Fuck that hurt! "Oh gods, this isn't a dream."

"No. They did it again to another person, about thirty minutes ago. She was on the same ship as me, but I didn't know her name. The things the Concords did to her were horrific. Watching them cut pieces of me away was bad, but what they did to her was worse." He shuddered.

"She's alive too? She was pregnant."

"I wouldn't really call her alive. They tossed me in the corner when whatever experiment they did didn't work. They removed the fetus from her corpse before doing the ceremony. Franklin didn't want to *muddy the waters*, whatever that means. I watched them do the ceremony, and whatever was in me was also in her. It left, though, as some black gas stuff. It floated back to the little pyramid thing. Then the woman went crazy. Ewing tried to call security before she died."

"Ewing's dead?"

"The woman tore her to pieces. Franklin ran out of the room and locked it. I barely got out of there, but the room has reinforced windows and they're all red. It's not pretty. While Franklin freaked out, I crawled in here and hid. When Franklin left, I searched around and found the directory. Only one Leti in this place."

"You're alive," Leti said. "This is real."

"It is. I'm cold and hungry too, and the woman's been banging on the door for a while. I'm afraid she'll get out."

"You said Franklin is gone?"

"Yeah. She left with five other people that looked like soldiers. They had a third body and the pyramid thing with them. I think she's going to try again."

"Okay," Leti said. "I have your coordinates from the call. We'll come get you."

"Thank you, Leti," the man said. "For everything."

Leti jumped up, clutching his comm, and started dressing frantically. "Oh fuck," he said, pausing. "What's your name? I don't know your name."

"Remy," he said, smiling. "Remington Forster."

"Okay, Remy," Leti said. "Stay on the comm, and we'll be there. I just need to hunt my friends down."

He ran into the hall, picking Abbot up on the way. Cuddling the big rabbit, Leti checked each room. Mo and Rizzie were already at school, but Hack wasn't in the office. He heard laughter from the kitchen and ran there. Shae fed Pepper, and Maia bounced Sami on her lap. Wolfe and Sebastian quietly stuffed food in their faces while Juniper flipped pancakes. Shit, he wouldn't have time to eat.

"Where's Hack?" Leti asked. He bounced from foot to foot.

"He's meeting with the Council about the artifact," Maia said. "He told us to let you sleep in."

"Thank you," Leti said. "I needed the sleep, but now I really need some help." He held up his comm. Remy waved.

Sebastian's fork clattered to the table. "Is that your guy, Leti? Blue Eyes?"

"It is," Leti said. "His name is Remy, and he's in the office next to Franklin's in the Medical Research Buildings. The other rescued prisoner is there too. She's violent and killed Ewing. I'll explain more later, but we need to get Remy to safety and find Franklin. She has Morrick and the element. She's probably with the last five Concords that were smuggled in."

Juniper flipped some bacon. "Okay. We need to do this fast, so here's what we'll do. Sebastian will stay with the kids and finish cooking breakfast. I'll call Finn and meet him at the docks. He'll update Hack and the Lord Admiral. We'll find Franklin. Leti, you, Shae, Maia, and Wolfe go to Remy. I'll call Nettle on the way, and we'll see who we can rally to meet you there."

"Hear that, Remy," Leti said, setting down Abbot and picking up a shrunken Princess. "We're coming." He grabbed one of his favorite snuggling blankets from the living room on the way out the door.

They separated from Juniper on the shuttle tram and quickly made their way to the Medical Research Buildings. Without stopping at the front desk, Leti followed the signal on his communicator and quickly walked down one of the halls. They came to the right door but couldn't open it.

"Damn it," Leti said. "Where's Beck when you need him?"

"We may be able to help," Nettle said, grinning. Fifteen security guards stood behind him, and one of them stepped up to the door. He typed in a code and the door opened. Security went in first, Leti and the others following close behind. Remy was still sitting on the floor, trying to cover his crotch. A pale pink blush spread over his white cheeks.

Leti rushed to his side, handing over his blanket. He started to kneel beside Remy, but Shae rolled a chair over.

"If you get down there, you'll never get back up," Shae said, smile shaky.

Leti sat and helped Remy wrap the blanket around his shoulders. Nettle knelt at the man's side, scanner at the ready. Shae watched the door to the other room warily, while the guards stood back, waiting for orders.

Blood covered the viewing windows and loud, violent bangs came through the door. Leti could already see where the woman's hits curved the door outward. That shouldn't be possible. If Death was inside the woman, he was adding to her normal strength.

"She's not there," Shae said. "There's absolutely no mental sign of her."

"I remember she seemed almost happy to die," Leti said. "The host for Death needs to want to live." He looked at Remy. "They also need to be whole. It may not seem like it now, but you should probably be glad about your legs."

"I think I get it. The thing that was in me wanted a host that could walk?"

"That's what we think," Nettle said, voice shaking. "You're fine. I remember you dying, and now, you're just a little dehydrated and malnourished. Fuck, that's all. I want to run more tests back in the office, but you're fine. Gods."

"We'll get him home after we deal with her. He can eat breakfast and get some rest. You know where we live if you want to come poke and prod him a bit, but we'll bring him to you tomorrow morning," Leti said.

"Sounds good," Nettle said and took a deep breath. "Lilah and I cook about as well as you, so we'll come by for dinner tonight. I'm sure Ma will be by to spoil the newest addition."

"She will," Leti said, then looked at the blood-smeared windows to the other room. "Now, what do we do with her?"

"Sir," a guard addressed Nettle. "Do we restrain her?"

"There's no point in it," Shae said. "She's not there anymore. Her mind is empty, and she's just a beast of violence. Pain and anger are all she feels."

"She doesn't deserve that," Nettle said. "Damn it. Shae, there's no retrieving her mind?"

"No," he said. "I don't think it came back when her body awakened."

"Try to detain her first," Nettle said. "We can at least make her death peaceful."

"She'll fight back," Shae said.

"When she does," Nettle said to the guards, "you may use deadly force. I don't *want* her to be needlessly hurt, but that doesn't mean we risk any of you."

"Yes, sir." The guard nodded.

Nettle and Shae helped Remy to the hallway, Leti trailing behind. He peeked back into the room. Wolfe had two small blades out and was crouched atop a desk in the corner of the room. Maia stood next to the door with her blade and phaser at the ready.

One guard unlocked the door and opened it, standing back. The woman was a blur of motion. Like Remy, she now had white hair and skin. Her eyes were completely blood red. She ran from the room and grabbed the closest guard, wrenching his arm. Leti watched as the woman was shot dozens of times. She didn't slow down, slinging the guard across the room and grabbing another.

Maia and the guards used their blades, trying to land a hit, but the woman was too fast. She threw another guard, and he landed hard against the wall with a snap. Wolfe vaulted over the guards and landed behind the woman, swinging his blade quickly. Blood sprayed and her head rolled across the floor. Her body crumpled.

Nettle rushed back in the room and checked the two fallen guards. "Fuck. Call the medics," he said, putting his bag down and getting to work.

"At least she threw them instead of tearing them apart," Remy said, shuddering.

Wolfe wiped his blade off and sat beside Leti. Leti took his hand and squeezed it, resting his head on the young man's shoulder. They waited for the medics to arrive.

24

"This is absolutely fascinating," Dr. Manning said for the fourth time. "Oh, I wish I'd seen Dr. Hackett's research earlier. The element could most certainly be housing a being, which would explain so much. Of course, it makes it far more dangerous to study, but still."

"So this is plausible?" Councilwoman Brinanda, a Fallon woman, raised her brow. "Truly? Insidious beings from a long-dead civilization are running the Concords?"

"Stranger things have happened," Councilwoman Rundel responded. She was an older Siren woman with a surplus of experience.

"Scientifically speaking," Dr. Manning said. "It really is possible. Gods, to think of the science behind it! I can't wait to get back to the lab."

"His research does seem extensive, and he's careful to qualify all his theories," Councilman Warren said. The older Havenite gentleman read his tablet in fascination. Hack had a feeling Dr. Manning wasn't the only one who wanted to get to a lab.

"Are we approving his dissertation or talking reality here?" Councilman Delino was a no-nonsense Cardinal. It didn't surprise Hack that Delino and Brinanda were skeptical. That was part of what made them good Council members.

"What if it is real, Delino, and we ignore it? The Concords are the largest mercenary group in the galaxy, and they hate non-humans," Councilwoman Jalina said. The dainty Grell's light pink face scowled.

"What do you think Lord Admiral?" the last Council member asked. Councilman Mitchell was human and usually the last to speak. The man liked to watch and observe before making a decision. Hack had to admit he respected him the most.

"I trust in his skills," Fasi said. "He is a skilled researcher and not prone to hysterics. Well, unless Hack eats the last of his chocolates."

The Council members snickered, sending winks and smiles Hack's way.

"At the very least," Fasi continued. "We should investigate it more."

"I'll immediately run some tests when I'm back at the lab," Dr. Manning said, nodding enthusiastically.

"Um, sorry to interrupt," Finn said, poking his head in the door. "General Hackett, we have a situation with Dr. Franklin."

"Come in, Finn," Fasi said. "We were just discussing the element."

Finn stood beside Fasi, swallowing nervously. The

poor guy had never been in front of the whole Council before. "It's a bit involved, but to keep it simple, Dr. Franklin was working with Ms. Ewing to keep Dr. Manning uninformed about Leti's theories," Finn said. "She's been experimenting on two of the missing bodies. Now Ewing is dead, and Franklin's trying to escape Charybdis Station with the artifact, Dr. Morrick's body, and five Concord mercenaries."

The Council stared at him in shock.

"What?" Brinanda half stood from her seat. "Who's stopping her?"

"Juniper is working with Station Enforcement to track her. Draif and others are waiting at the docks. We've notified Dock Security."

"You said Franklin experimented on two of the missing bodies?" Dr. Manning looked both horrified and curious. Hack understood the feeling. The thought of those poor people's bodies being violated was terrible, but he wanted to know what knowledge was gained.

Finn paled and shuddered. "The man, a young hybrid named Remy, was brought back. He called Leti from the suite next to Dr. Franklin's. The woman was too, but she's not coherent. Leti and some others went to investigate. We'll know more soon."

"Gods, that's unbelievable," Delino said, leaning back in his chair. Finn and Hack's communicators buzzed. "Hack, if you don't mind, can we hear your call?"

"Sure," he said, hooking it into the conference table. Juniper's face appeared.

"Whoa," he said, seeing the whole Council. "Did I call the wrong ID?"

"Nope," Hack said. "Report."

"Franklin's gone," Juniper said. "She had more help from the docks. Draif and his crew are in pursuit. Cordelia and I did get two of the Concords and the three men in the docks that helped her. The Concords have the Life tattoos, General."

"Fuck," Hack said, forgetting where he was. "Watch them closely and make sure no one says anything important in front of them. We don't know how much connection he has with them. Do we have any Sirens nearby? Shae's been able to read them a bit."

"I'll find someone, sir," Juniper said and signed off.

His comm buzzed again.

"Go ahead, son," Fasi said when Hack looked around the room.

Leti's face popped up this time, wearing a goofy grin. "Blue Eyes is alive, Will. His name is Remy and he's a nice guy. He's eating breakfast now." Leti flipped his comm, and Hack saw Remy sitting at the table with Sebastian, Shae, and Sami.

He'd frozen in place with his fork halfway to his mouth. "Uh, hi," Remy said.

"Fuck," Sami yelled, waving at Hack. The Council members snickered, and Hack blushed but waved back to his son.

Leti turned his comm again with a sheepish look. "Anyway, the other woman is dead. Again. Remy was used in the ceremony first, but Death left him because of his missing legs. Then, Franklin and Ewing used the woman, but the poor thing didn't want to live anymore so Death had to leave her. Where Remy is normal though, she wasn't more than an animal in pain. Shae didn't sense any sentient mental activity. We tried to detain her, but she almost killed two guards, and she did kill Ewing right after she woke up. Wolfe had to kill her."

"That must have been horrible. She was tortured, lost a baby, died, was brought back, then killed again," Rundel said.

Leti nodded, tears filling his eyes. "It really was. Shae doesn't think she was there anymore. He thinks her mind and soul refused to come back, which made Death move on to look for a new host."

"I hope so, for her sake," Rundel said. "So, Shae's been of help to you?"

"Oh, gods, he's the best," Leti said. "He helped us with our research, helped on the medical ship during attacks, and even helped rescue some of the Concord prisoners. He's able to give us a unique perspective on those influenced by Life too."

She smiled softly. "He's a good boy," she said.

Leti blew a kiss to Hack. "I'll let you get back to work. I just wanted to update you on what's happening here."

"Thanks, baby. Take care," Hack said, closing the call.

"Your mate is sweet, Hack," Delino said. "He's also apparently correct in at least some of his theories. Damn, this is not good."

Dr. Manning practically vibrated. "May I please be

dismissed? I want to go speak to Leti and check out Remy too. Please?"

Fasi laughed. "Go on, Orsla. We'll update you all on Franklin." The doctor ran from the room. Fasi shook his head. "I have a feeling Leti just made a new friend."

Hack's comm buzzed again, and Draif's face popped up. The man looked pissed off. "Draif, what do you have to report?"

"She's gone," he said. "We were on their tail when something froze the ship. It fucking froze the ship! Selene said it shouldn't be possible."

"What could do that?" Warren asked.

"I've not heard of any technology that comes close to doing that," Renee said from beside Hack. "Not even Half-Moon has something like that."

"Are you still frozen?" Sheiria asked from Hack's other side.

"No, we're working now. We set off after them again, and well, we found the two remaining Concord mercs."

"I thought they were on the same ship," Mitchell said.

"They were. Someone tossed them out the airlock."

"Damn," Brinanda said. "That's not an easy way to go."

"Fuck, fuck, fuck," Draif said. "We've been frozen again. Every time we get within range of the shuttle, something freezes us."

"Come back to the station," Fasi said. "We know they're going to the Crellic System, and they have to pass through the Silverlight System to get there. Cas and his fleet are right outside Union Station. I'll get them to hunt them down. Shouldn't be too hard. It's our shuttle, and we have a tracker on it. They may even have to stop for fuel unless the traitors from the docks stocked the ship."

"Yes, sir," Draif said and signed off.

"Well, this is really happening, so what are we going to do about it?" Delino propped his arms on the conference table.

"Don't forget, Grellweir now stands behind us in the war against the Concords," Jalina said. "They can certainly be of help."

"I spoke with Half-Moon this morning and told them about Wolfe," Renee said. "I have a feeling they may offer some support as well. The Guild Master is very concerned with keeping his brother safe."

Hack didn't understand it. Wolfe was the most capable fighter he'd ever seen. Why would he need to be protected?

"We continue fighting the Concords as we are," Fasi said. "In addition, we send scouts to the Crellic System. If Half-Moon would indeed help us, they'd be the ideal choice for this. Their ships are basically invisible."

"General Caspian can work on securing the element and poor Dr. Morrick's body," Mitchell said.

"Leti can continue his research as well," Warren said. "Then we can reconvene when we know more. I have the feeling we're on the edge of a very steep cliff. The more knowledge we have, the better."

"Agreed," Rundel said.

"While we're all here, how is it going for Beck and Xavier on Burnished Outpost?" Jalina asked.

"Well, their ships were in better shape than anyone thought they'd be," Hack said. "Chieftain Bowan is adamant about establishing alliances with the other planets and most of his people seem to be onboard with that idea."

"Grellweir and Cardinal Hold are both sending people out to teach them agriculture techniques, and I believe Fallow will send someone with a few herds. Haven and Siren's Lament are likely to contribute something too," Delino said. "I have to admit I love seeing our system come together."

"We're lucky," Fasi agreed.

Hack's comm buzzed again. He didn't even ask, just plugged them through. Finn sat next to Sheiria, sighing.

Juniper's face popped up with a big, fake smile. "General Hackett, sir," Juniper said. "How are you today?"

Hack smirked, used to Juniper's quirks. "What's the bad news, Juny?"

"Well, the three Concord mercs are dead."

"How did they die?" Rundel asked.

"They stopped breathing," Juniper answered. "Literally, they just stopped breathing. Didn't even blink as they turned blue and died."

"Life doesn't even need poison to kill them," Brinanda whispered. "Gods, this is horrible."

"They were listed in our records as higher-ranking officers for the Concords," Juniper said. "There's no way in hell the admiral of the Concords would send his favorites to do a basic infiltration job like this."

"He probably didn't make that decision," Hack said. "One of Leti's contacts said that Wendell Belcort was in charge of his Concord escorts. They weren't the ones giving orders." He sighed. "Thank you for letting us know, Juniper. Are the two wounded guards alright?"

"They'll recover, but it'll take a little time." He nodded and signed out.

"So," Brinanda said, nodding to Hack. "We'll see you at dinner then?"

$\mathcal{L}$eti leaned back in his comfy patio chair, his feet propped up on an ottoman. Sebastian sat in the chair next to him, reading his tablet. Sami stood beside the chair, head pressed against Leti's belly. He was growing obsessed with the baby. Rizzie knelt behind him, waiting her turn.

"I guess another boy won't be too bad," she said. "Xu is nice enough."

"Gee, thanks," Xu said, standing next to her.

"Oh Xu," she said. "You know you're my best friend."

"I know, but I'm a boy so you can't like me a lot," he said, giggling.

"It's the way it has to be," she said. She reached over and hugged him. "Still my best friend though. I don't care what the other girls say."

"You two are silly," Leti said. "You should like each other as much as you want to. If anyone has a problem with it, let Mo tell them what's what."

"I like your idea, Daddy Leti," Rizzie said. "You still need to have a girl next time. Okay?"

"As soon as this one's out, we'll talk about it," Leti said.

"I think it's a great idea," Hack said. He carried a couple of plates of food in one arm and a bouncy Pepper in the other. "Here you go, baby. Rizzie, Xu, you better go get some food before Nessa eats it all." The little girl did have quite an appetite. The two kids ran to the food table while they could.

"Juniper and Ma are the best," Leti said, grabbing the plate.

Hack sprawled in the grass and set the other plate down. "Come on, Sami boy. Food time."

"Foo, foo," Sami yelled. Leti's little boy loved his food.

Wolfe helped Silas onto the patio sofa across from Leti, then plopped down too.

"How you feeling, Silas?" Leti asked. He'd checked in with the man every few hours, but this was the first time Silas had been up and about.

"Better. I love my suite, but damn if I'm not happy to be outside." Wobble stuck his head over Silas's shoulder. "Yeah, yeah, I missed you too, Wobble," he said, petting the llama.

"We'll make sure you get more time outside," Hack said. "At least it never rains and stays a steady temperature."

"We could just leave you in the hammock indefinitely," Draif said, smiling as he sat on the grass, plate in hand. Lucas followed close behind, as usual.

He handed a plate to Sebastian, then sat close to Draif.

"Thanks, man," Silas said. "You're so kind."

"Aww, poor Silas," Shae said, walking up with his own plate. He bent and kissed the top of Silas's head before sitting on the grass next to Hack. "Give me my Pepper. I haven't had any patty-cake time today."

Leti looked around the yard. His family, friends, and pets were scattered throughout the yard. Remy sat surrounded by Orsla and the Council members, animatedly telling his story. Fasi and Renee cuddled in a chair next to the food, reminding him of Dru and Lerais. This was a happy moment. All it needed was a few more people.

"ARE you sure you want to call him?" Leti didn't like how worried Wolfe looked. No one should be nervous to talk to their brother.

Wolfe nodded, holding up his tablet. *I'll just type and you can talk. I don't feel like signing, and I want you here anyway. I've already sent him messages, but he wants to see my face. Stupid brothers.*

"Okay," Leti said and made the call.

A man that looked a lot like Wolfe popped up on the screen. The biggest difference between the two was that Wolfe looked delicate, while Guild Master Beol looked rugged. They had the same eyes, the same mouth, and the same growly expression. Wolfe just looked a little prettier.

"Wolfe," Beol said. "I'm glad to see you. Why aren't you home?"

Leti read Wolfe's words. "He says, 'Hi, big brother. This is Leti and he'll be my voice.'" Leti looked at Beol's raised brow. "That's me," he said and smiled. "Okay, so he says, 'I am at home. I just have a different home now. I don't want to come back.'" Leti wrapped an arm around Wolfe's shoulder. "Aww, we're happy to have you."

"What do you mean a different home? Am I not enough for you?" The pain in Beol's voice made Leti tear up.

"I'm sure that's not what he means. He says, 'You're more than enough family for me, and I love you. It's just that Union Station isn't home. It never has been. It's where we were trained, where they hurt us. I can't be happy there.'" Leti kissed Wolfe's head.

"Then we'll move," Beol said. "We aren't tied here. We can go wherever you want to go."

"You could come here," Leti said, excited. "Charybdis Station is a great place to live. How many people are in your Guild? Oh wait, Wolfe says, 'I don't want you to be unhappy. It'd be a lot of work to move the Guild.'"

"It's worth it," Beol said. "We couldn't be family before, because of *him*, but now we can. I need to be near you for that to happen, idiot."

"Charybdis Station is a fabulous place," Leti said, doing a tour guide impression. "It's an engineering marvel with plenty of space for your growing guild of assassins."

Wolfe silently laughed at him and reached down and picked up Abbot, gently petting the rabbit.

Beol's eyes softened. "You really are happy there." He nodded once. "I'll contact the Lord Admiral now. He wanted our help with something in any case."

"He wants to know what the Lord Admiral wants your help with," Leti said.

"I didn't see him typing," Beol said.

"Okay, so *I* want to know what the Lord Admiral wants your help with."

Beol smirked. "I'd hate to upset the Lord Admiral when I'm hoping to move my business to Charybdis. You'll just have to ask him yourself." He ended the call.

"Your brother really is annoying," Leti said.

I told you he was. He's a good guy when you get to know him.

"Well," Leti said. "He's moving here, so I'll get that chance. Oh, I bet Alois would let you guys have his house since he'll be living with Sebastian as soon as they get their heads out of their butts. You can also keep staying with me! Your brother could sleep on your couch. This is going to be great!" He tackled Wolfe for a hug and squealed. "Let's go bother Dad now."

The two left Leti's office, hand in hand, and headed to the kitchen. As usual, Juniper stood at the stove, cooking.

"I love you, Juniper," Leti said. "Did you know that?"

"Considering you tell me every morning? Yes, I did know that," Juniper said.

Sebastian sat at the table, already eating, and Sami sat in his highchair, feeding himself.

"You are such a smart little boy," Leti said, dropping a kiss on the top of Sami's head.

"You said he was chewing on Pax's foot this morning," Sebastian said.

"Well, he's still learning boundaries. Doesn't make him less of a little genius," Leti said. "Does Shae still have Pepper? He wouldn't let me get her ready this morning."

"He loves that little girl," Juniper said. "Enjoy the help while you have it, but he went up to visit with Silas."

Leti sighed. "I should be thankful, but I already miss Rizzie and Mo while they're gone to school, and Hack hogs Pepper when he's home. At least I have my little monster," he said, pulling on Sami's bare foot. His little boy giggled and stuffed more bits of waffle in his mouth. "We're going to Dad's office this morning. Anyone else want to come?"

"I do," Sebastian said. "My back is killing me, so a good walk should help."

"You sure you're not in labor?" Juniper eyed him warily. "I'm okay with patching up a wound or two, but I don't want to deliver a baby."

"No! I'm not in labor," Sebastian said, wrinkling his nose. "I still have two weeks to go."

"We'll be near the medical building just in case," Leti said. "We can go by and visit with Remy too."

In the end, everyone, including Silas, decided to go.

"It's not like you two will be walking fast," Silas said,

looking pointedly at Leti's belly. "Even injured, I still outwalk you and Sebastian."

A short shuttle tram ride later and they walked slowly to Fasi's office. His assistant nodded at them and let them in. Fasi and Renee sat at Fasi's desk, working on mysterious Lord Admiral things.

"Leti," Fasi said with a smile. He jumped up and gave Leti a gentle hug. Renee already had Sami free from the stroller and Pepper in her arms. "You've never visited my office before. Any problems?"

"No, just some questions," Leti said. "Wolfe and I spoke with his brother this morning, and we wanted to know if Half-Moon could move here. Please?"

Renee's jaw dropped. "Seriously? Do you know how long I've been negotiating with Guild Master Beol to get his help? One conversation with you and Wolfe and he'll move here?"

Leti shrugged. "He misses his little brother, and Wolfe is ours now." Leti pushed Silas into a chair. Stupid man wouldn't take care of himself.

"Does that mean they can come?" Shae asked.

"We'll work it out," Fasi said. "We can make the space, but I guess it depends on how much he'll compromise. One of the reasons the Guild is located on Union Station is because it's easy to maneuver the government. That wouldn't work with us. I'll talk it over with him, Leti. Don't worry."

"Okay," he said, trusting Fasi to do what he could. Trusting a parent was still a really odd feeling.

I'm going to go gather some of Half-Moon and head to the Crellic System, Wolfe typed.

"What! That's a big jump there, Wolfe," Leti said.

"I thought you wanted to stay here," Shae said.

I do, but we need to get someone out there. Beol told me that's what Charybdis was trying to hire them for. It'll give me the chance to get my stuff and get Beol moving. It'll also give us eyes on the enemy. The Concords may be patrolling the system, but we won't be seen. I won't stay long, just get patrols set up.

"If your brother approves it," Renee said. "Make sure you stay off the surface of the planets. We don't want to alert them, and we don't want to give Life access to any of our friends."

Wolfe nodded. Leti frowned, tears filling his eyes. He didn't want his new friend to leave. Wolfe was his, just like Draif was.

I'll go now. Leti, don't worry. I'll be back before you know it. Wolfe squeezed his hand, smiling. *You can learn sign language while I'm gone.*

"I'll make sure everyone does," Shae said. "I've already started."

Leti stuck his tongue out at Shae. "Kiss up."

Wolfe kissed Leti's cheek and left the room. Leti's lip trembled. He knew it'd be a while before he saw him again.

"Oh Leti," Fasi said, pulling him into another hug. "I love how much you love."

"Mo," Leti called. "What's Rosie's favorite color?" Hack's mate held two of his favorite quilts up. "Which do you think she'll like best?"

"Doesn't her room already have blankets?" Hack asked.

"Yes, but I wanted to make sure they both had something from me."

"Are you the one who keeps putting crocheted throws in my room?" Mo tried not to grin.

"Oh, like I haven't seen you wrapped up with them in the window seat," Leti said. "Which one would she like best? I'll give the other to Alex."

Mo grinned and pointed at the one on the left. Leti waddled out of the room, and Mo turned back to Hack. "I can't believe they're coming today."

"I know," Hack said. "How are you feeling about your mom and dad?"

Mo shrugged. "Honestly, I think that's the only way it could end. I've talked with Uncle Bowan. His mate was pregnant and Mom knew it. She wanted to kill him anyway. I'm glad Rosie was there. As for Dad, he's hated Uncle Bowan for as long as I can remember. Grandpa Moses and Uncle Bowan are the ones who taught us to hunt and spent time with us. Dad never seemed to care what we did."

"You are too mature for a kid your age," Hack said. "Too damn sensible."

Mo elbowed him. "Someone has to be the adult in this house."

"Hey now, that's me and Leti!"

"You chased Leti through the house last night. He was giggling and you were play growling. I don't want to know what happened once we all went to sleep."

"Well, adults do things like that," Hack said, blushing.

"None of the adults I know do that," Mo said, narrowing his eyes. "That's not even considering the pranks you and the crew play on each other."

"Laughter keeps you young," Hack said. He *had* switched Cordelia's shampoo with hot pink insta-dye last night.

"Exactly. That's why you guys are toddlers. I'm the responsible one."

"Really? Who organized a mock pet battle in the backyard last week?" Leti said, coming back in the room.

"Fluffle kicked ass," Mo said. Hack grabbed him and started tickling his sides. "Okay, okay, I may see your point."

"I THINK I'm going to puke," Hack said. They waited at the station gate as the incoming ship finished docking. Leti held his hand. His parents stood behind him, offering their support.

"This is going to be great," Mo said. "Alex and Rosie are going to love it here, and I know Grandpa Moses is going to be happy to see you."

"He's right, Will," Leti said. "It's okay to be nervous though. It's been a long time since you saw Moses, and you're meeting your siblings for the first time." He leaned up and kissed Hack's chin. "I love you, doofus."

"Love you too, baby."

"Gods, they say that all the time," Sebastian said.

"Bah, you and Alois will be just like that when he comes back," Shae said.

Sebastian sputtered and blushed. "We're just friends, Shae."

"Sure," Shae said, drawing out the word.

"Adults are weird," Rizzie told Xu. The two best friends held hands and waited with the others. Hack's sweet girl was eager to meet Mo's brother and sister.

"Just think, Sebastian," Nettle said. "Within the next few days, you'll have a baby, and in another couple of weeks, Alois will be home. When do you think you'll get married?"

"Friends! We're just friends," Sebastian yelled.

"Friends, my fine rear end," Cordelia huffed. Her hot pink hair looked great, but she had sworn vengeance on Hack.

"How's Quinn, Cordy?" Leti asked.

Hack saw Sebastian shoot him a thankful look.

Cordelia blushed. "How would I know?"

"Don't you talk to her every morning?" Lilah asked.

"Okay, everyone," Leti said as the cargo bay door opened. "They're coming."

Hack watched as Beck led a group of Burnished from the ship. There were about fifteen extra passengers, all young. Hack's dad had been surprised when Chieftain Bowan told him how many wanted to come. Almost all of them wanted to train to fly, but a few were interested in engineering. Bowan said he'd send more after the group returned.

One of the Burnished caught his eye. It'd been just over twenty years since he'd seen him last, but Hack would recognize Grandpa Moses anywhere. He was short for a Burnished and slim of build. Despite that, he was pure muscle and stubbornness. His hair was white now, and there were more wrinkles on his face than not, but that strength was still there.

As soon as his eyes met Hack's, he stopped walking. "Willard?"

"Fuck me, did he say Willard?" Finn tried to hold the laughter in.

"Yes," Selene said. "That's what he said. Willard, are you going to greet your grandfather?"

Hack ignored them and walked to Moses, dragging Leti behind him. Then he was there, right in front of him. "Grandpa?"

The old man crumpled, tears streaming down his face. Hack grabbed him, pulling him into a hug. Moses wrapped his strong arms around Hack, sobbing into his chest.

"You're alive. You really are alive," Moses said. "I'm so sorry, sweet boy. I'm so sorry."

"It's okay," Hack said through his own tears. "It's okay. We're here now. Together." He vaguely heard Mo reuniting with his sister and brother. Leti's voice filtered in and out, but all Hack was aware of was his grandfather's arms and tears.

"I swear to you, if you let me back into your tribe, I'll never abandon you again," Moses said. "I swear it."

"You're in, old man," Hack said, sniffing. He finally stepped back and pulled Leti forward. "This is my mate and husband, Leti Hackett."

Moses held his hand out to Leti, who grabbed it, then pulled the old man forward for a big hug. "I'm so glad to meet you Moses. When Mo told us about you and how you missed Will, I just knew he needed to see you again. We already have your room fixed up. It's directly off the kitchen." He leaned in and whispered. "Don't tell anyone how often I get night snacks, okay?"

"Your secret is safe with me," Moses whispered back.

"I have a few kids around here," Hack said. "Pepper, Sami, and Rizzie."

"Do you know what this one is yet?" Moses waited for Leti's nod, then reverently placed his hands on Leti's big belly.

"It's a boy," Hack said. "We haven't settled on a name yet, but we know it's just one."

"Why did you feel you had to specify only one baby

is growing in here?" Leti was getting really good at arching his brow. Moses chuckled.

"Will, come meet Alex and Rosie," Mo yelled.

"Oh, damn. I should go," Hack said. His feet seemed frozen in place. On the one hand, he needed to leave so Leti wouldn't yell at him for commenting on his size, but on the other hand, that was his brother and sister.

Leti took ahold of Moses's hand, waving encouragingly toward the younger Burnished. "Go on. They're just teenagers. Hmm, wait, that sounds ominous."

Hack rolled his eyes and followed Mo's voice. Standing beside his brother was a tall, broad-shouldered young man who looked just like Mo. He carried Rizzie on his back and smiled good-naturedly. With them was a young woman, around fifteen, with wild, black curls and a round face. She held Abbot in her arms, looking uncertain. Gravy leaned against her leg. She was the spitting image of his mother. Gods.

"Will," Mo said, pulling him forward. "This is Alex and Rosie."

Alex grinned and nodded, and Rosie smiled shyly.

"I told them about Princess and their rooms," Mo said.

"I can share a room," Rosie said. "I don't need my own."

"You're a growing young lady," Hack said. "My mom assured me that you do, in fact, need your own space."

"Your… mom?" she asked. Her shoulders slumped and any bit of confidence she had disappeared. Hack winced.

"That would be me," Renee said, stepping forward. She bounced Pepper in her arms. "Fasi and I adopted Will when he was found. I'm his mother. Will you come with me and Leti, Rosie? We'd like to talk to you a moment."

"Yeah, sure," she said and shuffled beside Leti. They stood a distance away, huddled close to Rosie.

"Grandma will make sure she understands she has nothing to feel guilty for," Mo told Alex. "Leti will too. He had a similar problem with his own parents."

Alex sighed. "I've tried to talk to her, but she's so stubborn."

"By the way," Mo said, "Alex said he wants to join Charybdis Station. Do you think he can serve in your fleet? If not, he can be in Uncle Cas's, right?"

"Well now, I can answer that," Fasi said, holding onto a giggling and wiggly Sami. Moses stood beside him, looking around in wonder. "What do you want to do in the fleet?"

"I want to be a fighter," Alex said. "Beck told me about the Concords and what they're doing. I want to help."

"Why am I not surprised?" Fasi said with a grin. "If Hack will have you, you can start training with Selene."

"I would be honored," Hack said, nodding to Alex. "Selene will work you hard, but trust me, she's the best."

"For now," Draif said, draping an arm over Selene's shoulder. "I'm still getting better."

"You do keep me on my toes," she said, then tilted her head. "I've gotten better too, Draif."

"Lucas! Come on, we need to go spar," Draif said, running towards the tram.

Lucas rolled his eyes and followed. "Thanks, Selene," he said. "There goes our whole day."

Rosie, Renee, and Leti joined the group again. Rosie's face was red, but she held Leti's hand, adoring eyes focused on Renee. Hack hoped they'd worked their magic.

Hack looked around. His friends, his family, talked to the Burnished and welcomed them into the station. They didn't have to be here, and he hadn't asked them to come. He hadn't had to. They came to help him and Leti. They came to offer their support.

Charybdis Station had a rough road ahead, but together, Hack knew they could handle it. Death, Life, it didn't matter. He had his friends with him, his parents and brothers behind him, and Leti and the kids beside him.

"General Caspian," Rundel said. "What do you have to report?"

Cas's face projected for all the Council to see. Leti noticed he looked paler than normal. "We easily traced the shuttle when it entered Silverlight System," Cas said. "Our fleet spread, hoping not to tip it off."

"Sounds good," Mitchell said. "It went toward the Crellic System?"

"No," Cas answered.

"No? Where did it go?" Fasi asked.

"Straight to Frost Veil. We tried to intercept, but anytime one of our ships got close, it was frozen."

"What about multiple ships?" Hack asked.

"Didn't matter how many there were," Cas said. "They all froze. The strangest thing, though, was how they reacted to the Concords."

"The Concords? They tried to take them?" Brinanda asked.

"Yes. Four of our ships were frozen and two small Concord fighters showed up."

"What did Franklin do?" Warren asked.

"I don't think it was Franklin," Cas said. "The ships just imploded. Completely."

"What did she fire?" Fasi seemed puzzled.

"Nothing. Just like when we get frozen. No missiles are fired. It just happens."

"If not Franklin, then who do you think did it?" Renee asked.

"They went to Frost Veil, not the Crellic System," Cas said. "Think about it."

"Why Frost Veil?" Leti knew the significance of the place to Dr. Morrick, but not to Franklin.

"Exactly, why Frost Veil?" Cas said. "Their ship landed illegally at Facility B194A. We hacked the dock's recording system. We've edited it to skip over the boring shit, but watch."

Cas disappeared, and a video popped up. It was daytime, and it wasn't snowing for once. The video showed the stolen shuttle landing. The angle from the camera showed straight into a window to the bridge. Blood smeared across the window and a pale face pressed against it. Dr. Franklin's dead eyes stared straight at them. From the looks of things, she'd been dead for a few weeks. The same amount of time it would have taken the shuttle to reach Frost Veil.

The angle jumped to the shuttle door. It slowly lowered and a figure walked down the ramp. He had bone white skin and hair, just like Remy. He wore a wrapped sheet around his waist but didn't seem to mind when his bare feet crunched in the snow.

The angle changed again to give a close up of his face. Leti cried out. Dr. Morrick. His plain face was as familiar as his own. It'd been haunting him for so long. His eyes, though, were no longer brown. They were completely black. No pupil, no cornea, just pure black throughout.

My beloved son,

Yesterday, you turned five years old. Your mother threw you a massive party and all your friends went. The neighbors, your mother's family, even my parents went. Your mother called me after the party, screaming. She said that you waited for me, all day. Instead of having fun and opening your presents, you sat at the door and waited for me to come. I didn't. I had meant to, but then I started researching a new virus. Before I knew it, your mother was calling me, and I had missed it. I don't know what to say. All I can see is your little face watching the door, waiting. I don't know what to say.

I want to make promises. I want to say, "When I'm done with this new virus, I'll make it up to you. We'll spend some time together, just the two of us, and I'll take you wherever you want to go." I know better though. I know myself. I have to make the galaxy a better place for you. I have to make sure you're safe. I'm afraid of what that means. I'm afraid it means I'll lose you. I may not be there, but know that you are the most important person to me. You are more important than any of my work, any of the other people I've saved. I wish I could gather the courage to tell you that.

I love you more than all the stardust in the galaxy.

-- Your father

The Blue Solace Series – science fiction/fantasy, mpreg

1. The Mercenary's Mate – https://amzn.to/2MAOFEH
2. The General's Mate – https://amzn.to/2G1abRE
3. The Soldier's Mate – https://amzn.to/2S7R6ng
4. The Lieutenant's Mate – https://amzn.to/2THZ47w
5. The Engineer's Mate – https://amzn.to/2HpI4vH
6. The Captain's Mate – https://amzn.to/2knP03W
7. The Rebel's Mate – *Coming Soon*
8. Fire's Mate – *Coming Soon*

The Hobson Hills Omegas – non-shifter, mpreg, omegaverse

1. Falling for the Omega – https://amzn.to/2BgWURV
2. Snow Kisses for My Omega – https://amzn.to/2TdDiol
3. Romancing the Omega – https://amzn.to/2UNENKD

4. Healing the Omega – https://amzn.to/2FNcXrY
5. A Pint for my Omega – https://amzn.to/2XItQf7
6. Unraveling the Omega – https://amzn.to/2xRCnRL
7. The Alpha's Christmas Wish – *Coming December 2019*

Hobson Hills Shorts – short stories from the world of Hobson Hills Omegas

1. The Beta's Love Song – https://amzn.to/2UrRPNN
2. Bennett's Dream – https://amzn.to/2GwSpG3
3. Justin's Journey – https://amzn.to/2DhW1t1
4. Grey's Gift – https://amzn.to/2BcjxXf
5. Hobson Hills Shorts: Volume One – https://amzn.to/2M3oGGZ

Holiday Omegas Shorts – holiday short stories from the world of The Silver Isles – paranormal, mpreg

1. Cauldron Cake Pops and a Witch's Kiss – https://amzn.to/33wMrhc
2. Sugar Cookies and a Witch's Love – *Coming December, 2019*
3. Candy Hearts and a Witch's Ring – *Coming in February, 2020*

The Silver Isles – paranormal, mermen, mpreg

1. The Guppy Prince
2. The Not so Little Merman – *Coming Soon*
3. The Sea Witch – *Coming Soon*

If you would like to keep up with releases, please like and follow me on Instagram (@c.w._gray) or Facebook (@cwgrayauthor), join C.W. Gray's Reading Nook on Facebook, or visit my website at https://cwgray-author.com.

Unedited excerpt from *The Soldier's Mate* – book three in The Blue Solace

The Blue Sparrow - On route to the Sugarworm System

"Sebastian said he's having a girl," Alois said. The Dedril looked pensive for a moment. "He's going to name her after his cousin, Nina." He sat sideways in his chair, legs hanging over one side and his head over the other. His expression turned wistful as he talked about his maybe-mate. "He's taking on translation work for a lot of Leti's university colleagues. Sebastian still doesn't realize how smart he is. He'll be bringing in a nice, steady salary soon enough."

Morgan Murray leaned back in his chair, his long legs stretched out in front of him. "That's nice," he said. "Have you told him you already started a college fund for the baby?"

Alois blushed. "Of course not. He's a bit skittish, so we're taking our time. I have to be cautious, so I don't scare him."

"You make him sound like a feral cat." Morgan brushed a strand of silky hair from his face and sipped his coffee. He watched the two young women circle one another on the mats. Quinn's chin dropped. He raised his phasor and quickly zapped her in the shoulder. He had it set extremely low, but he knew it stung. She winced, then started moving again, without the chin drop.

"I just don't want to fuck up. Sebastian is special. I

don't know for sure if he's my mate, but honestly, I don't give a damn. He's going to be mine."

"Aww," Morgan said. "It's so cute, the way you think it's your choice."

Quinn threw hit after hit, interspersed with the occasional kick, and Hazel blocked more than he expected. The young engineer was getting better. Hazel tapped her foot, readying a kick, and he zapped her in the shin. "Ouch," she squeaked, then carried through on her kick, this time without the foot tap. Quinn blocked it, then went on the offensive. The two got zapped three more times each before they finally collapsed on the mats.

"I still didn't get a fucking hit in," Hazel said. The young hybrid woman rubbed her pointed ears. He'd noticed she did that when she was stressed. Her light pink skin glistened in the light of the ship and her white hair hung limply, wet with sweat. The poor thing looked pitiful.

"You're getting better, Hazel," Alois said, giving her an up-side down smile from his chair. She smiled back, her grin infectious.

Quinn slowly moved to her feet. Morgan knew she had to be sore, but the woman sure as shit had some grit. He sparred with her himself this morning. She kept coming and coming, no matter how sore and tired she was. She would make a damn good fighter one day. Right now, she was an average one, and average fighters died fast. He didn't want that for the tough hybrid woman. She had already suffered so much at the hands of the Concord.

"You both still have too many tells," he said, standing smoothly. He paced around the women. "The expression on your face isn't the only thing your opponent sees. Quinn, you tilt your chin when you're about to attack, and your fingers twitch when you're about to throw a punch. Hazel, your face shows every emotion you feel."

Quinn groaned and dropped back to the mat, resting on her knees. "Any good news?"

"You're both getting better. Quinn, I only shot you four times. Hazel, you're down to eight. Yesterday I shot you thirteen times. I know it's a pain in the ass to break these habits, but it's necessary."

"Let's do one more round, Hazel," Quinn said, voice hard. She stood up and moved into position. "We have to be better if we want to stay alive long enough to help people."

"Okay," Hazel said, slowly getting to her feet. "One more round."

Morgan couldn't contain his proud grin. He had never wanted to be charged with training others – to make sure they were prepared to keep themselves alive and help others. It was a big responsibility, and he preferred being a simple soldier. Then Hack and Dru asked him to be the weapons specialist for the Blue Sparrow. Of course he had to agree. It was Hack and Dru. Now, he had three trainees and an ulcer. Responsibility sucked. There were his fighters, though. Getting ready to push through their pain to get better.

"Look at that proud papa grin," Alois said, fluttering his eyes. "Now who's cute?"

"Shut it," he said, growling. He turned back to the women. "Get moving."

Their next match was much slower. They didn't focus on speed, but on their tells. By the time Quinn had Hazel pinned to the mat, Morgan hadn't had to shoot either of them. "Much better," he said. "Slower, yeah, but better."

The women knelt on the mat, panting and smiling. "We'll get there," Hazel said.

"You will," Alois said, sitting up in his chair.

"Since you're making progress, we'll update your training a bit," Morgan said. "You'll both need to begin meditating. Plenty of people think it's a waste of time, but it will help you control your emotions."

Quinn whimpered. The woman definitely had trouble staying still and quiet. Meditation would be hard for her. "Meditating sounds better than sparring," Hazel said. The engineer-in-training had no problem with focus. She'd enjoy it.

"We're a week away from the Sugarworm System, so we'll get you both into a routine. First thing in the morning, you meditate right here for one hour then do your normal amount of cardio. After breakfast, you two spar until Hazel has to go train with Lerais in Engineering. Quinn, at that point, you'll start training with me, on the dummy, or with Linc if he's available. Then, you both meditate for another hour before lunch. After lunch, we pick it up again until you both drop. Got it?"

"We can do it," Quinn said, nodding. Hazel nodded too, eyes starting to droop.

"Great. Go clean up and get some dinner. I'll see you both after breakfast tomorrow."

The two women walked stiffly from the Training Room, limping towards the hot showers. Morgan watched them go, grinning. Quinn would be great by the time he was done with her. Hazel wasn't a natural fighter, she was an engineer, but her training was progressing faster than Selene and he had thought it would.

"You're doing damn good work, Morgan," Alois said, jumping to his feet. "Let's do a round. We need to stay in practice, so the trainees don't kick our asses."

They sparred, and he knocked Alois on his ass. This time anyway. Alois shot him dirty looks as they both worked through their own routine. He did join in with Morgan for thirty minutes of meditation to finish the night. Alois limped beside him. "When did you get so good? When did meditation become part of combat training?"

"I can't help it that I'm amazing, Alois. You slept too much during the last mission, so you missed out on my rise to glory."

"That's not how Draif described it. He said you got wounded again and again."

"Draif! What does he know?" Morgan grinned. He'd picked up meditation from Draif. The man had extensive combat training, but Alois didn't have to know that. Alois gave him a suspicious look and headed toward his room.

Morgan went to his quarters to clean up. His room on the Blue Sparrow was surprisingly just a little smaller than his space on the Blue Solace. It did have a nice sized window which was definitely better than the porthole he'd had before. He'd decorated in bold colors and crazy patterns. His walls were a deep blue, and a large abstract painting in purples and blues dominated one wall.

The hot water felt good on his tight muscles, and he hummed in pleasure as he showered. He used his favorite almond body wash and his special hair conditioner. After drying his hair and pampering himself, he dressed in soft, clean clothes and dropped into a chair. He called Selene. She picked up quickly, her still, expressionless face comforting to see. "Morgan," she said, voice as empty as her expression.

"If Dru asks you about shooting trainees with a phaser during training, just go with it, okay?"

"I don't shoot trainees with a phasor."

"It's for their own good, and I just zap them a little," he said, smiling big and fluttering his eyes. "Please?"

"Fine."

"How are things at the Station?" His home, Charybdis Station, was going through some changes as it shifted from a mercenary base to an independent planet. Selene and the others were right in the middle of it all.

"Politics are boring," she said. "I've been working on training Hack's soldiers and that's much more interesting."

Morgan snorted. "Of course you'd rather fight and train than sit through meetings." He pulled his long, blond hair into a bun at the top of his head. "Is Xu still enjoying school?" Selene had recently adopted a young orphan. People had been surprised, but Morgan knew his girl. She was a good mom.

"He is. He's very smart and likes to read," she said. "He's also already better at defense training than the other children his age."

"Proud mama," he teased her. "You're doing great with him, Selene, which is no surprise really. You put up with me."

"He's part of my family," she said. "You are too, Morgan."

"I know," he said, smiling tenderly. "I'm the little brother that likes to annoy you. At least Shae worships the ground you walk on. You don't have to deal with pranks from him." Shae was her biological brother and had recently moved in with her at Charybdis Station. He was a good person, just very young and sheltered.

"True," she said.

"How is he settling in?"

"He tried training with the fresh recruits. It… didn't go well. He isn't good at hurting others, even in training."

"Oh no," he said. "He had his heart set on being a soldier like you."

"Then he worked with Medical to become an assistant. That also ended badly. Apparently, he doesn't take orders well."

Morgan winced, feeling sorry for the young Siren. "What did he try next?"

"Diplomacy," she said.

"Oh fuck," Morgan said. The young man was way

too sarcastic to be a diplomat.

"Correct. Now he's working as Leti's assistant. He's actually very good at it."

"That's unexpected. I guess Leti can use all the help he can get."

"Morgan!" Dru came through his door without knocking. The Captain of the Blue Sparrow carried her Vexal newt, Monty, on her shoulder. "Are you seriously shooting at Quinn and Hazel every time one of their tells pop up? I overheard them talking in the Commons."

"It's a common technique, Dru," Selene said from the vid-screen. Morgan grinned. His big sister was the best. "He has his phasor on the lowest setting, and it really is for their own good."

"Fine," she said, narrowing her eyes on Morgan. "I got my eyes on you, Murray. I still remember when you first joined our crew on the Blue Solace. You put syrup on my pillow."

Morgan shot her a shocked look. "You think that was me? That was Lucas." His best friend had joined the crew at the same time as him.

"Bullshit, pretty boy. I'm watching you." She glared one more time, then spun and stomped out of his room.

"You were the one who put syrup on her pillow," Selene said.

"Your point? Lucas isn't here to defend himself."

The two chatted for a few more minutes and then ended the call. He stared at the walls for a minute then called Lucas.

"Hey, man," Lucas said. The Betonize-Cardinal hybrid looked good. He had lost an arm, an eye, and a leg on their last mission and was still recovering. Morgan didn't like to think how close he'd come to losing him.

"Have you married Draif yet?"

"The better question would be, have I even kissed Draif yet," Lucas said with a self-deprecating look. "We're getting closer every day, but it's slow going."

"You two will get there," Morgan said. "I spent a lot of time with him while you were being lazy. He has trust issues, and he's demisexual. Just be patient."

"Wow," Lucas said. "You were your normal insulting, asshole self right there *and* a mature adult. What's happening?"

Morgan stuck his tongue out at his friend. "I'm a kickass adult, man. Get it straight."

"Something's up with you," Lucas said. "I don't know what, but I'll figure it out."

"Oh, no," Morgan said. "I just got a message. Dru needs me."

"I'm looking right at you," Lucas said. "You're a fat-mouth liar."

Morgan leaned forward and *oops* the call ended. He put his shoes on, then left his room, unable to deal with the quiet room tonight. Usually it didn't bother him, but lately, being alone had gotten down right lonely. Stupid Lucas and his comments. He headed for the Bridge.

Buy Here: https://amzn.to/2S7R6ng

Carter loaded the last of his tools into his new work van and shut the door. His first day in his new profession was off to a good start. He had three clients to see today and eight spread out during the rest of the week.

Finally getting his plumbing license had been a good idea, even if his perfect, wealthy family hated the idea of him being a plumber.

Hell, they had also hated the idea of him being a soldier and of him moving out of state when he came back injured. They pretty much hated every decision he made.

The crisp fall wind was cold, but the gold, brown, and red leaves on the trees and ground made the cold worth dealing with. Autumn in Maine sure wasn't the same as autumn in Georgia, but so far, he was damn happy with the move. There was a peace here amongst the trees that he hadn't managed to find anywhere else.

"Hi, Mr. Neighbor!"

A child's voice came from behind him, startling Carter. He spun around, stumbling a bit on his prosthesis, and faced the little girl standing a few feet from his van.

She looked about five or six, with two black braids, caramel skin, and a freckled nose. When she smiled brightly, he saw a small gap between her two front teeth.

A black and gray miniature schnauzer sat at her feet, gaze stern and trained on him.

He looked around and didn't see any adults. His little half acre tract was quite a ways back from the road, nestled between a good-sized apple orchard on one side and a thick forest on the other.

Where the hell had this little girl come from?

"My name's Olive, and I brought you a welcome basket. I made it myself, but Daddy made you one too. He's gonna bring it tonight. I wanted you to get mine first, 'cause it's from me and then we'll be best friends." The little girl paused to take a breath. Her wide brown eyes sparkled and met his straight on, innocent and fearless. "We'll be best friends forever."

She didn't even seem to see the scars along the side of his face. The burn marks had already made two kids cry at the grocery store yesterday. Both times, the parents had been too embarrassed to apologize. They just grabbed their kids and ran.

"Uh, where's your daddy, Olive?" His voice was deep and cracked, broken by the scarring on his neck. Her adoring stare was starting to freak him out a little. He'd never really been around kids.

"He's at home," she answered and handed him the basket. "See what I brought you? Look, look, look."

"Do you know your phone number? Maybe we could give your daddy a call," Carter said, taking the basket from Olive. He pulled the small hand towel from the top and almost dropped the basket. "Is that a hedgehog?"

"Yep! That's Hodges the hedgehog. He wanted to

come visit too. Oh and this is Winston," she said and knelt to pet the small dog.

"Okay, your number?" He tried to keep his gruff voice kind. No sense in scaring the kid.

"Olive! Olive Persephone Wilson! Where are you?" A man's voice called from the orchard, full of panic and desperation.

"Uh oh," Olive said. She hurriedly looked around, then darted behind his van, Winston following her. "That's Daddy." She poked her head out and stared hard. "Tell. Him. Nothing."

She quickly hid again when a young omega rushed out of the orchard. He was her father, had to be. He looked just like her.

Carter suddenly couldn't catch his breath. The man in front of him was simply adorable. He was short and well formed, a little chubby. His black hair fell in curls around his face, and his wide hazel eyes contrasted beautifully with his caramel skin. The same freckles that decorated his daughter's nose, fell across his own. Where it looked cute on the kid, on her father... Bad thoughts, Carter! Bad thoughts!

"Have you seen a little girl? Black hair? Brown eyes? Miniature schnauzer with her? Maybe a hedgehog?"

Carter stared at the handsome man, mouth gaping, for too long.

The man frowned at him, tilting his head. "Are you alright?" His shy smile revealed the small gap between his front teeth.

Oh fuck, he was so damn perfect. He met Carter's eyes too, didn't even glance at the scars.

"Mister?"

Carter shook his head and did his best to pull himself together. He smiled, as best he could with the scar tissue, and nodded toward the van, holding a finger to his lips, encouraging the man to keep quiet.

Olive's father rolled his eyes and stomped around the van. A squealing Olive ran from her hiding spot and hid behind Carter, hugging him around the waist.

"Mr. Neighbor, save me!" Her giggling told him she wasn't too worried about her father catching her.

"Olive, you scared me to death running off like that." Her father really did look worried. "What have I told you about leaving the house without me?"

"But daddy," she whined. "I wanted to meet Mr. Neighbor. We're best friends now, and I gave him a welcome basket. I was being hospital."

Carter frowned. Hospital?

"Hospitable, baby girl, and it doesn't matter. You are too little to be wandering around by yourself and talking to strangers. No television time this week, and you have to clean out Pooka and Banjo's stalls on Saturday."

Olive gave a big sigh and leaned her forehead into Carter's leg. "Okay, Daddy, but it was worth it. I have a new best friend now."

The man met Carter's stare, a question in his eyes. Carter nodded and gave his best half smile.

"Well, maybe our new neighbor would like to come over for dinner one night? So that we can meet him properly," the man said.

"Yay! Mr. Neighbor, can you come tonight? Daddy's gonna make apple dumplins for dessert."

Carter smiled at the little girl and nodded. "Yeah, if it's okay with your dad."

The man smiled and nodded eagerly. "That would be great. I hardly ever get to cook for anyone but Olive." He gave a flustered look and held out his hand. "Oh, I forgot. My name is Elijah Wilson. I live in the farmhouse with the orchard. Of course, you've met Olive."

Carter shook his hand, touch lingering longer than it should. He was reluctant to release him but finally did. "Yeah, I'm Carter Benson. Just moved here from Georgia."

"Wow, so Maine's probably a bit different, huh?"

"Yeah, but all the colors on the trees? And ya'll actually have snow. I've never seen much of it."

"You say that like snow is a good thing." Elijah shuddered. "Well, welcome to Hobson Hill. I see Olive already gave you a welcome basket."

Carter looked back in it. "There's a hedgehog in there." His coarse voice was getting rougher as he spoke. He wasn't used to talking so much. Doctors said it was good for him to do though.

"I put cider in there for you. It's in my favorite big girl cup, the one with Moana. There's also butter from Pooka and some of Daddy's bread. It's so yummy!"

"Thanks, Olive. I appreciate it," Carter said. The little girl still hung on his leg, smiling up at him. She was a cute one, he acknowledged, even though she was clearly a little crazy. It was a good crazy though.

"Your alpha won't mind me coming," Carter asked Elijah.

The man winced and lowered his eyes. "I don't have an Alpha, so no, that won't be a problem."

Carter was surprised. Happy, but surprised. This adorable man had to be beating them off with a stick. Of course, some folks thought poorly about single omegas, and some alphas refused to even speak to them. Idiots.

"I guess I'll see you tonight. What time?"

"Oh, is six okay?" Elijah's confidence seemed to bounce back at Carter's question.

"That's fine. I better get to work."

"Yes, of course," Elijah said and pulled Olive off Carter's leg. "Come on, Olive. We better get back to the house. We need to get you to school."

"Okay. Bye, Carter, love you!" The little girl and her dog ran off through the orchard.

"I swear it's exhausting keeping up with her," Elijah sighed. Carter smiled and held the hedgehog out to him. "Thanks," he said, taking Hodges and smiling shyly. "See you tonight. Have a good day at work."

Carter stood frozen as he watched Elijah walk away. He was in trouble. Big, wonderful trouble.

Buy Here: https://amzn.to/2BgWURV